THE
BUTTERFLY
TATTOO

THE BUTTERFLY TATTOO

Barry Norman

Thorndike Press • Thorndike, Maine

This Large Print edition is published by Thorndike Press, USA and by Chivers Press, England.

The Butterfly Tattoo published in 1996 in the U.S. by arrangement with St. Martin's Press, Inc.

The Mickey Mouse Affair published in 1996 in the U.K. by arrangement with Orion.

U.S. Hardcover   0-7862-0723-X (Cloak & Dagger Series Edition)
U.K. Hardcover   0-7451-5384-4 (Windsor Large Print)

The text of this Large Print edition is unabridged.
Other aspects of the book may vary from the original edition.

Set in 16 pt. Bookman Old Style by Al Chase.

Printed in the United States on permanent paper.

British Library Cataloguing in Publication Data available

Library of Congress Cataloging in Publication Data

Norman, Barry.
    The butterfly tattoo / Barry Norman.
        p.   cm.
    ISBN 0-7862-0723-X (lg. print : hc)
    1. Large type books. I. Title.
    [PR6064.O722B88 1996]
    823'.914—dc20   96-12753

*For Bertie
and in loving memory
of Oliver.*

PREFACE

From the gallery the director's voice, crackling in her earpiece, said, 'Two minutes, Lacy,' and in the studio Lacy Jones, standing a little to the left of camera one, raised the first two fingers of her right hand, a swift, abrupt movement, the back of the hand facing the interviewer. It was a cheerfully vulgar gesture, not strictly speaking one from the floor manager's rule book, but it served its purpose. There were politer ways to let Kevin Rycroft know that he had two minutes to wrap up the programme — she could, for instance, have turned her palm outwards — but a V-sign was more fun.

From the corner of his eye Rycroft saw the two derisive fingers sweeping upwards and wished, as he had done many times before, that the bloody girl wouldn't do that. She knew perfectly well that sometimes, when he was caught off guard, it made him giggle and he wasn't supposed to giggle. He was television's arch interrogator, for

Chrissake, an inquisitor even, who turned up on screen once a week, forty weeks of the year, to give politicians and other shady characters in public life a ferocious grilling. He was famous for it.

He leaned forward in his chair, adopting the pose and the expression for which he was famous — eyes narrowed, chin jutting, lips curled into a thin, mocking smile. 'So, Minister,' he said, 'what you are saying is that despite the gloomy prognostications of the Bank of England and, of course, the Opposition, despite the worrying trade figures, what you are saying is that under this government and especially under your personal auspices, British industry is groping its way towards the road to recovery?' The mocking smile, the trick he had of making the question mark not just audible but almost visible gave the nod to his devoted viewers that he, Kevin Rycroft, didn't believe a word of it.

Across the table Archie Beckway, Minister for Industrial Development, nodded solemnly and raised his water glass to his lips. The water was tepid with a slight film of dust on the surface. What could you expect, he thought, tuppenny-ha'penny outfit like this — tiny studio, table top badly scratched, stains on the armchairs. Oh, it all looked elegant and spacious when you watched it on the box at home but the reality showed that for all its critical acclaim and, be honest, political clout *Speaking Out* was not a programme on which the BBC lavished much money.

Beckway didn't need the water but he, too, had seen the V-sign, was aware that camera two was zooming in on him and he was playing for time. Used to be easier in the old days, he thought, remembering how Harold Wilson, when he was Prime Minister, would duck an awkward question by knocking out his pipe, blowing through it, spraying dottle all over the place, refilling it, tamping it . . . Couldn't do that now, though. Only people who didn't mind being regarded as degenerates smoked on television these days.

He put the glass back on the table and leaned confidentially towards the narrowed eyes, the jutting chin and the mocking smile. 'Kevin,' he said, 'British industry is firmly *on* the road to recovery. Oh yes, oh yes, there are always gloom merchants only too ready to

9

knock the Government's achievements — remarkable achievements, I would say because that's what they are. Make no mistake about that. Remarkable. But I personally am sick of . . .' He stopped himself just in time. He was going to say 'I am sick of knockers' but then he realised what the Opposition press might make of that: 'Archie Says He's Sick of Knockers.' Government minister, sexual innuendo — mustn't give them the chance. They had nothing on him yet, though God knows they'd tried . . . He cleared his throat. 'I am sick of gloom merchants,' he said, lamely but safely. 'Under this government industrial recovery is 100 per cent on course. And let me just say this . . .'

He caught a glimpse of the floor manager signalling frantically. She had her head on one side, she had crossed her eyes, her tongue was protruding from the corner of her mouth and she was drawing an index finger horizontally across her throat. The message was clear: wrap up NOW. She was, he noticed as camera one moved in on Kevin Rycroft, a remarkably pretty girl. He remembered, suddenly, that he had thought as much the last time he was on the programme, three months ago, but she had been quieter then, not so vivacious. Maybe she'd had the curse or something.

Rycroft said, 'Thank you, Minister. No time to just say this, I'm afraid. That's all from *Speaking Out* for tonight. At the same time next week . . .'

Beckway relaxed, smiling benevolently for the closing two-shot. Not bad, he thought. He had got through the entire thirty minutes — or, allowing for the opening and closing credits, 29 minutes and 15 seconds — without saying anything of any significance whatsoever. The Prime Minister would be pleased. Kevin the Inquisitor indeed. Handle him right and he was just another neutered pussycat.

'Goodnight,' Rycroft said to camera one and turned to bestow a last thin, mocking smile on the Minister. Shifty bastard, he thought. The lights came up in the studio and on the wall the red 'Transmission' sign faded to darkness. 'Thanks, Archie,' he said. 'Went pretty well tonight.'

'Had me worried there at times,' Beckway said. 'We have to be on our toes when we come on your programme,

Kevin.' They unclipped their microphones and stood up, friendly smiles masking mutual disdain.

'You'll join us in hospitality, Archie?'

'Love to,' Beckway said, hoping the floor manager — what was her name? Lacy? Odd name for a girl; odd name for anyone, really — hoping she would be there, too.

The producer of *Speaking Out*, a lissom young man with blond hair which he wore long to show off its slight curl, came into the studio, arms spread wide as if in rapture. 'Well done, Kevin. Well done, Minister. Splendid programme, splendid. Lots of lively cut and thrust.' Beckway couldn't remember much in the way of cut and thrust; it had all seemed satisfactorily bland to him but he nodded acknowledgement of the intended compliment. Behind the producer Freddie Marcus, the Minister's publicity minder, smiled, winked and raised his left thumb approvingly. Now that, Beckway thought, *was* a compliment, confirming his own belief that he had slid through the interview without (a) imparting any real information whatsoever and (b) telling any lies that could easily be identified as lies. Keep this up, my lad, he thought and, come the next reshuffle, that seat in the Cabinet is yours.

They all ushered each other courteously out of the studio and together producer, presenter/inquisitor and government minister ambled down the drab corridor and took the lift to the hospitality room in the basement. Beckway was gratified to see that the floor manager was coming with them.

Hospitality rooms at the BBC's Television Centre in west London are windowless cellars painted in nondescript colours apparently chosen for their instant forgettability. Off-white, beige, a sort of pale green? Something like that anyway. There was a long table spread with finger food, sandwiches, sausage rolls, cold, grey chicken legs. Institutional chairs were dotted here and there and a white-coated barman dispensed drinks: beer, colas, fruitjuices, red and white wine.

'Hold on, Minister,' said the producer. 'We've managed to find a bottle of Scotch for you. Know your preference, of course.' From a plastic bag behind the food table he produced a bottle of blended whisky and poured the Minister a hefty slug. Beckway, whose preference was not actually for blended whisky but for single malts, accepted it anyway, added ice and soda and, ignoring Marcus who was chatting to one of the programme researchers, carried his drink to where the floor manager was sitting, a plate of sandwiches on her lap. Her short skirt had risen well above her knees, drawing Beckway's attention to her long, finely-shaped legs. He sat down beside her.

Across the room, where the drinks were, Rycroft said sourly, 'Marvellous, isn't it? Minister for Industrial Development, country's about as developed as bloody Somalia and all he seems to be interested in is getting his leg over.'

'So I see.' The producer tossed his curls like a girl in a shampoo commercial. It had become a habit; he hardly knew he was doing it. 'I thought he'd stopped all that. A few years ago . . . well, we all heard the rumours, did we not? But I thought he'd cleaned up his act, especially now he's a responsible member of the Government.'

'He's a what?'

The producer chuckled. 'All right, a member of the Government then. But if he's thinking of going back to his old ways, he's certainly made a beeline for the right girl.'

Twenty feet away the Minister was saying, 'That was naughty of you, Lacy. Giving poor Kevin the V-sign, I mean.'

Lacy grinned and Beckway thought this was the most enchanting sight he had seen for, well, for several days. She had a cap of pale, blond hair, hazel eyes and a straight little nose and when she grinned her whole face became a series of charming horizontal lines. Beckway, a movie buff, thought she looked like the young Shirley Maclaine. 'Well,' she said, 'you have to do something to relieve the monotony. What I always hope is that he'll corpse — you know? Burst out laughing? All these endless political interviews, you've no idea how tedious they can . . .' She stopped, blushing. 'Oh, not yours, of course.'

Beckway patted her knee — just above the knee actually — to show that he understood. 'Hey, come on' he said, 'don't knock my confidence. If my interview wasn't just as tedious as the others, I must have been doing something wrong.' She put her hand on his and squeezed it gently. He found the contact

15

disturbing; any physical contact with women he found disturbing. He lowered his hand to his lap so that she wouldn't notice how disturbed he was and thought, Stop this. Stop it now. Don't be a fool.

The producer, appearing suddenly behind them, said, 'Well, Minister, I hope you're not too unhappy with the, ah, grilling Kevin gave you.'

'No,' Beckway said. The interruption and Lacy's removal of her hand had calmed him down. 'No, not at all. I thought he was very fair — tough, of course, as one expects but fair.' He smiled pleasantly, his sharp politician's instincts making it easy for him to resist adding that in his opinion Kevin was an overrated prat.

'Yes, well, of course,' the producer said, 'he does give you people rather a hard time but then that's what he's there for.' He tossed the curls again and laughed.

The barman had eased up discreetly behind Lacy and was murmuring to her, 'It's reception, Lacy. Your sister . . .' Beckway couldn't hear the rest because the producer had embarked on another laugh. Lacy got up, put her plate and wine glass on a side table and walked to the door. Beckway was conscious of all her movements — the way she bent, stiff-legged, to put the plate down so that her neatly rounded bottom was thrust towards him, the slight sway of her hips as she glided away. At the door she turned, caught his eye, smiled. Her lips said, 'Back soon' and then she went out of the room.

'Now then, Minister,' the producer said, 'I wonder if I might ask a small favour. What we would like to do, the last two programmes of the series, is back-to-back interviews — leader of the Opposition one week, Prime Minister the next. Well, the leader of the Opposition, as you can imagine, is very keen but we're having trouble signing up the PM and I was wondering if you could perhaps use your influ— '

Beckway thought, Dammit, the girl's out there waiting for me, I know she is. One part of him was saying, Let her go. You don't need this — it's stupid, it's dangerous. Think what happened when the others got caught, the political careers that were ruined . . . But another, more urgent, more thrusting part was murmuring, What harm can it do?

You've been so good for so long, you've denied yourself, you need this, you deserve this . . .'

'Would you,' he said, 'would you excuse me for a moment? I'm rather desperate for a pee. Would you . . . ?'

'Of course, Minister.'

At the door Beckway said, 'I won't be long. We'll talk about it,' and then he plunged into the corridor. It stretched away endlessly, curving gently, deserted, round the circular shape of the Television Centre. The perfect location, Beckway thought, to film something from Kafka. He headed towards the lifts, confident that Lacy would be loitering there, expecting him. She wasn't. He walked back a few paces towards the women's lavatory, wondering whether she might be in there and, if so, hoping she wouldn't be long.

From another corridor adjoining this one at right angles a man appeared. He was big and broad-shouldered and he wore a Mickey Mouse mask. 'No, no, not there,' he said. 'That's for the ladies.' His voice, muffled a little by the mask, had a strong Northern Irish accent. 'This is the one you're looking for.' He put a hand on Beckway's shoulder and eased him towards the men's room. 'This is the place,' he said, sounding amused; 'this is where all the big nobs hang out. The old jokes are always the best, don't you think?'

An 'Out of Order' sign was hanging on the handle of the men's room door. Beckway said, 'No, look, it's not in use. And anyway I'm waiting — '

'Ah, you don't want to worry about that,' said Mickey Mouse. 'They don't mean a thing, these notices. I've used this loo already tonight. It's working perfectly.'

Beckway said, 'No, you don't understand. I — ' But he was too late because the firm hand of Mickey Mouse had already propelled him into the men's room. He just had time to notice that, curiously, there was a wooden chair beside the wash basin before he was suddenly, violently, shoved across the room to crash face-first into the metal door of one of the cubicles. He staggered back, his nose bleeding from the impact. 'What . . . what the hell are you doing? Do you know who — '

'Shut up, Minister,' Mickey Mouse said. 'Just shut the fuck up, do you hear me?' He grabbed the wooden chair

19

and wedged the back of it under the door handle. 'OK, all clear.'

The door of the second cubicle opened and three people came out, two of them men dressed, like Mickey Mouse, in blue sweatshirts, jeans and trainers. They, too, were big and broad-shouldered. One wore Goofy's head, the other Pluto's. The third person was a woman. She wore diamond-patterned black stockings, a dark coat, a Minnie Mouse mask and the kind of high-heeled shoes that, even in his already very perturbed state, Beckway thought of as fuck-me pumps. Pluto had a 35mm camera hanging from a strap around his neck.

Mickey Mouse nodded towards Goofy and Pluto and, before Beckway could protest, they had dragged his jacket off him. 'Right then, Minister,' Mickey said. 'Drop your trousers.'

'Dro . . . ? No, goddammit, I won't. Look, if it's money you want — '

Mickey Mouse moved close and punched him hard in the stomach. Beckway moaned and doubled over. Goofy said, 'Hey, what are you doing? This wasn't — '

'Shut up, all of you,' Mickey said. 'Are you listening to me, Minister? Do I have your undivided attention now? That's good. So drop your trousers —and your underpants while you're about it. I want to see you bollock naked from the waist down except your shoes and socks. I like the shoes and socks, they're a nice touch. Now do it.'

Beckway tried to appeal to Goofy, to Pluto, to Minnie Mouse. 'Please, help me. I — ' Mickey hit him twice more and he doubled again, retching the whisky and the remains of a grey chicken leg onto the floor.

Pluto said, 'Stop it, Mickey. This wasn't what we — '

'Belt up,' Minnie Mouse said. She put her hands on Beckway's shoulders and pushed him upright against the wall beside the urinal. Her voice was shrill and excited, the accent exaggeratedly Cockney. 'Come on, dahlin', let's 'ave yer strides dahn.' She fiddled with his belt, his zip, pulled his trousers and boxer shorts to his knees and took his shrivelled, flaccid, humiliated member in her hand. 'Dear, oh dear, this the best you can manage, duckie? I don't believe it, not what I've 'eard abaht you.'

Mickey said 'Pluto, for Chrissake get the camera ready. We don't have all night here.' He tugged the trousers and shorts down to Beckway's ankles and made him step out of them. 'Minnie, get on with it — what are you pissing about for?'

Minnie Mouse took off her coat. Beneath it she wore only a garter belt, suspenders and stockings. Her skin was smooth, faintly tanned all over and unblemished except for a colourful butterfly tattoo at the top of her left thigh.

Mickey put the heel of his hand under Beckway's chin and shoved his head hard against the wall. 'Right, on your knees, Minister, unless you want another good thumping. Pluto, have you got the camera ready at all? OK, good. Places everybody.'

Beckway's protest turned into a thin shriek as Mickey Mouse grabbed a fistful of his hair and yanked his head downwards. He dropped to his knees in front of the almost naked Minnie Mouse, his face only inches away from the crisp, dark thatch between her legs. Pluto shuffled back, focusing his camera. Goofy took up a position by the door, leaning against it so that the combination of his weight and the chair-back jammed under the handle would give anyone trying to get in the impression that the room was locked.

Mickey relaxed. 'Fine, fine,' he said. 'Now then, Minister, what I want you to do, I want you to ease up on the delectable Minnie and take a good mouthful of hair pie and just keep chomping away so Pluto here can get some decent snaps. I'll tell you when to stop, though maybe you won't want to, you'll enjoy it so much, a noted pussyhound like you.'

Minnie took Beckway's head in her hands quite gently, and turned his face up towards her. Behind the mask he could see only her eyes; the pupils were a deep, inhuman purple, as if she were some alien creature from another planet who had somehow inhabited this desirable female body. Her breathing was quick, excited. 'Come to momma,' she said and pulled his face into her crotch. He was aware of all manner of sensations — the flashing of Pluto's camera, the sound of Mickey's voice, the scent and feel of the woman.

'Go on, Minister,' Mickey said, 'put some effort into it, let's see the old tongue get to work. You like it, you know you do. And you don't have to worry about your health. She's a good, clean girl.' He thumped Beckway on the back of the head, pushing him closer. 'Use your hands, man, get hold of her buttocks. Grab a fistful of those lovely, silky buns. Ah, that's much better. Come on, Pluto, keep snapping away. That's it, that's good, ah, that's grand. Go on, Minister, you're doing fine there. Just turn your face a little towards us, will you, so we can get a shot of that noble profile. Oh yes, oh yes. Oh, my word, will you look at that? See how the little feller's standing up to salute the queen . . .'

To his horror, his shame, Beckway realised that despite his fear, or perhaps because of it, despite the sexual subjugation he was suffering, or perhaps because of it, he had an erection. He tried to pull away but the pressure of the girl's hands was firm on the back of his head and besides, he knew, humiliatingly, that it was only his mind that was telling him to stop; his body was suffused by a surge of voluptuous excitement that was almost uncontrollable. Then Mickey said, 'That's enough. Stop. Move away, Minister, move away. Come on, man, on your feet. We're going to do it the other way now. Ah, sure I'm sorry. There's nothing so totally, bloody frustrating as coitus interruptus, is there, even if the coitus is only oral? But . . . Be patient. Who knows, this could still be your night, after all.'

Beckway was pulled unsteadily, throbbing, to his feet and the girl knelt before him and took him in her mouth. Pluto's camera flashed and clicked until Mickey said, 'OK now? Have we got enough?' Pluto nodded. 'Right then, Pluto, off you go.'

Beckway, the girl's fingers and mouth all over him, was hardly aware of the door opening, of Pluto leaving the men's room. The thought flashed through his mind, 'A standing penis has no conscience'. The shame, the horror, had faded. All he wanted now was for this physical experience to continue to its logical, bursting conclusion. But even that, in the circumstances small, consolation was denied him for Mickey said 'OK, stop, stop. What's the matter with you, girl? You're not supposed to enjoy this work. Bad enough that he does, the horny little sod.' He caught Minnie around the waist and pulled her away from Beckway who, released from the soft, warm embrace of her mouth, slumped against the wall. 'Go on, girl, away with you.'

Minnie Mouse put on her coat, ran her hand gently over Beckway's groin and went out. He was suddenly aware that Goofy had gone, too, and that he was alone now with Mickey Mouse. Mickey said 'Let me guess what you're thinking, Minister. You're thinking now there's just the two of us maybe you should do something brave. Well, don't bother your head with that nonsense because you haven't a chance.' In his right hand he was holding a short, evil-looking cosh. 'Take one step towards me and I'll smash your jaw. Besides, what good would a punch-up do you? You're in a no-win situation here, Minister. Pluto's long gone and he's got the pictures and it's the pictures you have to worry about.'

Beckway said, 'What do you want from me?'

'You'll learn soon enough. We'll be in touch, I promise you that. Just expect a call sometime, any time, from your personal photographic service. Have you got that? Your personal photographic service.' He stepped closer to Beckway. 'Isn't sex a bitch when you can't finish it? I mean, look at the state of you still, all proud and ready to serve. Well, at least I can do something about that.' With a sudden backhand motion he slammed the cosh hard against Beckway's testicles, bringing him down to his knees once again. The pain was almost insupportable. 'A perfect cure for tumescence that, a good thump in the balls,' Mickey said. 'See, it's worked already.'

He put the cosh in the back pocket of his jeans. 'I'm going to leave you now, Minister, and I know you'll not try to follow me because you don't have your trousers. They frown on people wandering about half-naked at the BBC, unless of course you happen to be in one of their plays, in which case anything goes. There's far too much of that kind of stuff on the box these days, don't you agree? All that full-frontal nudity. And it's hardly ever men, have you noticed that? It's the poor actresses who have to give their all. And to what end, to what purpose? Just so that randy buggers like you can sit at home and get their rocks off. Shameful, it is, shameful.' He pulled the door open a little, then closed it again. 'Ah well, what the devil. Just to show you I'm not altogether a bad man I'll tell you where your trousers are. You'll find them behind the cistern in the first cubicle there. I'm afraid they may be a little crumpled but look at it this way — crumpled or not it's better to be wearing trousers than walking the corridors flashing that thing at innocent people.'

And then he was gone, leaving Her Majesty's Minister for Industrial Development kneeling half-naked and sobbing on the lavatory floor.

ONE

Near the bottom of White Hart Lane I drove into a sort of builder's yard. It was after seven o'clock on a Saturday night and the builders had long gone but there was a handwritten sign outside that said parking was available at a price. The price was high but less than the cost of being clamped or towed away. I nosed into a space by the wall and gave money to a villainous-looking pair who, in return, handed me something that had clearly started life as a cloakroom ticket and was now being asked to serve as a receipt for my car. And I took it — quite happily. Did these two rough and ready herberts own the builder's yard? Unlikely. Did they have any official right to operate the parking concession that night? I had no idea. And yet I took their ticket and walked away confident that my property would still be there when I returned a few hours later. Well, even in this wicked world you have to trust people sometimes.

At the high street I crossed the road and turned right towards the sign of the rampant cockerel that proclaimed the home of Tottenham Hotspur football club. It was summer and no football would be played that night. Instead there was to be a fight, a boxing match for one of the umpteen versions of the world welterweight championship, a British challenger against the American holder. The crowd converging like me on the Spurs' ground gave off a vibrant, faintly disturbing air of excitement barely suppressed. I kept my head down and walked fast. There was a time when everybody knew me. Well, all right, not everybody; I was never as famous as, I don't know, a TV weather forecaster — I mean, come on, these days that's real celebrity — but a lot of people knew me.

But that was then and this was now and now I wasn't recognised too often, though the people I was walking among that evening were those most likely to know who I used to be and I wasn't anxious to get involved with them. They were in groups and, as anyone who has ever enjoyed his fifteen minutes of fame will tell you, groups are dangerous.

Individuals are placid and ask for your autograph but groups can turn nasty and snap at your heels like jackals.

That night I pretty well got away with it. I was on my way into the ground before a man across the street shouted, 'Hey, Bob, makin' a comeback, are yer?' His companions, half a dozen of them, raised their beer cans to me. 'Yeah, get in there, Bob. Don't make 'em like you any more.' I was lucky; these were friendly jackals. I grinned and waved and went on in.

Tall, well-built young women in tight teeshirts, high heels and tiny satin shorts were directing us ticket-holders to our seats and parrying the sexist wisecracks with weary smiles. One of them led me upstairs to the Players' Lounge and hoped I would have a pleasant evening. She seemed a nice girl and I thought it a pity that she had to do this kind of work in this kind of company. Pretty women who are employed, as she and the others were, simply because they are pretty women can have a rough time of it when they're surrounded by excitable men on a big night out.

The Players' Lounge that evening had

been reserved by the fight promotor, Donovan, for the use of his personal guests — friends, business acquaintances, people he was using or hoped to use in the future. I got a glass of wine at the bar and helped myself from the buffet which Donovan, in his benevolence, had provided. It was early yet; there was no sign of Donovan and there were not too many people in the room but there was one group which, I just knew, was going to cause trouble.

Three men, flushed and chortling, already well into the booze. As I sat down, half turned away from them, the leader of the group, a man about my height, maybe a little heavier, in a dark mohair suit, began doing impersonations of a punch-drunk fighter, face slack, mouth open, arms dangling as if to drag his knuckles across the carpet. I knew this was for my benefit because they were all looking at me, eager to see my reaction, but I let it pass and started eating my food. They didn't like that. They wanted me to say something, do something, anything.

They paused to get more drinks and then the mohair suit started again. This time he moved around so he was almost in front of me. His friends thought he was very funny and the other people in the lounge were watching, too, and grinning. It was one of those situations where, you know, what do you do? Ignore it and kick yourself later? Pretend to join in the joke? Or . . .

The girl who had brought me there came into the room. She had a message for a Mr Clark and as soon as he saw the legs and the high heels I lost the mohair suit's attention.

'What's the message, darling?' he said. 'I'll take it.'

'Are you Mr Clark?'

'For you, darling, I could be. I could be anyone you want.' He smirked, playing to the crowd, and moved up close, only inches away from the girl. His two friends got in behind her, crowding her.

'If you're not Mr Clark I'd better come back later.' She was trying to smile but she looked a little scared.

'What do you want with Mr Clark when you've got us?' mohair suit said. 'Come on, relax. Have a bit of fun.'

'No, I'd better go.' She tried to leave but mohair suit put both his hands on her shoulders, then ran them up her neck and started stroking her cheeks.

One of the two men behind her must have goosed her because she suddenly flinched.

'Tell you what, darling,' mohair suit said. 'Give us a kiss then you can go.'

'No, please. Leave me alone — '

'Just a little kiss, no harm in that.' The other two were sniggering as mohair suit put his arm around her and tried to pull her face towards him.

'You don't want to do that,' I said.

I saw the look of surprise on his face as, for a moment, he stopped pawing the girl. Then he turned towards me; they all did but only the girl looked grateful for the interruption. She tried to wriggle away from them but the other two stooges had hold of her arms. 'What?' mohair suit said. 'Fuck's it got to do with you?'

I stood up and walked over to him. 'Tell them to let her go.'

'You what?' He laughed and turned to his friends, inviting them to share the joke. 'Oh yeah, I'm about to take orders from a punchy fucking hasbeen, I don't think. Who do you think you are?'

And that's when I grabbed him by his lapels and ran him backwards till he thumped against the wall. 'You know very well who I am,' I said. 'And that means you also know I can hurt you.'

He wriggled furiously, clenched his fist, drew back his arm — and then thought better of it. 'Charlie,' he said, 'Joe. Don't just stand there. Give us a hand, for Chrissake. Get this lunatic off me.'

Over my shoulder I said, 'Don't do it, fellers. Don't even think about it. It's not a good idea. Trust me.'

One of them said, 'Pete, I mean, what can I do? I just got out of hospital.'

Pete the mohair suit wriggled some more. I took a tighter grip on his lapels and lifted him slowly against the wall till he was standing on tiptoe. 'You're fucking mad,' he said. 'Look what you're doing to my coat. You ruin this coat and I'll sue you.'

I gave him my hardest, coldest stare. It's very good that hard, cold stare of mine. Pete looked at me, didn't like what he saw and decided to cut his losses.

'Let her go,' he muttered. 'Do what he says.'

I glanced back as his companions hesitated, shrugged and slowly released their grip. The girl rubbed her arms, smiled at me, said 'Thank you' and then hauled off and punched one of the men full on the nose. 'Keep your fucking hands to yourself in future,' she said and went out, head up and looking pleased with herself.

And then Donovan said 'Mind telling me what's going on here, Bob?' I hadn't seen or heard him come in but there he was, right behind me, peering curiously over my shoulder at Pete, the mohair suit. I let the man go and stepped back. There were quite a few men and a number of women in the room by now, all looking in my direction and apparently enjoying themselves but none of them had thought to interfere. Sign of the times — people just don't like to get involved.

'Nothing much,' I said. 'These three clowns thought they'd have some fun with one of your girls but she wasn't in the mood for it so I was politely asking Pete here to think it through again.'

'That right?' Donovan said. He took Pete by his mohaired arm and led him back to his friends. 'Out,' he said. 'All three of you, piss off.' They did, no questions asked, no argument. Donovan had that effect on people. When they'd gone he said to me 'The fights are supposed to take place in the ring, Bobby, not up here.'

'I know.' I sighed and shook my head. 'I can be a terrible bully sometimes.'

I'd not seen him for a while but he hadn't changed much — a big, burly man with a big, handsome Irish head and a mass of thick, curly grey hair. He still looked much younger than his years. I thanked him for the ticket, the ringside seat which he had sent me and which I had accepted out of curiosity as much as anything. Fight promoting was a comparatively new venture for Donovan, an honest — or anyway as honest as the fight game gets — addition to his other, usually more nefarious enterprises that included bookmaking, gaming houses, high-class brothels and practically anything else that might turn a profit, legal or otherwise, except drug dealing. Donovan had watched a nephew die of drug abuse and ever since had waged a personal vendetta against the dealers, some of whom had enjoyed premature funerals because of him.

We got ourselves drinks and he said, 'Now you're here why don't I get the MC to introduce you from the ring along with all the other old pugs? "And now a big hand, please, for Bobby Lennox, the retired undefeated, undisputed middleweight champion of Great Britain, the British Commonwealth and Europe." No, don't shake your head. Go down well, that would. You've still got a lot of fans out there.'

'Yeah, well, let them remember me as I was.'

It was some years since I'd retired from the ring and I'd rather lost interest in the fight game. Oh, it had been good to me; I'd earned a fair bit of money and with the help of a couple of partners, a stockbroker and a solicitor, I'd made it work for me. Some speculation here, a little dabble there, buying and selling at the right time. I was comfortably, very comfortably, fixed but though I was grateful to boxing, the original source of this affluence, it no longer held much attraction for me. Nothing had happened to change my view that the only good thing about the fight game was the fighters. Like every other boxer I'd known my share of dishonest managers, incompetent judges and referees, bent promoters and various other parasites who made their livings by exploiting brave kids with little between the ears but with hearts a lot stronger than the Bank of England. I'd put up with them because I had to but I wasn't about to seek their company once I'd finally hung up the boots, the gloves and the protective cup. Besides, though I still admired the skill, the strength and the special courage that I know boxers have there was a part of me which, even when I was still active, despised myself for enjoying the fight game and despised others for enjoying it, too. I saw the darkly primitive instincts that a blood-spattered fight unleashed in the crowds and I knew those same instincts were at least straining against the leash in me. So I didn't go much to boxing matches any more.

'What it is,' I said to Donovan, 'I don't really like fight fans.' I gestured vaguely in the direction of the ring, set up in the middle of the football ground. 'At this very minute some of the nastiest people in London are taking their seats out there. You think they've come to see skill, the noble art of self-defence? Bullshit. They've come to see blokes knock each other's brains out and if they don't see that they'll probably tear the place apart.'

Donovan shook his head sadly. 'Know your trouble, Bobby? You're a snob. Those people out there, my customers, salt of the earth they are — ordinary, decent people carried away by a natural blood lust and the desire to see grievous bodily harm legally inflicted. Where you went wrong, you should never have gone to university. Education ruins fighters. Makes 'em think too much.'

He was wrong on at least one count — education had given me the nous to get out before I really got hurt.

A couple of fight managers breezed up, trying to catch Donovan's attention and as they moved in I started towards the door.

'Hold on,' Donovan said to the managers, 'don't crowd me, all right? Bobby, case I don't get a chance to talk to you while the fights are on, come back here afterwards, will you? Something I want to ask you.'

I grinned at him. 'Fight tickets are like lunches, are they? There's no such thing as a free one. OK, I'll see you later.'

I went down the stairs and along the

tunnel past the footballers' changing rooms, which tonight were being used by the fighters, and out onto the pitch. A roped-off pathway covered with carpet to protect the turf and guarded every twenty yards or so by a hefty steward led to the ring. It was a warm, still evening and so far the crowd was in a good mood. Quite a few people called to me as I made my way towards the ringside. I smiled and waved and hurried on.

It was the usual kind of undercard for a big fight night — wannabes versus hasbeens, nothing to get excited about. Just before the main event a man I knew dropped into the seat beside me. Throughout my career in the ring he had been the chief boxing writer for a daily paper, a small, plumpish man with a full head of hair and a slightly hunched look as if he had been designed by nature to play Richard III. I hadn't seen him since my last fight when, with a lack of success that still made my jaw and ribs ache whenever I thought of it, I had challenged for the undisputed middleweight championship of the world.

'You're looking bloody fit,' he said as

we shook hands. 'Thinking of a come-back, perhaps?'

'Not even if they let me wear knuckle-dusters instead of gloves. What are you doing down here, Ted?' I waved towards the press seats. 'Shouldn't you be up there along with the other hacks?'

'Too old for that lark. I'm a columnist now. I don't report, I pontificate with all the benefit of hindsight. It beats work-ing. See?' He took a business card from his top pocket and handed it to me — 'Teddy Davies, Columnist, *Daily Journal*, it said. I made appreciative noises. 'Keep it,' he said. 'Now, what do you reckon tonight? Think our boy's got a chance?'

'Maybe. If it goes the distance he might sneak it on points.' I'd seen him fight a couple of times on TV; a good boxer with fast hands and feet. 'I'd fancy him more if he had a decent punch.'

There was a dimming of the lights, a fanfare and the British boxer ducked through the ropes into the ring. He had the supple, smoothly muscular body of a small Muhammad Ali and the tense, drawn look that betrays the excitement and apprehension that hits you every

42

time you walk up those steps to the ringside. Then another fanfare and the champion arrived: shorter, stockier, more powerful and exuding the confidence that comes simply from being the champion. Both men were sweating heavily from their warm-ups in the changing rooms.

We all stood for the national anthems and after that a handful of ex-champions were introduced from the ring, gave the crowd the boxer's salute — both hands clasped above their heads — and went to each corner to wish the combatants good luck. Then the MC did his stuff, the referee summoned the boxers to the centre of the ring to remind them of the rules they already knew by heart and the fight began.

It was a good one, too, not spectacular but always interesting. The American moved forward, chin tucked in, hands held low, looking for a chance to land the big punch. The British fighter boxed on the retreat, picking up points with a neat left jab, ducking and weaving away from his opponent's obviously more dangerous hooks and uppercuts. For the first half of the bout there wasn't much in it either way.

In the ninth round the challenger did some of his best work, urged on by the unashamedly partisan spectators. 'Go on, Jackie, my son,' yelled a voice from just behind me, 'kill the black bastard,' an exhortation which, assuming he heard it, must have bewildered Jackie quite as much as it encouraged him, since he was no less black than the American.

The champion came back strongly in the tenth round, stronger still in the eleventh as the effect of his body punches began to wear the challenger down and took the twelfth and final round by a clear margin. It was no surprise when the three judges made him the winner by a unanimous decision but the fact that justice had clearly been done did nothing to satisfy the crowd.

They had come for a British victory and even more for blood and mayhem and they had been disappointed on all counts. There were no knock downs and no cuts. What they had seen was a well-balanced contest between a boxer and a puncher at the end of which both men were conscious and able to leave the ring under their own momentum. The onlookers felt bitterly let down so, just as I had warned Donovan, they saw it as their duty or even their God-given right to tear the place apart. From all sides they rose up, yelling and snarling, and surged towards the crush barriers, thoughtfully bringing their seats with them to use either as weapons or missiles, depending on how the mood took them.

A couple of chairs flew over my head and landed, bouncing, on the hard turf between me and the ring. Teddy said 'Time to go, Bobby. I shouldn't be at all surprised if things turned quite nasty in a minute.'

As we got up to leave, crouching to protect our heads from flying chairs, a steward who recognised me said 'Stick close to me, Bob. I'll get you out of here.'

Teddy said 'Don't worry about him. He used to be a fighter, he can look after himself. I'm a middle-aged man with a dodgy Bakewell tart. I'm the one you should be protecting.'

The steward grinned and led us at a brisk trot back along the carpeted pathway towards the players' tunnel, pausing only to flatten a skinny youth who was misguided enough to leap in front of us brandishing a chair. 'I enjoyed that,' the steward said when he had returned us to safety. 'Hammering little turds like that is what I'm paid for.' He pocketed the fiver Teddy gave him. 'Ta, mate. Not necessary but ta anyway.' And then he plunged back into the fray looking for more little turds to hammer.

Teddy said, 'That's enough excitement for one night. I'll wait here till the fighters get back. Give me a call sometime, Bobby. We'll have a drink, talk about the old days.' I said that would be nice and returned to the Players' Lounge where Donovan was holding court surrounded by the usual collection of bookies, secondhand car dealers and the like who turn up at the big fights.

'You wanted to talk to me,' I said.

He nodded. 'Get out of my way,' he said to the car dealers and the bookies. And when he'd cleared a little space around us he said, 'I'm a bit tied up at the moment, Bob. The Yank's manager is giving me some aggro. Says I haven't paid his fighter enough. Look, come to my house tomorrow morning. About elevenish. You know the address?'

'Yes. What's this all about, Donovan?'

'Mate of mine's got himself into a spot

of bother. I think you might be able to help. Like to talk it over with you anyway.'

'OK. What's his name, this mate?'

'Beckway. Archie Beckway. Politician. Know who I mean?'

I said I did and left him to his car dealers and the angry manager. The villainous-looking pair had gone by the time I got back to the builder's yard but my car was still there.

I drove home wondering what sort of bother Archie Beckway could have got himself into.

TWO

I had known Donovan since I was a boy and he was already the established organiser and mastermind of almost every criminal activity that originated in the area of south London around the street where I grew up. Neither of us had lived there for a long time now and indeed it was unrecognisable these days, the little terraced houses and shops replaced by stained, neglected tower blocks that looked like a mouthful of decaying teeth.

When I was going to school and learning to box Donovan had appointed himself as a kind of surrogate father to me, partly because my own father had died but mostly because he fancied my mother. I think she rather fancied him, too, and somewhere down the line they had probably got it together now and then, not that they ever said as much to me, nor that I ever asked them about it. It was none of my business after all.

Over the years Donovan's interests, legal and illegal, had thrived and expanded. He had no criminal record — he had never even been arrested — but he was probably the biggest and most powerful crook in London, a lot bigger and more successful than any of the City villains for whom, anyway, he had almost as much contempt as he had for drug dealers. Robbing small investors, stealing the savings of old age pensioners and preying on addicts was not Donovan's style. Greedy businessmen, banks and insurance companies were more his targets, though he was equally content to separate wealthy mugs from their spare cash in his gambling clubs, betting shops and whorehouses. He was also happy to kill, or arrange to have killed, people who got in his way or otherwise upset him. Fortunately for them the majority of those likely to incur his wrath, rival gangsters or drug dealers foolish enough to trespass on what Donovan regarded as his domain, were aware of this little peccadillo of his and usually took pains to avoid offending him.

All in all he was a thoroughly disreputable character and I liked him a lot. There were times, certainly, when I disapproved of him and I'd had no difficulty resisting all his offers to join his firm. But we were products of the same environment, the Street — its actual name doesn't matter; the Street is what we called it — and if you grew up there, then you grew up surrounded by crime and villains of all kinds and sizes. In the Street an honest crust was what you earned, or otherwise procured, without actually hurting anyone who couldn't afford the loss, and Donovan exercised a strict code of conduct in that area.

That I had grown up comparatively law-abiding was due to genetics. I had inherited my mother's brains and at her insistence had gone to university to read English and it was the fact of my having a degree that had made Donovan anxious to take me into one of his businesses. I think he had a wistful dream that I might be groomed to become his heir. Nothing unusual in that, I suppose; every robber baron wants to pass his empire on to somebody and Donovan had no children of his own. He had never married; he wasn't the marrying kind. But I had no wish to work for him, much to my mother's relief, incidentally. She was convinced that one day the law would pounce on him and he and all his close associates would spend the rest of their lives in prison. I think and have always thought that she was wrong: Donovan owned too much of the law for the rest of it to have even an outside chance of catching up with him.

Increasing affluence had taken him away from the Street to a moated Tudor mansion in Norfolk and a succession of flats and houses in the more desirable parts of London. Now he owned an elegant house in Mayfair, just off Berkeley Square, and I fetched up there, dead on eleven o'clock, on the Sunday morning. The sun shone, the traffic was muted, the streets were nearly empty, God was in his heaven and, for the seriously rich, all was right with the world.

Donovan's double-fronted house was in a quiet, narrow road and set back a few yards from the pavement. I rang the bell beside the big oak door and waited. A young Filipino woman holding a soft-looking poodle on a scarlet leash walked by and gave me a shy smile. I smiled back and we were still looking at each other when she rounded a corner and

51

disappeared. Just one of those pleasant, meaningless encounters that made us both feel good. We had each checked out the equipment and discovered that we were still fanciable. These things are important.

The door was opened by a tall, slender young woman with glossy brown hair and big, dark eyes. She was in her late twenties and wore blue and white trainers with blue and white laces and a pale blue, velvet track suit with the Christian Dior logo on her left breast. I assumed at once that she was Donovan's latest bimbo.

'Hi,' she said. 'You must be Bobby. I'm Anneke but my friends call me Annie.' She had the long legs, bouncy bottom and wide mouth that were common to all Donovan's women but there was something else that set her apart from the usual run of his identikit girlfriends, a glint of humour and sharp intelligence in the eyes that were even more attractive than the physical attributes.

She led me into a square, carpeted hall with a wide staircase at the back that curved gently up towards the first floor. 'Dining-room there,' she said, doing her tourist guide bit. 'Kitchen back there, just beyond the stairs, lift on the right.'

'Lift?' I said. 'You have a lift?'

'It's four flights to the roof garden and Donovan has to preserve his strength for the more important activities these days.' She grinned wickedly and took up an exaggerated model girl pose, hands on hips, pelvis thrust forward. 'How about you? Another candidate for the lift or can you still manage the stairs?'

'How far do we have to go?'

'One floor up.'

'Then lead me to the stairs. I'm a lot younger than Donovan or hadn't you noticed?'

She looked me over appraisingly, mockingly. 'Well, yes, now you mention it.' She took me by the hand and ran me up the stairs, always one step ahead of me. Her fingers were long and slim but though the contact was pleasantly intimate I knew there was nothing personal in it. Just as the Filipino girl and I had done she was simply checking out the equipment to be sure it was still in working order.

Donovan was rich and powerful

enough to provide himself with a constantly changing supply of bimbos. Each would last for a few months, maybe a year, then he'd grow restless, consult the bimbos' *Exchange and Mart* and swap her for another, later model. When I was seeing a lot of him I kept aloof from his live-in women because, for some reason, they doted on him so much that when the inevitable time of redundancy came I could find myself, if I knew them too well, sharing their pain. But I instinctively liked this one, this Annie, and I rather hoped he might keep her for a bit.

Donovan was waiting for us in a first-floor sitting-room expensively furnished in keeping with the eighteenth-century style of the house. I gave it a long, slow examination and nodded appreciatively.

'Like it?'

'Love it,' I said. 'Must have cost an arm and a leg — someone else's arm and leg naturally. Or did it all fall off the back of a lorry?'

'This kind of stuff?' Donovan snorted derisively. 'Do me a favour. Anyway, I wouldn't have anything like that, anything wasn't kosher, not in my home. I entertain honest, responsible people here, you know — politicians, bankers, City men.'

'And some of them are honest and responsible, are they? Good to hear that.'

Donovan chuckled. 'Annie, love, get us some coffee, will you? Coffee all right for you, Bob, or you want something stronger?'

'Coffee's fine.'

Annie poured it from a Georgian silver pot into porcelain cups that were almost translucent. Donovan said, 'Thank you, darling. Now I'm sure you got things to do somewhere else . . .'

Annie gave a huge, exaggerated shrug and rolled her eyes at me. 'Oh, yes, master,' she said, bowing deeply to Donovan, 'me got many things to do. Me go do them now, leave master and friend to grown-up pow-wow.'

'Get out, you cheeky mare.'

She went, swinging her hips and bottom and pouting at us over her shoulder. Donovan watched her, smiling fondly.

'Had her long?' I asked.

'Good few months now. Met her at some theatre party, West End musical I'd put some money into. She was in the chorus. Lively little cow.' I couldn't think of any West End musical with that title so I assumed he was talking about Annie. 'Don't suppose you knew I'd become an angel, did you?'

'Hard to imagine you in that role, Donovan. I always think of angels with harps and wings, not stocking masks and sawn-off shotguns.'

'Same old Bob,' Donovan said heavily. 'Quick as a flash and witty with it. No, thing is I've got a lot of what you might call legitimate interests now. Nice chunk of one or two commercial television companies, that sort of thing. And once you're going legit it doesn't hurt to put your money about a bit — support the arts, drug rehabilitation, some of the charities the royals are involved in, give a few quid to the right political party. In this country, people think you're respectable you can get away with murder.'

Which in his case, of course, was literally true and I was about to say so when another, quite wondrous, thought struck me. 'Good God, Donovan, you're not after a knighthood, are you?'

'It's on the cards,' he said, smugly. 'Marvellous country this, Bobby. You can get anything you want, you set your mind to it and spend your money wisely. Besides, I deserve a little something, true blue patriot like me. I've done my bit for my country as you well know. I mean, fucking Sicilians tried to move in on the West End gambling, who saw them off?' He prodded his chest with a thick forefinger. 'Me.' Oddly enough it was true — he was true-blue English and patriotic. Despite his name, his looks and his obvious antecedents he saw himself as a Londoner, a Cockney. He liked the Irish and indeed employed many of them but he could become quite incensed if anyone accused him of being Irish himself.

I said 'You should aim higher. A life peerage, why not? Lord Baccarat of Roulette, that'd be a good title for you. Or Lord Pander of Bordello. Or — '

'Watch it, Bobby.' We finished our coffee and he said, 'What I asked you to come here about, this friend of mine, Archie Beckway's got himself into something that's beginning to look a bit heavy and I thought you might be able to give him a hand.'

'Why me? He's what, Minister for Industrial Development? I don't know anything about industry — or politics, come to that, except that on the whole it's an occupation that makes brothel-keeping look honest.'

Donovan waved this away impatiently. 'Spare me the political irony, Bobby. I've heard it all before. No, where I thought you might come in is you done, did, a good job with that California business last year. Regular little sleuth you turned out to be so I reckoned you might fancy another go at it.'

'I'm not a private eye, Donovan. I used to be a prizefighter. Now I'm a businessman. Of sorts. I'm not Sherlock Holmes.'

'Archie doesn't want bloody Sherlock Holmes. He doesn't want any kind of private eye. He wants someone he can trust — I want someone he can trust. Listen, this is a very delicate matter I'm talking about. One word of it leaks out and Archie's politically dead. That's why I'm asking you to help, because you're a mate and I trust you.' He shook his head irritably. 'You free? Got anything on today, I mean?'

'My time is yours.'

'Good. Then let's go see Archie now.' He got up and put on his jacket. It may have been Sunday and I may have been wearing jeans, Reeboks, an open-necked shirt and soft leather jacket but Donovan was in a dark Savile Row suit with white shirt and MCC tie. These potential knights can never let their standards slip.

'I'm going out, Annie,' he called up the staircase. 'See you after lunch.'

She put her head over the banisters two flights up. 'Don't hurry back. I'm thinking of getting a lover in. I might even get two.'

'Get your arse tanned, you talk to me like that.' Donovan blew her a kiss and we walked side by side down the staircase. 'How's your mum these days?'

'Haven't seen her for a week or two but I think she's fine. I'll tell her you were asking after her.'

'Yeah, do that.' He opened the front door. 'Your car or mine?'

'Mine's handy if you don't mind that it's not a Roller.'

He said generously that he didn't mind and we got into my car. 'Heard anything from Linda lately?' he asked.

I was silent for a moment. 'No. And if it's all the same to you we won't talk about that.'

'Poor old Bobby. Never have much

luck with women, do you? Take a tip from me, my son — slip 'em the old pork sword whenever you get the chance but whatever you do never give them your heart.'

'Well, thank you, dear Marje,' I said and shoved the car savagely into first gear.

THREE

Along Piccadilly going towards Hyde
Park we discussed last night's fight.
Donovan said the evening had turned
out pretty well, financially and otherwise. The rioting had stopped soon after
I left with most of the damage done to
the rioters themselves, courtesy of
Donovan's enthusiastic stewards, and
the argument with the disgruntled
American manager had also turned out
to Donovan's advantage.

When things had become a little
heated the American was asked
whether he really wanted to be carried
home on a stretcher because if he did
he was in luck — there was an ambu-
lance waiting in the car park, mostly in
case any of the fighters was seriously
hurt but easily able to accommodate
damaged managers as well, and the
nearest intensive care unit was on alert.
Donovan himself he was assured,
would send flowers and just hoped the
American would have enough nose left
to smell them with.

'Feisty little bugger,' Donovan said, with grudging admiration. 'Just trying it on, of course. I'd given him a bigger purse than he'd ever get in the States but he thought he was dealing with some hick. He carried on effing and blinding until I began to think I'd really have to do him some harm just to shut him up. But then, I don't know how it came about, I mentioned a couple of blokes I do business with in New York and Vegas and as soon as he heard their names he turned sort of thoughtful and quietened down. After that he gave me no more trouble.'

We went through the Park into Parliament Square and turned right along the Embankment. In the summer sunshine the Park, the Palace of Westminster and the Abbey were all looking their best for the tourist trade.

'How do you come to know Archie Beckway?' I asked.

'We did some business together, oh, way back when, before he even became an MP.'

I nodded. 'He's bent then.'

'I wish you wouldn't say things like that, Bobby. Of course he's not bent. He's a Minister of the Crown, for Chrissake.' Donovan ignored my hollow laugh. 'All right, I'm not saying he hasn't cut a few corners in his time, maybe done a few dodgy things, and I'm not saying he doesn't go wherever his John Thomas leads him — or used to, anyway — but he's not what I'd call bent.'

'So what's this bother he's in then?'

'He'll tell you that.'

'Why can't you tell me?'

'Because it's his story and he tells it better. I might leave out some of the juicy bits and that'd be a shame because I'm talking really juicy here.' He put his hand on my arm. 'Here we are, next turning on the right.'

Beckway had a two-bedroom flat in Dolphin Square, a discreet, comfortable compound of residential blocks which gives the impression that nothing much has changed since the 1930s and that the people who live there mind their own business. Even so it was an unexpected place to find a man like Beckway.

'I thought he was pretty well off,' I said, as we got into the lift. 'Couple of houses here and there, that sort of thing.'

'This isn't his home,' Donovan said. 'Good God, no. He's got a place in Hertfordshire and a town house near me. He took the flat here when his London house was being done up and he just kept it on as a sort of fornicatorium, where he comes to be private like when he's got a bit of pussy with him.' We got out at the third floor and Donovan pressed Beckway's doorbell. 'See how nicely situated it is?' he said, grinning. 'Right opposite the lift. Smuggle the pussy in, smuggle the pussy out and nobody any the wiser. Well, that's how he used to do it anyway. They tell me he's cleaned up his act these days.'

Beckway opened the door himself. He was about 45, my height give or take an inch, with a trim figure and the kind of looks that probably made him a shoo-in with the more susceptible female voters. His eyes were blue and long-lashed; his hair, swept back at the sides, was thick and luxuriant and iron-grey. Well, I thought it looked iron-grey but he probably called it gunmetal-grey, gunmetal sounding more macho than plain old iron. He wore expensive slacks and a sports shirt and a slightly worried look about the eyes.

Donovan introduced us saying, 'Archie, this is the feller I told you about, Bobby Lennox, good bloke.'

Beckway shook hands, a hearty, over-firm politician's handshake, oozing sincerity. He gave the impression that if I'd been holding a baby he'd have kissed it. 'You don't look like a fighter,' he said. 'The build, yes, but facially . . .'

'Only bad fighters look like fighters,' I said. 'The good ones stay unmarked. Look at Sugar Ray Leonard.' Actually, after I retired I'd had some plastic surgery to restore my nose to its original shape but I saw no reason to tell him that and the fact that I'd never been in Sugar Ray Leonard's class wasn't any of his business either. As far as I knew he didn't want me to punch anyone out for him.

The flat was soft colours and thick white carpet, armchairs big enough for two to cuddle up in, lamps strategically placed to give the most flattering light. It looked like a man's flat designed with women in mind.

'Please,' Beckway said, 'make yourselves comfortable.' We sat; he stood, fidgeting and ill at ease. 'I've got some sandwiches and wine. Not much of a

Sunday lunch, I'm afraid . . .'

We assured him that sandwiches and wine would be acceptable and he pottered in and out of the kitchen, burbling about the weather and bringing food, drink, plates and glasses. On closer examination he was not quite as dashingly handsome as he had first appeared. Certainly he had the authentic matinee idol's profile but there was something about the eyes and mouth — the eyes a little too anxious, the mouth not quite firm enough — that suggested a rather too eager desire to be liked. To me it all denoted weakness, though I daresay women would have given him the benefit of the doubt and interpreted it as vulnerability.

With growing impatience Donovan watched him flitting around. 'For God's sake, Archie,' he said, finally. 'Sit down. Talk to us. We haven't got all bloody day.'

Beckway sat down and sank a glass of Sancerre in one long gulp. Then he stared at the carpet for a bit and said, 'This is very awkward, very embarrassing. I don't . . . I don't quite know where to start.'

Donovan grunted. 'Then I'll start. Somebody's got to, for Chrissake.' He twisted round in the big armchair and addressed himself to me. 'Last Tuesday Archie's at the BBC Television Centre, Shepherd's Bush, right? He's on that political programme. You know the one? Kevin Whatsisface — Rycroft, Kevin Rycroft. Anyway, afterwards he goes down to the hospitality room, nips out for a leak and these three blokes pounce on him in the loo.'

I looked sympathetically at Beckway. 'What? They mugged you, assaulted you?'

Beckway shook his head. 'No, no. Well . . . Yes, in a way.' He took a deep breath. 'All right, I'd better tell it . . .'

So he did and as Donovan had promised the juicy bits were there. But he told it in a dull, flat voice in which the pain, the shame and the humiliation broke through. I listened attentively, ignoring the suggestive winks and grimaces Donovan threw my way as Beckway told us what the girl had done to him and he to her. When he had finished I said: 'What did you do then, after they'd gone?'

He shrugged. 'I got dressed and went back to the hospitality room and then . . .'

Well, then everyone had looked at him rather strangely for he had been away a long time. Kevin Rycroft and his producer were smirking, as at some private joke, and he could guess what they were thinking. They had seen him follow Lacy out of the room and assumed that something had happened between them, probably in his dressing-room.

Only Beckway's minder, Freddie Marcus, had seemed at all concerned. He said, 'Are you all right, Minister? I went looking for you but the nearest men's room was out of order and I'm afraid I couldn't find you.'

'Good of you, Freddie. I . . . I, er, I've been rather sick. Something I ate, I think.' The irony of what he was saying was not lost on him even at that bleak moment.

The producer said, 'Oh dear, I hope it wasn't anything we gave you. The chicken or . . .'

'No. No, it was probably something at lunch. Prawns. I had some prawns . . . Do excuse me but I think I'd better go home.'

They bustled solicitously around him and escorted him to the car, Marcus protectively holding his arm and trying to make light conversation to keep Beckway's mind off whatever it was that ailed him. As he eased the Minister into the back seat of the limousine Marcus murmured something, something bright and chatty. Beckway, only half listening, said, 'Not now, Freddie, if you don't mind. I'm not feeling at my best. Tell me tomorrow.'

'Of course, Minister,' Marcus said and closed the door.

As the chauffeur drove slowly from the forecourt Beckway, glancing through the back window, saw Rycroft and the producer still smirking after him.

I said, 'So you didn't tell anyone what had happened? Not even your minder?'

'Christ no. Do you think I'm mad? If a story like that got out . . .'

'And you didn't notice anything, I don't know, different, suspicious, when you went back to the hospitality room?'

He thought about it. 'No, nothing.' Then doubtfully, 'Well, the girl wasn't there.' And when, in chorus, Donovan and I said, 'What girl?' he said, 'Lacy, the floor manager, I mentioned her. She . . . Well, I wasn't actually going to the loo, I was following her. She was very pretty, very sexy and I thought she was coming on to me.'

Donovan said, 'Shit, you might have mentioned this before. When did you tell me about it, the rest of it? Wednesday, was it? You never said a word about chasing a bit of skirt out of the room.'

Beckway flushed, looking guilty. 'I haven't done anything like that for a long time now. I mean, the way the tabloid press are looking into politician's private lives like the fucking Inquisition . . . Well, you know all this, Donovan. I've been using the girls at your place in Mayfair. But this one, this Lacy, I don't know, she kind of got to me and I knew she was keen and, OK, when she left the room I followed her. But nothing happened. I never saw her again. It just didn't seem important.'

I said, 'Not important? You follow this girl, who's been giving you the come-on, then a man shoves you into a lavatory, all those other things happen and when you get back the girl's gone and you don't think that's important?'

Beckway said, as if the thought had never occurred to him before, 'You mean . . . You mean, she might have had something to do with it? She might have been the girl in the men's . . . ? No, that's impossible. Same sort of height and build, I suppose, but . . .' He shook his head firmly. 'It was coincidence. It must have been. She works for the BBC.'

Donovan nodded. 'She works for the BBC and that makes her kosher. Is that what you're saying? You don't think villains have ever worked for the BBC?'

Beckway put his head in his hands and stared at the carpet again. 'I don't know what to think. I'm not even sure I'm thinking straight at all. I'm worried, Donovan. Jesus, I'm more than worried — I'm terrified, especially after what happened on Friday.'

Donovan and I looked at each other and he said, 'Friday? You mean there's something more? What the fuck happened on Friday?'

Beckway told us that, too.

FOUR

Friday had begun as a normal sort of day at the Ministry of Industrial Development. Beckway had turned up at about ten o'clock and, guided by his Civil Servants, had shuffled bits of paper around, signed a document or two and been briefed on a couple of questions that would arise in Parliament that afternoon.

Then, at midday, he received a phone call, just one of many that day but crucially different from the rest. In the first place it didn't come through the switchboard but on his direct line, his private line.

And in the second place the caller, who had a strong Northern Irish accent, said, 'Good morning, Minister, this is your Personal Photographic Service and how do I find you this fine afternoon?'

It was the call Beckway had been expecting and dreading and yet it still came as a shock, almost like a blow in the pit of the stomach. He said, 'Sorry? What, what did you say?'

72

The Irishman sighed, tolerantly. 'Ah, come now, Minister, you know perfectly well what I said. Did you really think we'd be forgetting you after the jolly evening we spent together?'

Beckway's secretary put her head round the door. He mouthed 'Get out' at her and then he said, 'What do you want?'

'Oh, dear, oh, dear. Straight down to business, I see. No hello, no chat about the weather. The social niceties have vanished, have you noticed that? The pace of life is too fast these days, Minister. You'll have to learn to relax or you'll be getting yourself an ulcer.'

'Just tell me,' Beckway said deliberately, 'what the fuck you want.'

There was a chuckle at the other end of the line. 'So be it, Minister. I'll get straight to the matter in hand: if you go to your Dolphin Square apartment tonight there'll be an envelope waiting for you. Sure, there'll be nothing in it to surprise you but I think you'll find the contents interesting.'

Beckway said, 'I ask again: what is it you want?'

'That you'll know soon enough, believe me. In the meantime just enjoy what's in the envelope and be glad it didn't fall into other hands. You'll hear from me again, Minister, have no fear about that, but for the moment, pleasure though it always is to be talking to you, I'll say goodbye.'

And then the line went dead.

'OK,' I said, 'so what was in the envelope?'

Beckway moved heavily, like a much older man, to a desk in the corner of the room, unlocked it and came back with a plain manila envelope, which he handed to me.

It had been addressed to A. Beckway Esq. and posted in central London. In it were two photographs. Both featured a half-naked Beckway and a nearly-naked girl. One showed fellatio, the other cunnilingus. Donovan, perched on the arm of my chair, said, 'Bloody hell! Well, at least we know the photos came out.'

I said, reproachfully, 'Donovan, please.'

'What? What did I say? What?'

I examined the pictures carefully; they were, after all, quite interesting. Beckway was instantly recognisable in both of them but his companion in sex was shot in such a way that she could have been almost any shapely young woman. 'What about the girl?' I said. 'Could she be somebody you know?'

Beckway shrugged, shook his head. Donovan said, 'Unlikely, Bob. She's probably a girlfriend of one of the blokes or maybe some old tom they hired, some tart with a tattoo. I mean that thing on the top of her thigh there, what is it — some kind of fucking moth?'

'Well, a butterfly anyway. A Red Admiral, I think.' I looked at the pictures again. 'Now that's interesting. Come here.' Donovan and Beckway clustered around me. 'Look at this.' I pointed first to the cunnilingus photo, then to the fellatio. 'See that? In the second picture the butterfly's lost half a wing. It's not a tattoo at all, it's a transfer.'

'You must have licked it off, Archie,' Donovan said.

Beckway gestured impatiently at him. 'So what does that mean?'

I said, 'That it was a disguise, I suppose. Like the purple eyes. They were probably contact lenses. So, all right, a disguise for whatever that's worth. It could mean she is somebody you know

— one of the whores you've been using at Donovan's club perhaps.'

'Hostesses,' Donovan said. 'We don't mention whores at my place.'

'Whatever. On the other hand it could mean anything. Maybe Donovan's right, maybe she was just some tom they'd hired who was being very careful. After all, if you here doing what she was doing you'd probably go to quite a lot of trouble to make sure nobody could identify you. Look at the photos again, Archie, see if you recognise anything.'

Beckway got a magnifying glass from the desk and pored earnestly over the pictures. I'm not at all sure he didn't enjoy it. But in the end he shook his head and said, 'I don't know, honestly. She's got a great figure but . . . I know a lot of women with great figures.'

Donovan and I took it in turns like serious scholars to study the photographs through the magnifying glass. The publisher of a hardcore porn magazine would probably have paid a fortune for them but they offered no particular revelations to either of us. If there was any telltale sign on Minnie Mouse's body, like a strawberry birthmark, she wasn't showing it.

I put the pictures back in their envelope. 'So the next question is: who are these people?'

'The IRA?' Donovan said. 'A Loyalist outfit? Some of those crazy buggers haven't given up the fight even now. I'm not talking politics here, I'm talking organised crime because that's what a lot of them are into — protection rackets, that sort of stuff.'

Beckway shook his head. 'What would people like that want with me? I mean, it'll clearly come down to blackmail in the end, but for what? If it was simply money they'd surely have said so by now.'

I said, 'Right. If they don't want money, what do they want? OK, Mickey Mouse comes from Northern Ireland but not everybody up there still hankers for sectarian warfare. On the other hand . . . Archie, is your ministry involved with anything in Ireland that would — '

'Just a couple of very small projects,' Beckway said. 'Besides, if anyone over there wanted to muscle in they could easily do it without anything as . . . as elaborate as this.'

Donovan helped himself to more wine.

'All right,' he said. 'Where does that leave us?' He started ticking points off on his fingers. 'We don't know who these bastards are and we don't know what they want. That doesn't leave us much to go on, does it?'

We agreed, Beckway and I, that it didn't. 'And that being so,' I said, 'what the hell am I doing here?'

Donovan and Beckway discussed that and what they agreed was that Beckway should take me on as a kind of personal assistant, someone to watch his back, to act as go-between — if that should become necessary — between him and his persecutors, to deliver the blackmail money if that was demanded and generally to sniff around and see what I could discover. It was a pretty vague brief but I was happy enough to take it on. I had little else to do at the time and my private life right then was a void in contemplation of which I had already spent far too much time these past few weeks. I needed to keep myself busy, to keep my mind occupied, and messing about on the fringes of politics seemed at least to offer something unusual.

It was Donovan who urged all this and who negotiated my fee while I sat back and listened. Beckway simply agreed, listlessly, to whatever was suggested, giving the impression that he didn't think anything good could come of it but that, on the whole, action — or anyway some kind of movement — was better than nothing.

He put all these doubts into words when he said, 'All right, fine, but where do we start?'

That, I thought, was the easy bit. 'Let's find out about the girl, Lacy, see what she knows. She fancies you so, OK, call her, invite her to dinner.'

Beckway said, 'Oh yes? Where am I supposed to take her? Have you any idea how awkward it is for me to be seen dining out with young women? It's almost landed me in trouble before with the tabloid press.'

'So bring her here. Who's going to know? I'm not asking you to invite the press —just me. I'll be your beard, your chaperon, to make sure your spotless reputation isn't compromised.'

He regarded me darkly, narked by the sarcasm, but eventually he agreed. He also agreed that I should go to see him the following afternoon in his office at the ministry where he would introduce me around and get his staff used to the fact that I might be dropping in occasionally. Then he looked at his watch and said, 'Right. See you tomorrow then.' All at once he was the politician again, the brisk man of important affairs. 'In the meantime I have to get back to Hertfordshire. My daughters are home for the weekend and I've hardly seen anything of them.'

He led us down to where his car was parked, a dark, anonymous, family model Ford which seemed as incongruous for a man of his wealth and position as the Dolphin Square flat.

Donovan said, 'Still got the old Pussymobile, I see.'

Beckway grinned, a sudden, rather charming smile. 'Yes, well, I'll probably get rid of it soon, reformed character that I am. Be a shame, though. It has a nostalgic hold on me, this car.' He waved and drove away and we watched him go.

'If that car could talk,' Donovan said, 'it could sell its memoirs to the *Sun* and name its own price.' He glanced up at the building we had just left. 'Same thing applies to the flat, I suppose. You couldn't even imagine what Archie used to get up to with women.'

'So what stopped him?' I asked, as we wandered over to my own car.

'Same thing that stopped all the other horny buggers in Parliament. Too much newspaper interest. MPs having their toes sucked, other MPs fathering illegitimate kids all over the place — newspapers were full of them. Well, Archie took note of all this, reckoned that if he carried on the way he was it'd be his turn next and put a padlock on his flies.'

We headed back down the Embankment towards Mayfair.

'So?' Donovan said. 'What do you think?'

'About Beckway? Hard to say. I've only just met him. But from what you tell me he sounds like a fairly considerable shit.'

Donovan made an impatient gesture. 'Of course he's a shit. Given a free rein Archie would make your average tom cat look more or less celibate. But he's a likeable shit.'

'I'll have to take your word for that. As for the bother he's in, who can tell? Until we know what exactly Mickey Mouse wants it's anyone's guess.' I manoeuvred carefully round Parliament Square to avoid running over half a dozen Japanese tourists who had decided that the best place from which to take decent photographs of Westminster Abbey was slap in the middle of the traffic lanes.

'Look at the silly bastards,' Donovan said, disgustedly, as the photographers skipped out of the way, bowing and smiling and apologising. Donovan doesn't like the Japanese; he doesn't like the Germans; he doesn't like anybody Britain used to be at war with. He does have his good points, trust me, but against that he has others that you'd have to be a member of the Ku Klux Klan to appreciate.

I said, 'Why did Beckway come to you for help?'

'Well, put yourself in his place. You're a member of the Government, you're in deep shit and you know me, so who else are you gonna call? The Prime Minister? What do you say to him — "Oh by the way, PM, there's this photo going the rounds of me giving some tattooed tart a right plating, can you help?" I can't see that getting a standing ovation in Downing Street.'

'I take your point.' I turned off Berkeley Square into the street where Donovan lived. The Filipino girl was walking the poodle again. I waved and smiled; she smiled and waved back.

'Who's that?' Donovan said. 'Tasty little number.'

'Just an admirer.' I pulled up outside his house and gave two loud blasts on the car horn.

He jumped a little at the unexpected noise. 'What did you do that for?'

'A little warning to Annie. Give her time to hide her lover in the wardrobe.'

He leaned back against the car door and gave me a long, thoughtful scrutiny. 'There are times I wonder about you, Bobby. Whose side are you on?'

'Yours, Donovan, always yours. But I worry about your bimbos, too. It seems to me you don't always treat them very nicely.'

He sighed. 'Look at me,' he said. 'Take a good look. I'm an old fart, right? I'm overweight and I got more lines on my face than British Telecom. So what do these girls of mine — these bimbos as you so elegantly call them — what do they see in me? Animal magnetism? Bollocks. What they see is a rich and powerful man and for some women, not necessarily bad women, there's no such thing as an unattractive rich and powerful man. I mean, give him a few quid and the power to tell other people what to do and Quasifuckingmodo would be beating women off with a stick. Now, OK, I accept that. So what I have with my girls is a working arrangement. They're good to me and I'm good to them — while it lasts. And I decide how long it lasts because I'm the rich and powerful one. But when it finishes, when I reckon it's time for a change, I pack 'em off with a tidy sum in the bank and you'd be surprised, Bob, how fast their tears dry up when they pop into Barclays to check the state of their deposit accounts.' He turned his gaze away from me and looked up towards his house where Annie waited for him. 'You get what you pay for in this life, son. I pay in my way, the girls pay in theirs. It's a business deal, you care to look at it that way. They're happy and I'm happy. You want to come in for a cup of tea?'

I shook my head. 'Things to do. Give my love to Annie.'

'Certainly not. Might put ideas in her

head. You're a lot younger than me, Bobby, and in your way you're not a bad-looking bloke. While Annie's with me I want her undivided attention — I don't want her mooning about the place sighing over some broken-down pug with a pretty face.'

He climbed out of the car, grunting, and I said, 'That's the nicest thing you've ever said to me, Donovan.'

'Yeah, well, it's my silver tongue. Men and women, it wins 'em all over in the end.' He shut the passenger door and stooped to look in through the open window. 'Keep in touch. On the Archie business. I don't want anything bad happening to Archie. He's too important to me.'

He was still standing there on the kerbside looking at his house as I drove away around the corner.

FIVE

I have a flat in Chelsea, a big one with a terrace from which I can look out over the Thames. I bought it when I was still boxing and it cost a small fortune even then. But that was before the property boom made its value soar and now, even allowing for fluctuations in the market, it's still the best investment I ever made, though some of my pleasure in it vanished when Linda walked out.

That had happened quite recently, recently enough anyway for her absence to be almost tangible when I got home after dropping Donovan. Every time I walked in I still half-expected to find her there or to find some sign that she had been there a moment ago and would be back soon — a scribbled note on the pad by the telephone perhaps, a hint of her scent in the air, a book left open on the sofa, a lipstick-smudged glass in the kitchen sink.

There was nothing like that. The place was just as I'd left it that morning, comfortable enough, even elegant in, as

I like to think, an understated way. And empty. There was no sign of Linda, no sign that she had ever lived there; not surprising really since I'd gathered up all the inconsequential bits and pieces she had left behind and locked them in a cupboard in the spare bedroom. The debris of a broken relationship, out of sight if not out of mind.

I looked up the number of Teddy Davies's newspaper and rang it.

'Ted? Bobby Lennox. That drink we said we'd have, you don't fancy having it tonight, do you?'

'Bobby, my boy! I didn't expect to hear from you so soon. You must want something.'

'Ah. Obvious as that, is it?'

'Of course.' He chuckled. 'Where do you want to meet?'

'The Ivy, 7.30, dinner, I'm buying.'

'Nothing wrong with any of that. What's my contribution to the evening?'

'Anything you can tell me about Archie Beckway.'

He gave a little murmur of surprise. 'The Minister? You're not thinking of going into politics, are you? Bobby, please tell me you're not thinking of going into politics. You're an intelligent man — you could hold down a decent job, a useful job.'

'No, no. Things aren't that desperate. It's . . . well, I'll tell you about it at dinner.'

What I told him at dinner was that I was making enquiries on behalf of a friend. OK — a lame story but lame stories sometimes have that ring of truth just because they are lame.

'A woman,' Teddy said, nodding and chewing smoked salmon with equal vigour. 'This friend's a woman, right?'

'Why do you say that?'

'Bound to be. Oh, we all know about Beckway, all of us in Fleet Street, or what used to be Fleet Street until the great newspaper diaspora. Trouble is, we can't nail the bugger down. Every now and then the tabloids get a shot of him with some woman and throw out the usual insinuations but there's never any real scandal. He covers his tracks well, I'll say that for him.'

'Any insinuations lately?'

He shook his head. 'No, come to think of it. Not for a year or so, not since that wonderful period when you could hardly open a newspaper without reading about yet another adulterous MP.

Those were the days. I remember I was covering a fight and one of the boxers took about six counts and I said he was up and down like a Cabinet Minister's trousers. Good line, that.'

I cut the reminiscences short and spun him a tale about an accountant friend of mine, male, who'd been offered a job with Beckway's firm. I'd decided on this line because one of the few things I knew about Beckway was that he controlled a very big industrial publishing house. This friend, I said, was greatly flattered by Beckway's interest but before uprooting himself from the very agreeable job he already had in advertising he wanted to know what kind of a person he would be working for.

Teddy didn't believe a word of it. 'I should have thought a bloke in advertising could have found out all he needed to know for himself.'

'Well, yes,' I said, 'but I think he was hoping for some inside information.'

'Dirt, you mean.' Teddy signalled to the waiter that another bottle of Chablis was urgently required. He wasn't paying, after all. 'Is there likely to be a story in this? Because if so I want it exclusively for my paper, okay?'

'If there's a story, it's yours. That's a promise. So tell me . . .'

Swiftly Teddy outlined Beckway's potted biography: only child of elderly parents, father a well-to-do builder in the Home Counties. Minor public school, engineering degree from Durham University. Inherited the family firm on his father's death when he was in his mid-twenties and quickly earned himself a reputation as a whizz kid by building it up into one of the biggest companies of its kind in the country.

He was a millionaire several times over by the age of thirty, at which point he became involved in local politics and married into the aristocracy.

'The Hon. Felicity Parslow,' Teddy said, 'only child of Lord Watton, the fourth baron. Good marriage for both of them, I suppose. Shoved Beckway up the social ladder and injected some much-needed cash into the Watton family. The old boy was a bit of a drunk, well, a right piss-artist actually. Never earned a penny in his life and had just about boozed his way through everything his old man left him when Archie came along. Virtually all he had to his name was the family seat, nice little Elizabethan manor house in Hertfordshire.'

'Not exactly a love match then? More of a business deal?'

Teddy shrugged. 'Who knows? They're still together, though I imagine that must have been touch and go for a bit . . .'

In the first three years of marriage the Beckways had two daughters, now both in their teens and, in Ted's delicate phrase, 'found out what was causing it and stopped there.' Just before the birth of the second child Lord Watton died, gloriously drunk, in his sleep. There being no male heirs the family home passed to Felicity. Six months later Beckway was involved in a divorce action instigated by an irate husband.

'Reading between the lines,' Teddy said, 'it could have been a very messy one, too, only I think a fair bit of money changed hands.'

'Archie bought the guy off?'

'Looks like it. According to our lobby correspondent — incidentally, I hope you notice how much research I've been doing on your behalf, young Bobby . . .'

I showed my gratitude by refilling his glass and in turn he drank deeply to show his appreciation.

'Anyway,' he said, 'it turns out the woman involved was the Hon. Felicity's best friend. Isn't it always? Apparently she and Archie had been going at it like rabbits on amyl nitrate for ages. How Felicity found out I don't know. How do wives ever find out? But when she did the shit hit the fan and things turned quite nasty. The best friend said Archie had promised to marry her, Archie denied it, the best friend tried to kill herself and her husband went after Archie with a shotgun.'

'He did what?'

Teddy grinned smugly. 'Thought you'd like that bit. Yeah, well, it seems the husband charges off to Hertfordshire, chases Archie out of his own house, through the garden and over a couple of fields and then, just as he's got him cornered, the gun jams. After that there's an undignified struggle for possession of the gun, which Archie wins, followed by a lot of weeping, mostly by the husband, then they sit down and talk and by the time they get back to the house they're like David and Jonathan. A little while later the best friend finds herself divorced and her ex-husband comes into enough money to set himself up with a smart little restaurant in the Cotswolds. You figure it out.'

I thought about it. 'Presumably none of the juicy bits came out at the time.'

Teddy shook his head. 'Quite a lot of it was known about, I gather, but, no, it didn't come out in court.'

'Ted, where do you get all this stuff?'

'I told you — our lobby correspondent. And he got it from the ex-husband. They were at school together.'

Still, there was a raunchy enough whiff clinging to the divorce case to hold Beckway's political ambitions in check for a few years during which time he concentrated on growing even richer. He profited hugely during the property boom of the 1980s and was shrewd enough to sell his building firm before the recession destroyed the market. In the meantime he had acquired and expanded an industrial printing house which also controlled enough national magazines and provincial newspapers to make its support important to whichever political party had the owner's sympathy. Beckway, dispensing his patronage wisely, duly entered Parliament in a profoundly safe seat thanks to a convenient by-election.

'He's very close to the Prime Minister, of course,' Teddy said. 'They reckon that's why this new office was created for him, Minister for Industrial Development. Provides a job for the PM's chum without rocking the boat, which would have happened if he'd landed an established post that should have gone to somebody more senior, and also gives the impression that the Government is interested in supporting industry, which is a fucking joke really. But what you have to remember is that it's only a start. Archie's after a Cabinet job and he'll get one, probably in the next reshuffle.'

Was I surprised by any of this? Not really and certainly not by Beckway's political ambitions. When a man is unassailably wealthy by the time he is thirty the only thing left for him is power — not just the power over individuals that money can buy but the power over a nation that politics can bestow. The fact that his very hunger for it made him immediately suspect in my eyes was neither here nor there. I just have this theory that in a well-ordered society power should automatically be denied to anyone who actually wants it; that the very last people who should be entrusted with running a country are professional politicians.

'Tell me about the wife,' I said. 'The Honourable Felicity. Why did she stick with Archie?'

'Who can tell?' Teddy pushed his dessert plate to one side and lit a cigarette. 'Maybe she really loves him. Maybe she just likes the thickness of the butter he spreads on the family bread. Maybe she stuck around for the sake of the children. Your guess is as good as mine. But by all accounts that wasn't the first time Archie had popped up in the wrong bed and I'm damn sure it wasn't the last either.'

I tried to conjure up a mental image of the Hon. Felicity. Big-boned and gawky, I thought. Hearty. Tweeds, pearls and twinsets. Long-faced with large white teeth and a tendency to neigh when she laughed. 'What does Felicity look like?'

Teddy said, surprising me this time, 'A touch gorgeous. Tall, slim and a great figure. She was on the stage for a while before she met Archie. Put it this way

— I wouldn't climb over her in bed to get at Demi Moore.'

'Not saying a lot. Demi Moore isn't my type.' Still, Teddy's description had piqued my curiosity, making me wonder even more why such a woman would stay with a libertine like Beckway.

'So what's it all about then?' Teddy said. 'I mean, really?'

'Like I told you.'

'Bullshit. But we've still got a deal, right? If there's a story I get it first.'

'Absolutely. Though I can't really see why a sports columnist should be interested in what a politician gets up to.'

'I'd get a lot of Brownie points at the paper if I could present them with a good front page exclusive.' He sighed. 'I tell you, Bobby, journalism's not what it was. The old characters — the bevvy merchants, the skirt-chasers — they've all gone. Sometimes I think I'm the only one left. This new breed, the young guys, they're all so earnest. Don't drink, don't screw. They'd rather go to the gym for a workout than get laid. Old timers like me are on our way out . . .'

It was getting to be that time of night, the maudlin time. Teddy had reached it early. I got him another brandy, paid the bill and poured him into a taxi. As the cab pulled away he was still chuntering on about the dullness of modern young journalists who watched their weight, drank diet Coke, drove bloody Volvos and, he darkly suspected, probably practised safe sex even when they were masturbating.

SIX

The Ministry for Industrial Development was housed in a great, grey concrete slab just off Marsham Street in Westminster. The uniformed commissionaire in his cubby-hole checked my name against a list on his desk, gave me a visitor's pass, told me where to go and directed me across the glum foyer to the lifts.

I got out at the fifth floor where a plump young woman was plucking her eyebrows at the reception desk. I told her who I was and said the Minister was expecting me. She murmured something into one of the phones on her desk, told me to take a seat and said Beergut would look after me.

I said, 'Who?' She giggled, said, 'Beergut. You'll see,' picked up her handbag and trotted off down the corridor to the ladies' loo. It was suddenly very quiet out there in the anteroom, no sign or sound of life anywhere, and I was just beginning to wonder whether I had stumbled into some governmental ver-

sion of the *Marie Celeste* when the door
to what were presumably the ministerial offices opened and a very fat man
came out. He looked at the deserted
desk, paused and hesitated.

I stood up. 'Beergut?' I said.

He turned towards me. 'What?'

'Are you Beergut?' And my voice was
faltering because even as I spoke I was
thinking, Jesus, no he isn't, he may
look like it but he isn't, and cursing
myself for taking any notice of what the
girl had said.

His face had been pretty red to start
with but now it turned crimson. 'How
dare you? How bloody dare you?'

'Look, I'm very sorry. I . . . The secretary — '

'Not that it's any of your business, you
insulting bastard, but I happen to suffer from a seriously underactive thy-
roid.' He whipped round, if a man built
on the general lines of an ocean-going
tanker could ever be said to whip, and
went back whence he had come. I
dropped back into my chair, hot with
embarrassment. A few minutes later
the door opened again and a tall, blonde
young woman came through.

'Mr Lennox?' Her voice was soft,

educated, a little husky.

I nodded.

'I hear you've been very rude to the Minister's PPS.'

I said, shakily, 'What?'

'His Parliamentary Private Secretary. He's very upset.'

'Is that who it was? Oh God. I thought — '

She offered a slim hand which I took and shook somewhat limply. 'I'm the Minister's personal assistant.' She gave me a cool, appraising look — not approving, just appraising. 'I'm also Beergut,' she said.

'You?' The one thing she didn't have was a beergut. Well, she didn't have a goitre or a hump either but she certainly didn't have a beergut. If she had any spare flesh on her at all it was in the places where it did its best work.

She pointed towards the deserted desk. 'The fat little trollop who occasionally sits there, in the rare moments when she's not redecorating her spotty face in the loo, is the one who calls me that.' She stared moodily at the receptionist's empty chair. 'She's leaving on Friday, getting married, can you believe that? Why any man would want to marry . . . Aha.' Her lips curved slowly in a malicious grin. She walked over to the desk and paused, looking down at a polystyrene cup beside the blotting pad. Then with the middle finger of her right hand she gave the cup a sharp flick. It teetered for a moment before falling backwards and about half a pint of cold tea spread like a small tidal wave over the Filofax on the blotter, soaking it thoroughly before saturating all the other papers on the desk and finally trickling over the edge onto the seat of the receptionist's chair. 'Oh dear,' she said. 'What a shame.' She looked upon her work for a moment or two and, presumably finding it good, turned back to me with a bright smile. 'Shall we go and see the Minister?'

I had watched all this with bemused interest, reckoning that if such behaviour was par for the course around here life in a government office must be a lot more exciting than I'd thought. 'Why does she call you Beergut?' I asked.

'It's the ignorant little slag's idea of a joke. My name is actually Birgit, after my maternal grandmother. She was German, you know. This way, Mr Lennox.'

She opened the door into the ministerial offices and ushered me through. We went first into what was clearly her own office — white painted, grey carpeted; a desk with a row of phones, a word processor and a vase of red roses. I noticed a few well-tended indoor plants and two or three good prints, landscapes mostly, before she knocked on another door, opened that, said, 'Mr Lennox, Minister,' and ushered me through there, too. As I walked in the fat PPS passed me on his way out. He didn't say anything, just glared balefully and shut the door with a bang behind him.

Beckway's office was on the luxurious side — a deep, plum-coloured carpet, panelled walls, a large, uncluttered mahogany desk, leather armchairs and a matching sofa, oil paintings including one of the Queen and framed photographs of Beckway with various other prominent layabouts, among them the Prime Minister.

'Minister,' I said.

He got up, shirtsleeved and tie loosened, from behind the desk to shake hands. 'Please. Carry on calling me Archie and I'll call you Bobby, if that's all right.' He made a vague sort of gesture with his free hand. 'All these diminutives. How very British. But if we're going to struggle through this bloody awful mess together we might as well be informal about it. Tea?' I shook my head. 'No, thanks.'

'Don't blame you. We really do drink far too much of the stuff in government offices.' He pointed me towards the leather armchair, which sighed gently as I sank into it, while he resumed his place behind the desk.

Here in his power base, surrounded by the trappings of an important man, he was more impressive than he had seemed the previous day. There was a confidence about his movements, his body language, that had been missing before, yet even so there was something a touch illusory about this apparent assurance for there was still that flicker of uncertainty in his eyes. There was still the too-ready, too-eager smile as if no matter how high his own opinion of himself he was never entirely sure that everyone else shared it.

'How do you want to play this?' he asked.

'Well, to start with, who knew you

were going to be at the Television Centre that night?'

'Apart from various people at the BBC?' He frowned. 'Practically everyone around here, I suppose. So that's, what, a dozen, maybe two dozen people? My activities — my official activities — are hardly a secret in this place.' The frown became a little deeper. 'Sometimes I wonder about my unofficial activities as well.'

It didn't help much. Mickey Mouse and his team had obviously known where Beckway would be but it looked as though they could have got that information almost anywhere.

'What about whatshername, the floor manager?'

'Lacy Jones? Ah, yes, well she's coming to dinner tonight at Dolphin Square. Eight o'clock.' He grinned, deprecatingly. 'She seemed quite eager, positively delighted in fact. I, er, I didn't tell her you'd be there, too. No point in spoiling her anticipation of the evening.'

'Thanks very much. But shouldn't you be in the House of Commons tonight?'

'Oh, no problem. There's only routine stuff going on and, anyway, I've paired myself with my shadow on the Opposition benches. He jumped at the chance of a night off, wants to go and see his mother apparently.' He shook his head, seemingly amazed that anyone should wish to waste a free evening visiting his mother. 'Anything else?'

I gave it some thought but very little came to mind. 'I'd better meet your immediate staff, I suppose, get them used to me. What have you told them?'

'Very little. I just said you were a business associate, a friend, and you might be dropping in occasionally.' He got up and opened the door. 'Birgit, bring the others in, will you?'

The others came in, half a dozen or so assorted civil servants from the Permanent Secretary down, the people who were in closest contact with Beckway. None of them was Irish; none had the physical build of the men Beckway had described. Nobody wore a Mickey Mouse mask. They shook hands, made small talk for a few minutes and left. The fat PPS wasn't among them but, as Beckway said, 'I gather you've already met and offended him. Unfortunately, he didn't know about Birgit's nickname, though considering his shape it probably wouldn't have helped if he had.' He shuffled some papers about on his desk. 'You don't think any of them, any of my people, is involved do you?'

'Could be. At this stage it's anybody's guess.' I got up to leave. Beckway didn't bother to see me out.

'Until tonight then,' he said from his desk. 'About 8.30 if you don't mind. Give Lacy time to settle in, feel relaxed.' I had noticed before that whenever he mentioned her a little gleam came into his eyes. I was beginning to get the uneasy feeling that his loins if not his head were hankering for the old days and the libertine ways he claimed to have renounced. If she could have that effect upon him at a time like this, I thought, the Lacy woman should be worth meeting.

At the door another thought struck me. 'One person I haven't met,' I said, 'and that's the minder who was with you at the TV Centre that night.'

'Freddie Marcus? Ah, yes, well he's not around, I'm afraid. He had some very bad news that same night, as a matter of fact. When he got home he heard that his son had been rather badly hurt in a car crash in France. Lyons, Avignon, one of those places.

106

The boy works there apparently. Anyway, Freddie got the news and he and his wife dashed off immediately to look after their daughter-in-law and the grandchildren. I've no idea when he'll be back.'

'Find out, will you?'

'You mean now? Why?'

I shrugged. 'I've met everyone else around here.'

'OK.' He got on the phone, talked and listened for a while and when he had hung up, he said, 'He'll be back tonight. About seven. Seems the son's recovering nicely. Freddie's wife is staying over for a while but Freddie will be in the office tomorrow. Are you planning to see him?'

I nodded.

'Be bloody careful what you say,' he said, anxiously. 'What do you want to talk to him about anyway?'

'I don't know. Anything he might have seen, heard, while he was roaming the corridors looking for you.'

'He didn't mention anything. He chattered a lot while he was walking me to my car. Trying to cheer me up, I suppose, because he thought I wasn't feeling well. But I don't remember him saying anything that might be . . .' He stopped. 'Yes, he did. As I got into the car he said, what was it now? That's right, he said, "You'll never guess who I saw in the corridor this evening".'

'Did he say who it was?'

'No. He was going to but I wasn't in much of a mood for chitchat.'

'Pity.'

We stared at each other. Beckway said, 'Hey, come on. It was probably some old mate of his, someone he was at school with. You don't think . . .'

'Nothing to be lost by asking him,' I said. 'Where does Freddie live?'

In the anteroom the plump receptionist, her face stained with tears, was saying, 'I'm ever so sorry, Miss Cassidy, really I am. I don't know how it can have happened. My Filofax is all ruined.'

Birgit, looming sternly over her, said, 'Serves you right, you clumsy girl.' She swapped her scowl for a dazzling white smile and turned it upon me. 'Goodbye, Mr Lennox. So nice to meet you. I look forward to seeing you again.' When I got to the lift and looked back she was still watching me, still smiling. I waved; she waved back. I had no idea what to make of her.

SEVEN

Freddie Marcus owned a smart terraced house in Westminster. It struck me as a bit upmarket for a publicity minder but then I remembered that this was an area that had been gentrified, that once upon a time these had been council houses, provided at subsidised rent for the needy. But a few years back the council had sold them off and quite a few people in and around politics had been able to buy them at particularly favourable prices. Lucky for some — among them, I assumed, Freddie.

At a little before 8.30 the road was quiet, the householders indoors eating supper or watching the telly. A mile or so away Beckway was probably feeding gin and tonic to Lacy Jones and not feeling remotely sorry that I had forsaken dinner with them in order to come and see Marcus.

'You'll never guess who I saw . . .' It could mean anything; it could mean nothing, but it was at least worth following up. Whoever the person was, he or she was someone known to Marcus and very probably to Beckway and, presumably, someone whom Marcus had not expected to see roaming the corridors of Television Centre in the late evening.

Well, as Beckway had said, it could have been anyone. It could have been Beckway's cleaning lady, moonlighting at the BBC; it could have been, for heaven's sake, the Prime Minister and I wondered what he would look like in a Mickey Mouse mask, sweatshirt and jeans. No, not the Prime Minister, I thought. He didn't have the build for it.

But whoever it was, it was worth checking out, if only because right then I couldn't think of anything else to check out.

Marcus had been expected home about seven and I'd given him an hour or so to settle in before springing myself upon him. I had with me a note from Beckway to introduce me and to assure the publicity man that he could speak to me freely and in confidence.

Which was all very well but what was I going to say if Marcus asked me why I wanted to know whom he had seen that night?

I locked my car and walked the few yards to Marcus's house. What would I say? Something like, 'I am not at liberty to reveal my motives?' Or, 'My lips are sealed?' Or, 'Mind your own bloody business?' Or . . .

The front door was open — not all the way open but slightly ajar. It didn't worry me, not right then; it just surprised me. People in London didn't leave their houses open even on a summer evening, not if they were smart.

I rang the bell and heard it sounding sharp and clear in the hallway. Nobody responded. I rang it again and then a third time. Still nothing. I called his name. Nobody replied.

So then I pushed the door open and walked in, thinking we'd be getting off to a lousy start if the irate householder suddenly appeared and demanded to know what the hell I thought I was doing, a total stranger, marching unbidden into his home and —

The householder, not irate — just dead — was lying, face down, at the end of the hallway. The back of his head had been smashed in. A heavy, blood-smattered brass vase lay beside him, the flowers it had once held strewn around him like some premature funeral offering.

Gingerly I raised one limp arm and checked his pulse. The body was still warm but he was dead all right.

I went back and closed the front door and looked around. At the foot of the stairs there were two suitcases with Air France baggage tags. In the sitting-room to the left of the hall I found the telephone and the answering machine, one of those old-fashioned numbers that was sophisticated enough to cut in after so many rings but not sophisticated enough to cut out if somebody then picked up the receiver. I'd owned one myself, oh, back in the dark ages, at least ten years ago. It didn't know what was important and what wasn't, so it recorded everything it heard. The red light on Marcus's machine was blinking.

Quite a few of the callers had been Marcus's friends and colleagues, asking after his son, offering sympathy. Some were hang-ups, no message left.

There was only one call that interested me. A woman had picked up the phone and said, 'Hello, who's that?' And a Northern Irish voice had asked, 'Is Mr

Marcus there?' The woman had said, 'No, he's away I'm afraid. He won't be back till Monday evening. Can I take a message? I'm the cleaning —' And then the Irishman had rung off.

I played the tape through to the end but there was nothing else.

Marcus was still lying at the back of the hall and I left him there while I went out to my car. He wasn't going anywhere.

On my carphone I called Beckway's Dolphin Square number. The answering machine clicked into play. 'I'm afraid there's nobody here to take your call at the moment. If you care to . . .'

'Come on Archie,' I said, 'pick up the fucking phone. This is important. I know you're there — talk to me.' Wherever he was, whatever he was doing he either couldn't hear me or chose to take no notice.

So then I went back into the house and called the police.

They didn't hang about, I had to grant them that. First a couple of uniforms turned up in a Panda car and when I told them who the dead man was they were swiftly followed by a detective inspector and his sergeant and then the scene of crime officer with a whole bunch of technicians.

The DI and the sergeant led me into the dining-room, the room nearest the front door, and we sat round a dark, polished table while they took my statement. I said I'd come to deliver a message from Beckway — best wishes, glad the injured boy was recovering, Marcus not to hurry back to the office if he still had family business to clear up, that sort of stuff.

The DI nodded. 'Why didn't Mr Beckway come himself?'

'Too busy, I suppose. He's a government minister, he's got the country to run.'

Another nod. 'Yeah, but see, what I don't understand is why he sent you. I mean, you're a fighter, aren't you?' He was a tall, cocky blond, about my age, with cynical eyes.

'Was. Now I'm a businessman, an associate of Mr Beckway's. I'm, er, joining his publishing firm.'

'Know all about publishing, do you?'

'No, but I'm a quick learner. Look I've known Archie Beckway on and off for a good few years, he found out I was at a loose end, looking for something to do, so he offered me a job and I took it.'

'Hmm.' He tapped on the table for a moment or two with a ballpoint pen. 'You know what else bothers me a little, Mr Lennox? You don't look very upset for a man who's just discovered a murder. Does he look very upset to you, Clive?'

The sergeant said, 'No.' He was clearly the strong, silent type because this was the first word I'd heard him speak.

I shrugged. 'I used to be a fighter, remember? I'm used to seeing blood.'

'Yeah, well, you spilt quite a lot of it yourself, didn't you? In that fight with Willie Slate, for instance.'

'Thanks for reminding me.'

A uniformed constable put his head round the door and beckoned to the DI. 'Guv? Can I have a word?'

The DI went out into the hall and shut the door behind him. Clive and I sat in silence until he came back and resumed his seat.

'Now, here's a funny thing,' he said. 'We've been talking to the neighbours. Nobody saw anyone come into this house but the lady across the street, she did see someone come out. You. Why?'

'Why? Well, I . . . Like I told you, the front door was open, I walked in, saw the body and . . . I don't know, it's stupid, I suppose, now I look back but the first coherent thought that came into my head was that I'd left my car unlocked, so I went to check. All right, it wasn't very logical, I know, but . . . well, maybe I was more upset than I thought. Shock can make you do funny things.'

'You buy that, Clive?' said the DI. Clive just shrugged.

'There is another explanation,' said the DI. 'What if you came in here, killed Mr Marcus, realised as you left the house that the lady across the road had spotted you, went to your car, thought it over and then instead of driving away came back in here, called us and played all innocent?'

'Why should I do any of that? I didn't even know Marcus.'

He sighed. 'It was just a thought and, who knows, you might have coughed. Never that easy, though, is it?' He picked a bit of fluff off the sleeve of his navy blue suit. 'Something else you might help us out on. We can't seem to locate Mr Beckway. Do you know where he is?'

I shook my head. 'I last saw him two,

three hours ago in a wine bar near the House of Commons. I imagine that's where he is now — in the House of Commons, I mean, not the wine bar.'

'Well, he isn't. Is that when he asked you to drop in on Mr Marcus?'

'That's right. I was on my way home and, well, this isn't very far out of my way.'

'Why didn't he just telephone his message?'

'I don't know. Why not ask him?'

He leaned suddenly across the table, the cool, cynical manner deserting him for a moment. 'Because we can't fucking find him. I just told you.' He sat back in his chair again. 'I don't know. There's something about you that I don't like, Mr Lennox. It's this story of yours, I suppose. I just don't believe it.'

'Sorry about that.'

'Yeah. I just hope for your sake you're telling the truth.' There wasn't much comfort in that for a man who was telling anything but.

They let me go soon afterwards. They'd checked me out, they said; they knew where to find me if they wanted me. The way they said it, it sounded like a threat.

As I was leaving the house I said, 'Do you think you'll get him, whoever did this? Do you think you'll find him?'

'Will we what?' the DI said, 'Will we find him? Is a bear Catholic? Does the Pope shit in the woods? Oh, we'll find him all right.' And that sounded like a threat, too.

EIGHT

I called Beckway twice on the short trip to Dolphin Square. Still the answer-phone, still no pick-up.

I left the car beside the entrance and dashed into the building. The lift was God knows where — not on the ground floor anyway. I ran up the stairs, all three flights, hit the landing breathless and hammered on Beckway's door. He was slow answering so I hammered again and then, at last, his voice somewhere in the recesses of the flat . . . 'All right, all right, I'm coming, for Chrissakes.'

A pause, then his voice again on the other side of the door. 'Who is it?'

'Archie, just open the bloody door, will you?'

He did. He was wearing a white towelling robe and, as far as I could make out, nothing else. 'What the hell do you think you're doing?' he said. 'With all that ruckus I was just about to call the police.'

I pushed past him, kicking the door

shut. 'Don't bother. They're on their way.'

'What?'

I told him about Marcus, about how the police were anxious to talk to him, Archie, about how I'd explained my relationship with him. 'If they know about this place — '

' — they do.'

' — then they'll be here any minute. Is the girl still here?'

'Yes. She's in there.' He gestured towards the main bedroom.

'Oh, shit. Look, we've got to get her out of here fast. We — ' The doorbell rang, a long, loud, oddly menacing sound. 'Great! The bastards are here already.'

Archie said, whispering, panicking, 'What are we going to do?'

I pulled him towards the bedroom and opened the door. There was a flash of naked, female limbs plunging onto the bed and then a flurry of sheets. Outside, the bell rang again, a longer, more persistent sound this time.

A girl, a young woman, now lay in the bed, all blonde hair and big, angry eyes, the sheet pulled up to her chin. I said, 'Listen to me: the police are here, I'll explain why later. Archie's going to let them in — he has to. I'm going to stay here with you until they're gone. All you have to do is keep quiet, OK? Not one sound.'

The doorbell rang for a third time. 'Archie, let them in but don't bring them in here. You're alone, right? You've been alone all night — working, wanking, whatever. And turn this light out on your way.'

He left us, switching off the light, closing the door behind him. I put my finger to my lips, muttered 'Shhh' at the girl and listened, my ear pressed to the door.

I heard Archie let them in, heard the familiar voice of my friend the DI say, 'Mr Beckway? I'm Detective Inspector Mason and this is Detective Sergeant Clark. I'm afraid we have some very grave news for you.'

'Grave . . . ? Oh, please, come in.'

I pictured him taking them from the door and into the sitting-room. What they were saying became indistinct except, suddenly, an exclamation from Archie . . .'Freddie? Freddie Marcus? Oh, dear God. Oh no, oh no. Dear God — Freddie?' He was good. He almost convinced me. Then more muttering, more droning voices until — and at this time they must have been standing just inside the sitting-room, near the hall — the DI, Mason, said, '. . . fighter named Robert Lennox. Bobby, they call him. Claims he knows you.'

Archie now. 'Bobby? Oh, good Lord, yes. I've known him, oh for some time. He . . .' The voices faded again as they went back further into the room.

I looked around me, my eyes grown accustomed to the darkness in the bedroom. The girl still lay motionless, the sheet clutched to her chin, her gaze following me balefully. Clothes were strewn around the room — Archie's clothes, her clothes, though of hers there were very few. A skimpy top, a black miniskirt, a black suspender belt and black, diamond-patterned stockings, black high-heeled shoes. There was no sign of underwear and I knew, from the glimpse I'd had of her as I came into the room, that she wasn't wearing any in bed, so presumably she had arrived dressed not so much for dinner as for after dinner.

She sat up, still hanging on to the sheet. 'What the hell's going on here?' she hissed.

'Shut up,' I hissed back, 'or I'll shove your face into that pillow.'

Voices outside now, just beyond the bedroom door. DI Mason saying, 'And this room, sir?'

'My bedroom,' Archie said. I heard him lean his back against the door. 'I was having a nap when you arrived. That's why I was some time answering the bell. Room's a frightful mess, I'm afraid.'

They moved away. More indecipherable murmurings from the sitting-room. Then they were at the front door and Mason was saying, '. . . to have been the bearer of such terrible news.'

'Yes. Such a, such an awful shock,' Archie said. The door was opened, there was a swapping of 'good nights' and the door closed again. I went out into the hall. Archie was standing there, shaking his head. He looked haggard.

'Thank God you got here before they did,' he said.

The girl came out of the bedroom, zipping her skirt. She had forgotten to tuck in her top and it had ridden up at the front, showing an inch or two of smooth, slightly tanned midriff. Her stockings and suspender belt were draped over one shoulder.

'Now will someone please tell me what's going on here?' she said. 'Archie, darling, who is this person and what were the police doing trampling all over your flat?'

'Oh dear,' Beckway said. 'Do forgive me. Of course, you two haven't met . . .' He introduced us; we shook hands. She didn't look very happy doing it; nothing about me seemed to make her happy.

'You threatened to shove my face into the pillow,' she said. 'That wasn't very nice.' In her high heels she must have been about 5' 8" and even with her lipstick a little smudged, even with her hair bedraggled — bed-raggled more likely — she was very pretty.

'Yes, well, it seemed like a good idea at the time,' I said.

'You don't have very nice friends, Archie,' she said. She moved up close and kissed him on the mouth, her left hand slipping inside his towelling robe, quite low down. He had the grace to look embarrassed and stepped away from her.

'Bobby, would you mind explaining this . . . this bizarre situation to Lacy? I'm not sure I'm up to it and, besides,

I think you have a better grasp of the details than I have.'

So I told my tale again — the tale I'd told to the police. I didn't mention the real reason I had gone to see Marcus. By the time I had finished she seemed to have warmed to me a little.

'Good job you came to warn us,' she said. She giggled. 'It would have been too awful if the police had found me here as you found me. Think of the scandal. Wow!'

Beckway thought of it and shuddered. 'Perhaps, in the circumstances, we should call it a night. I'm awfully sorry but — '

'No, you're right.' She picked up her handbag. 'I'm out of here.'

'No, you're not,' I said. 'Not for a while anyway. The police could be keeping an eye on the place, just to see if anyone comes in or out.'

Beckway said, 'Why on earth should they do that?'

'Because they're policemen. They're paid to be suspicious. It's what they're good at. Archie, make us some coffee, will you? No, better still get us a drink. I'll have a large Scotch — on the rocks.'

It was well after midnight when Lacy

Jones finally left and by then I'd found out something about her, not a lot but something. She was in her late twenties and had joined the BBC about six years ago after a stint in the theatre as an assistant stage manager with repertory companies. Married, no kids, her husband a freelance TV camera-man currently on a long location shoot somewhere in the Far East and not expected back for a couple of weeks.

She sat beside Beckway on the settee, showing a lot of leg, her arm linked in his, her hand resting on his thigh and occasionally stroking it. There was something possessive, almost trium-phant, about this open display of inti-macy, as if she were making a point for my benefit, as if she were saying, 'See? He's mine.'

Beckway didn't seem to mind, al-though he did ease her hand gently away when it strayed a little too high. And, give him his due, despite the pres-sure of her still bare leg against his he kept his mind sufficiently above his lap to realise what information I was after and to help me get it.

'Lacy works on Kevin Rycroft's pro-gramme, you know,' he said. 'That's where we met last week.' He turned to her, teasingly. 'I thought we were getting on rather well until you walked out on me. I must say I was a little surprised. Couldn't understand it. That's why I hesitated so long before calling you. I wasn't at all sure you'd want to hear from me.'

'Oh, I know,' she said. 'It was so infuriating. I thought I'd never see you again. But, Archie darling, I didn't walk out on you. I'd never have done that. Well, you know that, don't you, silly? No, what happened . . .'

What happened, apparently, was that the barman who had whispered in her ear had told her she was wanted at the reception desk: her sister had called in to say she would meet her there in ten minutes. Since this sister lived in Leeds and had said nothing about coming to London, Lacy had been concerned that something might be wrong. But when she reached reception there was no sign of any sister and nobody on duty had even received a phone call from a sister. On the other hand, one of the women on the desk had just, only a minute ago, gone off for her meal break and perhaps it was she who had taken whatever message there had been. So Lacy had gone looking for her and when, eventually, she had tracked her down to the canteen and discovered that she knew nothing about sisters either much time had passed. Even more time passed while she phoned her sister and discovered that she was tucked up at home in Leeds and hadn't even attempted to contact Lacy.

'So when I finally got back to hospitality, Archie, you'd gone.' She frowned, irritably. 'It must have been somebody's idea of a practical joke. What a stupid thing to do.'

I said, 'You didn't notice anyone hanging around in the corridors, did you? Anyone unusual, unexpected?'

'No. Why?'

I made a vague gesture. 'I don't know. I just thought maybe the joker was lurking about and . . .' I let the words tail away.

She shook her head. 'No. I suppose there must have been a few people around, there usually are, but I didn't notice anyone.'

'How easy is it to get into the Television Centre? For an outsider, I mean, someone who had no real right to be there?'

'Well, it's not very easy but it's not impossible either. All sorts of people drift in and out — messengers, taxi drivers, interviewees and their hangers-on. It's pretty nearly impossible to keep tabs on everyone.'

Which really got us nowhere. Presumably, with a little observation, Mickey Mouse and his friends could have worked that out for themselves.

Lacy left soon afterwards. Beckway walked her to the door and I poured myself another drink while I listened to them kissing goodnight. It took a while. When he came back to the sitting-room he was fastening the belt on his bath-robe. 'Well,' he said, 'what do you think?'

'Of Lacy?' I hadn't actually liked her a lot but it seemed tactless to tell him that. 'She's very pretty. I hope you practised safe sex, though. You can never be too careful these days.'

'You don't approve.' He smiled and shook his head. 'I understand that. I don't really approve of myself either. But she's extremely attractive, she was more than available and I just couldn't help myself. Women are my hobby, you see, and it's a hobby I haven't pursued for quite a while. I think I've been suffering from withdrawal symptoms.'

I knew there was a quick, cheap joke to be made there but I didn't even let myself think about it. Instead I said, 'Maybe it's time you went to the police, Archie. We could be getting well out of our depth here. Blackmail, or possible blackmail, is one thing but murder . . .'

'Marcus? You think Freddie's death is connected?'

I said, 'Do me a favour. What — you think it was coincidence? Just sheer chance that an Irishman was asking when he'd be home and now he's dead? No, that night at the TV Centre Marcus saw something or someone that he shouldn't have seen and that's why he was killed. I think the police should be told.'

'No.' He shook his head, much more vigorously this time. 'No way. Bring the police in on this and that's my career finished. If it's too much for you, if you want out, then go. I'll find someone else.'

'Oh, I'll stick around for a while, though what I can do . . .' I glanced at my watch and stood up. 'Good God, look at the time. I must go home.'

130

'What about Lacy?' he said. 'Do you think she's involved in all this?' He was staring at me anxiously, as if willing me to say no.

I shrugged, wearily. 'At this point, Archie, I haven't the faintest idea. I'll try to find out tomorrow.'

NINE

It was the motive that bothered me. Blackmail, yes, almost certainly. But what was the motive behind the motive? As Donovan had suggested, the Irish connection pointed towards politics — some disaffected IRA splinter group perhaps, determined to have no truck with cease-fires or truces, but I couldn't really buy that. What would their reasons be? And whatever they were, why pick on Beckway? His department had little to do with Ireland unless . . . Unless what mattered was not the department he controlled but the simple fact that he was a member of the Government. And if that were the case, if what the IRA or whoever wanted was to get a hold on a member, any member, of the Government then the answer to the question, Why Beckway? wasn't too difficult to find.

His interest in women, quiescent though it may have been of late, would hardly be a secret to anyone with a strongish interest in politics. Not that this made him unique, of course. If you lumped together all the politicians who, in recent years, had been caught with their trousers off in the wrong bedrooms you could form a coalition government. But what made Beckway particularly vulnerable was that he had not simply had an affair in the past, he had had affairs. Plural. And for that reason he was a better target, more easily compromised than most of his colleagues.

Right then. Mickey Mouse knew Beckway would be at the Television Centre that night; loads of people did. Mickey Mouse also arranged for Lacy to be called to reception, which meant at the very least that he also knew she was the kind of woman to perk Beckway's interest. But after that . . . Well, after that it was surely all down to luck. Nobody could know with absolute certainty that Beckway would follow her out of the hospitality room unless . . . Well, unless Lacy was involved in the plot and had given the Minister to understand that he was on such a firm promise that he would be a fool not to follow her. Either way I thought nothing would be lost by talking to her again.

The news of Marcus's murder had missed all except the latest editions of the morning papers but was given extensive coverage on the radio and TV. My name, I was relieved to find, wasn't mentioned and that was no doubt due to Beckway's influence or even a little pressure from Downing Street. A direct link between the discovery of the body and Archie would have had the Press scurrying around and very likely sniping at the Government again. It had been doing a lot of sniping lately and seemed to have acquired a taste for it. Not this time, though. The police statement said only that the body had been found by a messenger who was not under suspicion. The motive for the killing, it was suggested, was robbery. All very neat and simple. Such a comfort, I thought, to live in a country that practised open government.

I didn't hear from the police that morning but I did hear from Donovan. He wanted to know how things were progressing, so I told him and when I had finished he said, 'Jesus, poor old Freddie.'

'You knew him then?'

'Oh yeah. Well, I'd met him a few

times. At posh dinners and things with Archie, usually when Archie was making a speech. Bit dull but a nice enough bloke. So what do you reckon?'

I told him I reckoned the police should be called in but Donovan went along with Archie on that. 'No, we don't want the filth in on this, Bob. Be the end of Archie, that would.'

'You're very solicitous of him, Donovan.'

'Yeah, well, all heart, aren't I? Known for it.'

About midday I called Beckway at the Ministry and Birgit answered the phone.

'Mr Lennox!' she sounded delighted to hear from me. 'What a pleasant surprise. I do hope you weren't too upset by that awful experience last night.'

'What?'

'Finding poor Freddie's body like that. It must have been dreadful. Such a shock for you.'

'You know about it then.'

'Of course. Archie told me and anyway we've had the police here most of the morning asking questions. Did they ask you questions, too?'

'Yes. Look, can I speak to Archie?'

'Certainly. I'll put you through. Oh, by the way, I'm sorry you missed the dinner last night. I gather there was delightful company though, alas, not enough to go round.'

I said, 'How do you know all this? You're very well-informed.'

She laughed. 'Aren't I though? Perhaps one day, if you're very good, I'll let you into my secret.'

Casually, not really thinking about it, I said, 'Well, maybe I could be very good one night over dinner.'

And she said, 'Lovely. I like Langan's Brasserie, don't you? Shall we say tomorrow night at eight o'clock? That would be perfect. I'd better book the table. If they don't know you there they're inclined to put you upstairs and *nobody* eats upstairs at Langan's. I'll use the Minister's name. That always does the trick. Ah. I can put you through to him now. Till tomorrow night then.'

I barely had time to glance in the mirror and wonder whether it was my bright blue eyes or chiselled profile that had caused the lovely Birgit to take this sudden interest in me before Beckway was on the line. He sounded tired.

'God, what a bloody awful morning. The Prime Minister was none too pleased that Freddie's body was discovered by an apparent employee of mine. I had some difficulty explaining you away, I might add.'

'I can imagine. What did you tell him?'

'Much the same story that you told the police. I think he bought it but he was still a little puzzled that I should even know someone like you.' He sighed. 'And then, of course, we had the fuzz all over the place. I don't like that detective inspector, that Mason fellow. He has a knowing sneer.'

'I've noticed. Listen, Archie, I want to go and watch the recording of *Speaking Out* tonight.'

'Go by all means,' he said. 'But I have to warn you — you'll be bored out of your mind.'

'I know that. I've seen it on the box. I was bored then. All I really want is to get into the Television Centre and look around, study the layout. I don't know, something might come to mind. Anyway, I want to see Lacy again.'

'What for?' he asked, sharply.

'What . . . ? Oh, come on! Not for that reason. I don't want to chat her up, I just want to talk to her. It was sniffing around her that got you into this mess in the first place, or have you forgotten that? I just think it's a good idea to find out how much, or how little, she's involved.' He started to butt in but I talked through him. 'So what I want you to do is ring her up and ask her to invite me over.'

'I can't do that. It's impossible. I simply cannot, in my position, go around making phone calls to young women at the BBC. I did it yesterday at your request — '

'Did you more good than it did me,' I said but he ignored that.

' — but I won't do it again. I'm happy to give you her number and do, by all means, tell her that I suggested you call but you'll have to phone her yourself.'

I left a message for Lacy and she called me back about four o'clock, sounding impatient. They'd been having a run-through with all kinds of technical problems and now she was on her tea-break and wanting to put her feet up for a few minutes. If I had been anyone but a friend of Archie's, she said, she probably wouldn't have phoned.

I told her how grateful I was and said that, actually, it was at Archie's instigation that I had rung her. He thought it would be a good idea for me to see the programme being put together.

'Good Lord, why?' she said, wonderingly.

'Well, I'm working with him now. A kind of personal assistant. He reckoned I should have some first-hand knowledge of the sort of thing he gets involved in.'

'Well . . .' She still sounded doubtful.

'He listens to me a lot, you know. Says he values my opinion.' I paused. 'On all sorts of things.'

She let that sink in for a moment. Then . . . 'Well, all right. If it's for Archie. Look, I don't mean to be rude. I don't know what we'd have done without you last night. I'm grateful really. It's just that I don't have much time to hold people's hands when we're recording.'

'You don't have to. I'm a big boy now. Sometimes, when I concentrate hard, I can even tie my own shoelaces. I just want to sit quietly in a corner and watch what's going on. OK?'

'OK,' she said. Some of the frost had gone out of her voice but not all of it. I couldn't understand it. I was younger than Archie, better-looking than Archie and I just knew I'd cut a much more dashing figure in a white bathrobe than he did.

On the other hand he was a government minister and I wasn't. Maybe that had something to do with it.

TEN

I took a cab to the Television Centre. The security men on the gate had been told to expect me and there was no trouble getting in. We drove into the semi-circular forecourt past a long, orderly queue of people lined up outside a door on the lefthand side of the building. I went in through the main entrance on the right and one of the receptionists called the studio to let Lacy know I had arrived.

She appeared through double doors at the end of the reception area. Faded blue jeans, a denim shirt, crisp white jogging shoes. The jeans did no more to disguise the length of her legs than the miniskirt had done the previous night. I moved forward with the intention of planting a demure kiss of greeting on her cheek but she evaded that and offered her hand instead.

'This way,' she said and led me out through the main door again and along the walkway which skirted the circular lawn with its huge bronze sculpture of

Helios, the Sun God, all gold and well-hung and separated from his busy, hippy black hand-maidens, Vision and Sound, by the slender phallic symbol of the column whereon he stood busily being, as was his nature, all-seeing.

I said, 'Who are those people in the queue over there?'

She gave them a cursory glance. 'Studio audience. Not ours, of course, we don't have one. They've come to see that game show, *You'll Be Sorry*, and I expect they will once they've watched it. Serve them right. There's a lot of recording going on tonight — us, the game show and *Shoot to Kill* — do you know it?'

'Cops and robbers, isn't it?'

She laughed briefly. 'I think they prefer to call it a police drama series but, yes, it's just cops and robbers when you get right down to it.'

I said, 'How do you go about choosing a studio audience?'

She paused and looked at me. 'My, my, a real little seeker after knowledge, aren't we? Is Archie going to give you a test on all this?'

'No. I'm just curious, that's all.'

'Well, it's not a matter of choosing,

really. Mostly people write in to the ticket office and ask if they can come along. They turn up in groups quite often.' Which seemed to provide a possible answer to how Mickey Mouse and company had got into the place.

We went through double glass doors, down a short stretch of curving corridor, through a canteen area where a few people were dotted about drinking tea and into a studio with the rehearsal light glowing outside. 'In the old days,' she said, 'we used to have a much smaller studio, a sort of broom cupboard really, on the fourth floor. We don't need a lot of space, you see, because there's just Kevin and at most three guests. But they closed our old studio down so here we are in one of the big ones, just like real, grown-up television.'

It was a huge, high barn of a place. You could have staged a battle scene in there, let alone *Speaking Out*, whose modest set, lights, cameras and monitors occupied only a small, distant corner.

As we walked in Kevin Rycroft, who had been perched on the arm of a chair reading his script, glanced up and said something to a tall, lissom young man with longish curly hair. They both turned, grinning, to look at us and started in our direction.

'Oh, Christ,' Lacy said crossly, 'fucking Kevin Rycroft — that's all I need. You've caused me a lot of embarrassment today, I hope you realise that.'

'Me?' I said. 'What have I done?'

'Kevin wanted to know who you were and why you were coming in tonight, so I had to tell him about Archie and that set the pair of them sniggering, Kevin and Leonard.'

'Who's Leonard?'

'The other prat, the one with the curls. He's the producer.'

Lacy introduced us in a perfunctory sort of way as if she and I were in a hurry and had no time to hang around exchanging social niceties and tried to move me on. But Rycroft seemed to be in the mood for a chat. 'Lacy tells me you're a friend of Archie Beckway,' he said. I smiled non-committally. 'Slippery customer, old Archie. Very hard to pin down in an interview.' My smile carried on being non-committal. 'So, ah, what brings you here tonight?' He took a sly, sideways glance at Lacy.

'Looking after Archie's interests, are you?'

'What does that mean?' I didn't like Rycroft much on the box and I liked him even less in person. He was giving me his famous thin, mocking smile so I gave him my hard look in return, the one that had once prompted someone to say that I had the coldest eyes he had ever seen. His smile was no match for my look and the faint flicker of alarm that crossed his face gave me a moment of childish pleasure.

The producer, Leonard, noticed his presenter's discomfiture and moved in to distract my attention.

'Delightful to see you, of course,' he said, giving the curly locks a toss, 'but we were a little curious about why you — or perhaps it was Archie — made the approach through Lacy.' He smiled inquiringly, his head cocked to one side as if the act of tossing his curls had ricked his neck.

Lacy said, 'What are you getting at?'

'Nothing, sweetie, nothing at all. It's just that as a friend of the Minister Mr Lennox could have made the approach through me. After all,' he blinked disingenuously at her, 'I'm sure I know

Archie better than you do.'

Rycroft uttered a small, choking sound so I turned and gave him the look again and he said, hurriedly, 'Well, better get the show on the road,' and moved away.

Leonard was still smiling at me, waiting for an answer. I said, 'I know Lacy; I don't know you. Does that satisfy your curiosity?'

He spread his arms expansively. 'But of course. Perfectly reasonable.' I felt a grudging admiration for him. My hard look may have caused Rycroft to throw in the towel even before anyone had said 'Seconds out' but Leonard seemed impervious to it, simply returning it with a bland smile. He looked at his watch. 'Ah me, duty calls. Must have a word with tonight's guest before we wheel him into the studio. I'll see you later then.' He half-turned to go, then paused. 'Oh, by the way, such tragic news about Archie's minder, poor Freddie Marcus. I suppose you don't know if there've been any developments?'

I shook my head. 'Pity,' he said and left us.

'What a pair of bastards,' Lacy said, watching Leonard spring nimbly up the iron staircase that led from the studio to the producer's gallery.

'Do they know you were with Archie last night?'

She grunted contemptuously. 'Of course not. Do you think I'm mad? But they know he phoned me yesterday. Everyone knows. It's impossible to keep a secret in this place. And now you turn up. So naturally that pair of old women are putting two and two together.'

'And finding it adds up neatly to four,' I said. 'Awkward, isn't it?'

'Whose side are you on?' she said angrily, echoing Donovan. Good question and this time the answer wasn't so easy. I held no particular brief for Beckway or her. I hardly knew either of them and Beckway, I thought, was a fool to get himself involved with her.

'I'm on the side of truth and justice,' I said.

She grunted again. 'I'm asking for help and comfort and all I get is a load of pious shit. Thanks a bunch. Come on.'

She led me up to the gallery where Leonard welcomed me affably enough, introduced me to the studio director, the vision mixer and various other people who were operating a control panel that looked like the flight deck of Concorde and directed me to a seat at the back. Through the monitor screens I watched Rycroft and the studio guest, a Shadow Minister from the Opposition benches, being miked up and a few minutes later the programme began.

Beckway was wrong — or, at least, only partly right — when he said I would find it boring. The interview was fairly boring in that it was predictable. The Shadow Minister attacked the Government's handling of the National Health Service which, he said, was being perilously rundown and starved of money and Rycroft, playing the traditional interviewer's role of Devil's advocate, talked about money spent 'in real terms' and spouted other bits of political jargon which sounded impressive but didn't actually seem to mean a lot.

But watching the people in the gallery was fascinating in the way that seeing someone else at work always is. The director and the producer's assistant muttered instructions to Lacy and the cameramen in the studio while Leonard, who was in direct contact with Rycroft's earpiece, would murmur every now and then, 'We're not getting anywhere with this angle, Kevin. Ask him about . . .' I listened to all this and watched the monitors on the wall, which showed what was on-screen now and what would be coming on next.

With fourteen minutes of the programme still to run I stood up and muttered, 'Sorry. Must find the loo.' Leonard glanced at me irritably but a plump young man, who had been introduced as the programme's chief researcher, took me outside to the first floor landing and pointed the way. When he had returned to the gallery I went down the stairs to the ground floor.

The *Speaking Out* studio was in an area called Green Assembly; a young woman bustling by with a clipboard told me the game show, *You'll Be Sorry*, was being recorded in Red Assembly. I seemed to have struck lucky — she was the floor manager on that show. And, she added sternly, if I was a member of the studio audience I really should be in there by now; they couldn't have people wandering in and out as the whim seized them.

I assured her that I had nothing to do with the game show, though I did wonder what time it finished recording. About ten o'clock, she said, sometimes later if the host fluffed his lines a lot which, she added bitterly, he usually did. Last week, I said, striding along beside her towards Red Assembly, what time did they finish recording last week?

'Last week? Who can remember last week? But . . .' She puffed out her cheeks with the effort of remembering, then shook her head. 'Must have been about the same as usual, I suppose. We never finish early, I can tell you that but on the other hand we haven't been drastically late since, oh, sometime last month.'

So the studio audience was released at ten or thereabouts but Beckway's encounter in the men's room had happened around nine o'clock, which suggested that if Mickey Mouse and company had been watching the game show they must have slipped out early. Well, it surely wasn't impossible — they were only escaping from a TV studio, after all, not a maximum security prison.

'The audience weren't given fancy dress or funny masks to wear last week, were they?' I said.

She pulled up suddenly as we turned into Red Assembly's snack bar area. 'Funny masks? For the audience? Are you serious? Our genial host is supposed to be the comedian, if you'll pardon my using the word loosely, and he certainly couldn't stand competition from an audience wearing funny masks. I mean, have you actually *seen* our show? No, obviously not . . .' A flicker of alarm crossed her face. 'What's with all these questions? This isn't some BBC time and motion study, is it?'

'No. I'm not with the BBC, honest. I was just wondering.'

'Well,' she said, darkly. 'Way things are round here these days you never know who might be spying on you. Look, I've got to — Oooh!'

A tall young man had come up behind us and planted a great sploshing kiss on the top of her ginger head. 'Hi, gorgeous,' he said.

She wasn't gorgeous — a nice looking girl certainly but not gorgeous — and she probably knew it but it obviously thrilled her to be called gorgeous by this dark, handsome hunk who had now put his arm around her shoulders and was squeezing her affectionately.

'Roger,' she said, blushing with pleasure. 'Hi. How's it going?'

'Fine,' he said. 'Great. Sorry, can't stop and chat. Got to get to make-up.' He flashed a smile that embraced both the girl and me and headed towards the studio entrance on the right of the canteen area.

'Isn't he marvellous?' the girl said, though she seemed to be talking to herself as much as me. She shook her head as if emerging from some reverie. 'Look, I must go now. 'Bye.' She hurried away towards another studio on the left.

I was about to find my way back to the *Speaking Out* gallery when a woman, drinking coffee at one of the tables, said, 'Bobby? What on earth are you doing here?'

She was about my age, small, fair, plump and I didn't recognise her at first. She stood up, smiling a little sadly, as I walked towards her. 'Why is it that time is so much kinder to men than it is to women? It's not fair. You haven't changed a bit while I've turned into an old bag.'

She was unkind to herself there. She was neither old nor a bag but . . .

Mentally I took a few years and about fifteen pounds off her and said, 'Rachel?'

'Well, at least you got there in the end. How are you? It's been, God, I hate to think how many years.'

Rachel Grant. I hadn't seen her since the day we graduated from university together. A brainy girl, I remembered — got a first in history. And now . . .

Well now she produced the cop show, *Shoot to Kill*, and she'd sneaked out for a cigarette and a coffee during a recording break. She was married — to a stockbroker — two children, lived in Hampstead.

We had been good friends at university, though nothing more, and she had followed my career in the boxing ring with affectionate interest while wondering from time to time why I'd felt it necessary to get a degree in English as preparation for knocking people about for a living and she had winced and suffered on my behalf the night I'd tried for the world middleweight championship and taken an awful beating from Willie Slate.

'That's when I packed it in,' I said. 'That night, as I lay in hospital with a broken jaw and a couple of cracked ribs, I thought, "This is a mug's game. I shouldn't be at all surprised if I got hurt one day".'

'Yes, well,' she said, dryly, 'you were always quick on the uptake.'

A production assistant came over to say everyone was ready to start recording again and Rachel and I quickly swapped phone numbers and promised we'd do lunch one day, both of us meaning it and both of us knowing it probably wouldn't happen. Then she clapped her hands and said, 'Come along, children, time to get back to work.' A troupe of young men and women, all in make-up and some in police uniforms, got up from the surrounding tables and followed her into the studio to the right of the snack bar.

When I got back to *Speaking Out* the programme was over and Rycroft, Leonard, the studio guest and the researchers were all congratulating each other on what a lively and sparkling show it had been. I, having missed half of it, was not encouraged to join in the mutual back-slapping and I stood in the background alongside Lacy, who was shaking her head and muttering sourly to herself.

After a while we trooped down to the hospitality room in the basement, Lacy and I trailing a little behind the others.

'Good programme was it?' I said.

'Good?' She snorted contemptuously. 'Good? That was one of the dullest shows we've ever done. You didn't see all of it, did you? You were lucky. I used to work on an arts programme before I came here and, OK, that was always a bit boring, too. But I think arts programmes are supposed to be boring; I think the theory is that if people actually enjoy an arts programme then something's gone wrong and the audience hasn't been forcefed enough culture. That's culture with a capital C, incidentally. Or even a capital K . . .'

The hospitality room, she said, as we helped ourselves to sandwiches and wine, was the one they always used. Maybe it was my presence, or maybe not, but I noticed that apart from saying hello and then moving on, nobody seemed keen to stop and talk to Lacy. Since she was by a long way the best-looking woman in a room largely occupied by young men it struck me as odd. They all seemed wary of her and not just in the unself-confident way that young men are often a little nervous of pretty women.

After a while I left her, saying I had to find a men's room. Leonard stopped me on the way out.

'Forgive my asking,' he said, 'but have you known Lacy long?' He tossed his curls and smiled, a faintly knowing, faintly ironic smile.

'Not very long. Why?'

'Oh, nothing really. Interesting girl. Beautiful, of course, and, ah, very adventurous. Can I get you a glass of wine?'

I thanked him but said he couldn't because I was on my way to the loo.

'Again? Ah, weak bladder,' he said, sympathetically. 'My father had the same complaint.'

His father! Bloody cheek, I thought, plunging into the corridor and reflecting that I was, at most, three years older than Leonard. But my grudging admiration for him increased; Rycroft was nothing but his producer was obviously a doughty adversary.

The men's room, the one in which Beckway had been attacked, was just a men's room; the offices, or whatever, around it were locked; the corridors were empty. The stairs nearby led to an equally empty corridor on the ground floor. As a reconaissance trip my visit to the Television Centre hadn't turned out to be a lot of use. All I seemed to have discovered was how Mickey Mouse and his companions might have got into the building that night.

When I returned to hospitality Lacy said, 'I've told everybody that you and I are going off for supper, OK?'

I shrugged. 'Fine, if that's what you want.'

'Good. I've ordered a cab for us. It should be waiting now. Shall we go?'

She came with me as I said my good-byes to Rycroft and his cohorts. 'Have fun,' Rycroft said with the knowing grin that viewers throughout the land, me among them, wanted to slap off his face. And then, spitefully, to Lacy, 'When does Phil get back from the Far East?'

'Fuck off, Kevin,' she said. 'Just fuck off and mind your own business.' And in that moment, as I saw the look of cold, venomous fury in her eyes, I felt rather sorry for Rycroft. I would have felt sorry for anybody who upset her.

She was silent, brooding, until we got into the cab and I said, 'Where are we going?'

She shrugged. 'You can go wherever you like but I'm going to Dolphin Square to see Archie.'

'Oh, I see.' You were right, Rachel, I thought ruefully — real quick on the uptake, me. 'So I'm the beard, am I?'

She looked surprised. 'What else? Isn't that why Archie sent you along tonight?'

I caught a glimpse of myself in the side window. I didn't look like a pander but then how do I know what panders look like? I said, 'Last week, you knew that Archie would follow you out of the hospitality room, did you?'

Surprised, she said, 'Well, of course I did.'

'How?'

'How?' She shook her head. 'I thought, from what you said earlier, that he confided in you.'

'He does. I'm like the Sphinx. I do a lot of inscrutable grinning and say nothing.'

'Yes, well, he didn't confide this to you, did he?' She reached into her handbag and produced a sheet of notepaper and handed it to me. It was thick, expensive paper with letterheading that had been inked out. On it was typed: 'Dear Lacy, My friend and I have a bet. I say you'll have Archie Beckway eating out of your hand tonight. He says you can't do it. There's a lot of money on this so go for it.'

There was no signature.

'So?' I said.

'It was waiting for me, along with the most marvellous bunch of flowers, when I got to work last Monday.'

I read it again. 'But who was it from?'

She made an impatient gesture. 'Who do you think?'

'Archie? You think Archie sent this?'

'Hold it up to the light,' she said.

I did so, holding it to the reading light in the back of the cab. The address at the top, not so heavily inked out as it had first seemed, was The House of Commons.

'Oh, come on,' I said, 'do you really think Archie would send you anything as naff as this?'

'Yes, I do,' she said, fiercely. 'And maybe it's not as naff as all that. Think about it — Archie had nothing to lose. Nobody could prove he sent it. He had no real idea how I would respond, though I imagine he could guess, so this way he was making a pass at me without actually making a pass. If I'd ignored it and him, he was covered. Even if I was the kind of girl who'd give this to the Press, there was nothing they could do. If they accused Archie of sending it he could deny it and threaten a libel action. You think it's naff, I think it's rather clever. I knew it was from him as soon as I saw it.'

I read it again. It still seemed naff to me. I said, 'But what made you so certain?'

She gave me one of those serene, female looks. 'Because I knew he was interested in me. He was on the programme three months ago and I noticed the way he looked at me then. I knew it was only a matter of time.'

'Have you asked him about this?'

'Certainly not. When I've known him longer maybe.' She took the note back and returned it to her handbag. 'And don't you mention it to him either.'

As we neared Dolphin Square she did some running repairs to her make-up, restoring her lipstick, powdering her nose and cheeks, undoing a couple of buttons on her denim shirt to give Beckway a hint or two that she wasn't wearing a bra. It was like a Red Indian putting on the warpaint and pretty as she was I was glad it was Archie she had in her sights, not me. Married mistresses could be bad news if you were single; but if you were married yourself then it seemed to me that married and — how had Leonard described her? Adventurous, that was it — adventurous mistresses like this were potentially disastrous.

The cab drew up outside Beckway's block of flats. Lacy thanked me perfunctorily and got out and I, the unwitting pander who had delivered the lady to her lover, gave the taxi driver my own address and went home chastely to my bed, convinced that whoever had sent that note to Lacy had, at some time last Monday night, also worn a Mickey Mouse mask.

ELEVEN

When I woke up the next morning I felt like hitting somebody, so I went to the gym.

It was in Kensington, a mile or so down the road from me, and for the most part it was patronised by yuppies and their wives to get themselves into shape for the beach. I mean, hey, you don't want to hang around Barbados with half an inch of fat around your waist. But the owner was an old fight manager and in the back room he had fixed up a real gym where boxers could train. Men like Lennox Lewis and Chris Eubank had been known to work out there and that was the room I always used.

I'd been in a foul mood when I got home the previous night, cursing Beckway for the way he had used me to deliver Lacy to his bed. What did he think I was, for God's sake — some kind of amenable pimp? I had phoned him to complain and warn him never to do it again but all I got was his answering machine: 'There's no-one here to take your message now . . .' So I hung up and called Donovan instead and got an answering machine there, too. This time, though, I left a message — a bitter precis of the evening's events in the course of which, I remembered afterwards, I had called Beckway 'a randy sonofabitch' twice and that annoyed me even more because I hate repeating myself.

It was early when I got to the gym and I had the back room to myself. I spent an hour skipping and doing weights then I moved on to the good stuff — hitting the heavy bag. It was Beckway I had wanted to thump when I woke up so I imagined the bag was him and I liked the feeling. The jabs, hooks and uppercuts thudded into the heavy padding with such sweet power and timing that I could feel the impact all the way up to my shoulders. By the time I moved on to the speedball I was streaming with sweat and I had worked off the anger so thoroughly that I wasn't even thinking of Beckway any more.

The speedball and I had got into a nice, fast rhythm when a voice just behind me said, 'God, I wish I could do that.'

I gave the ball a final burst and stepped away, leaving it rocking back and forth.

'It's not that difficult,' I said. 'Just a matter of practice.'

The man who had spoken to me was tall, dark, handsome, a hunk in a sweatstained tracksuit. Not a boxer — I could tell that from his build — more of a yuppy in very good nick.

'Roger Kale,' he said, offering his hand. 'We sort of met last night at — '

'I remember.' I touched his hand with my training mitt. 'You work for the BBC.'

'Yes and no,' he said. 'I'm an actor. I'm in that cops and robbers series. *Shoot to Kill?* You probably don't — '

'I know the one. Haven't seen you here before, though.'

'No, well, they usually restrict people like me to the other bit.' He jerked his head in the direction of the yuppy section of the gym. 'But I saw you come in and when I'd finished my workout I thought I'd just sneak in and see how real fighters do it.'

'You know who I am then?'

'Oh, yeah. Big boxing fan. I saw you fight three or four times. Not the Willie

Slate fight, though. I missed that one, don't know why.'

I warmed to him; I always warm to people who didn't see Willie Slate beat hell out of me that night. It wasn't the only fight I lost in my career — there were two others — but it was the one that carried the most painful memories.

'You want to learn how to hit a speed-ball?' I said. 'Come on, I'll show you. Start slowly. and keep your eye on it at all times because if you miss and you're standing close it'll probably knock you out.'

He wasn't at all bad — a lot of strength and good co-ordination — and he only lost his rhythm when he grew over-confident and his punches became too vicious and too ragged. At that stage I decided it was time to stop and we went off, showered, changed and had coffee together in the gym's cafe.

We talked mostly about boxing and Rachel, his producer, the only two interests we really had in common. He was good company because unlike most actors he could boast without obviously boasting. He cottoned on quickly to the fact that I had never seen his TV series but by talking about it amusingly, self-deprecatingly, he made it clear, without actually saying so, that he was its star, the main reason why it was always in the top half-dozen in the ratings. And, more engagingly still, he spoke enthusiastically of Rachel. OK, he was an actor and it was no secret that I liked her, so maybe his apparent affection for her was just an act but if it was he did it well, which made him a good actor if nothing else.

'Next time you visit the TV Centre,' he said, as we parted, 'let me know. Come and see our show being recorded — not all of it, you don't need that. Just drop in, say hello. I'll introduce you to the rest of the cast.' He rolled his eyes in an exaggerated, actorish sort of way. 'There's a couple of very pretty girls you might care to meet.' Then he winked and we walked away in opposite directions towards our respective cars.

On my way home I stopped off at Harrod's food hall, then browsed a while in the book department and when I got back to my flat it was my turn for a message on the answerphone.

Beckway in a state of great agitation. 'Bobby? For Christ's sake why aren't you around when I need you? Meet me at the House of Commons at half-past twelve. I've had fucking Mickey Mouse on the phone again.'

TWELVE

I was late getting to the House of Commons and lost another few minutes going through the security procedures at the St Stephen's entrance so, what with one thing and another, it was close to 12.45 by the time I reached the Central Lobby, the circular foyer where MPs meet their guests. Beckway was already there, prowling agitatedly between the statue of William Gladstone and the post office situated discreetly, but still somehow a touch incongruously, at the back of the hall.

He whirled to face me as I came in, St Andrew on the stained glass window behind him and all the kings and queens of England in their niches on the wall no doubt sharing his disapproval of my lateness.

'Christ,' he said, by way of greeting, 'where have you been?'

'I got held up. I'm sorry — '

'Come out on the terrace.' He set off so fast down the corridor that I had to jog a few paces to catch up with him.

'What's all the panic?' I said.

He stopped and took a deep breath. 'Sorry. It's not, it's not really panic. It's just that the bastard is getting to me . . .'

The call had come through on Beckway's private line at the Ministry around 11:30 and had begun with Mickey Mouse saying, 'Tut, tut, tut, Minister. I'm sure I don't have to tell you who this is tutting at you, do I? But are you at all curious to know why I'm tutting in this sorrowful way?'

Oh, Jesus, Beckway thought.

'I'm tutting because I'm very disappointed in you, Minister, very disappointed indeed. My spies tell me you've hired some weary old prizefighter to sniff around on your behalf. Now I put it to you, Minister, was that a friendly act on your part? I'd go even further and ask you this: was it at all a sensible act, a man like that with his brains all scrambled? Ah, it's a terrible business, prize fighting, don't you agree? It inflicts dreadful damage on a man. You'd have been better off employing the Keystone Kops, so you would, unless . . . Well, unless I have hold of the wrong end of the stick altogether and your man isn't an investigator at all but just a pimp, because didn't he deliver your lady friend to you, all gift-wrapped, last night?'

Beckway said, sharply, 'How do you know that?'

'Tut, tut, tut again, Minister. Did you really think for a minute that I wouldn't have my eye on you at all times? If you so much as pick your nose I know about it.'

Beckway let his breath out slowly and said, 'Can we stop pissing about? I'm really not all that impressed by your sarcasm. Why don't you just tell me what you want? Money? OK, fine, you tell me how much you want, I'll tell you how much I can afford and we can start negotiating.'

Mickey Mouse chuckled. Beckway found that as irritating as the sarcasm. 'It's not your money we're wanting, Minister, though God knows you have enough and to spare. No, we're not common blackmailers, not at all, nothing as crude as that. Besides, demanding money is not very businesslike in the long run. I mean, just think about it. You'd pay up the first time, sure you would, and maybe once or twice after that but, ah well, you know how it is. We'd start getting greedy and asking for too much too often. It's bound to happen, it's human nature, am I not right?'

Beckway grunted.

Mickey Mouse said, 'You agree with me, sure you do. And the thing of it is you'd start hurting financially or you'd find it difficult to explain to your wife where all the money was going and then there'd come a day when you said, "Ah, the hell with it, I can't go on like this. Better to be disgraced than to be bled white." And at that point you might be desperate enough to go to the police. Well, I don't want that and, be honest now, neither do you.'

'So all right,' Beckway said, 'if it's not money what is it?'

'A favour, that's all. It won't cost you personally a single penny.

'A favour? Just one?'

Again the irritating chuckle. 'Well, just one to start with anyway. We may come back for more later, I'm not saying we won't. After all, we — and your good friend Minnie Mouse in particular — would like to think of this as a pleasant, ongoing relationship. Can you truly say

171

that's unreasonable now, when you remember how intimate you've been with
Minnie? She's not the kind to kiss and
run and we'd like to think that you're
not either, though I daresay there's
many a woman might say otherwise
about you. Some women have wicked
tongues, isn't it a fact?'

'Cut the bullshit,' Beckway said.
'What sort of favour are you talking
about?'

'Why, the simple sharing of a little
information, that's all. As to the precise
nature of that information I'll let you
know later on.'

'But — '

'Enough for now, Minister. You'll be
hearing from me again, never fear. And
as for your prizefighter, keep him
around by all means. He doesn't bother
us at all.'

And at that point Beckway snapped.
As he said later, he'd taken enough shit
for one morning; it was time to hand
some back. 'Then maybe you should be
bothered,' he said, 'because he knows
that you killed Freddie Marcus.'

There was a long silence at the other
end of the line. Then . . . 'What was
that you said, Minister?'

'You heard. He knows why you killed him, too.' And just for once it was Beckway who slammed the phone down.

We were standing at the far end of the terrace, out of earshot of the groups of other MPs and their constituents who shared the place with us. A riverboat full of tourists went slowly by, cameras clicking, the sun turning the vessel's spray into a shower of glittering silver. One or two of the MPs waved at the photographers; Beckway just glowered and turned his back on them.

'What's he playing at, this Irish bastard?' he asked. 'What's with all these bloody phone calls?'

The answer seemed clear enough. Mickey Mouse wasn't playing *at* anything; he was playing *with* his quarry, sawing away at his nerves, wearing him down and the tactic seemed to be working. Beckway was jumpy, close to the point at which he would be biddable enough to do anything the Irishman asked of him. As he recounted the details of the phone call the only time the dull monotone of his voice was infused with a bit of life was when he reported Mickey Mouse's description of me —

weary old prizefighter, scrambled brains — and then for a moment I detected a note of sour pleasure.

He turned back to stare gloomily at the river, his elbows resting on the parapet. 'I ought to thank you for last night,' he said. 'Bringing Lacy to the flat.'

For a moment the anger stirred again but then I let it go. 'Just don't expect me to do it any more. I'm not a procurer.'

'Touchy.'

I said. 'I'm not sure it was altogether wise to tell the Irishman that I know about Freddie Marcus.'

'Why not? Let him worry for a change. And I'm pretty damn sure I did worry him at that.'

Which made two of us who were worried — the Irishman and me. Because if he knew that I knew . . . Well, it did seem to make my position kind of dicey. If, as seemed reasonable to assume, he had killed Marcus to protect himself, what was to prevent him killing me, too? And if he decided to do that, how was I to protect myself? I had no idea who he was, for God's sake.

I said, 'Thanks a lot, Archie. You realise he might come after me now to make sure I don't tell the police?'

'Good. Draw the bastard out. That's what you're here for, isn't it? Get him into the open and then we can nab him.'

An MP waved from further down the terrace; Beckway waved back. There was no warmth in the exchange. 'That man is a prat,' Beckway said. 'And he hates me. He's about my age, he's been in Parliament four years longer than I have and he thinks I'm holding down a job that ought to be his. He's not alone either. That's why I don't need all this drama with the Irishman. I've got enough problems guarding my back against the people in my own fucking party. Did you learn anything useful at the BBC last night?'

'Not really.' We moved away from the parapet and sat at a table for two in the sunshine. I made an effort to stop thinking about the Irishman and what he might do to me and said, 'Tell me about Donovan.'

'Like what?'

'Like how you met him, how closely you're associated with him, that kind of stuff.' I shrugged. 'Who knows — maybe this present business has something to do with way back when.'

He looked at me thoughtfully for a while, then said, 'OK, why not? I mean, Christ, you know Donovan as well as anybody. He fixed a building contract for me, big block of council flats in one of the London boroughs. It was, oh, a long time ago, before I was married, when I was still trying to move my construction company into the major league.'

'Where'd you meet him?'

'One of his casinos. I gambled quite heavily in those days and I'd dropped a few thousand quid that night. Somebody introduced us, I can't remember who. Tell you the truth, I think Donovan arranged it. I was a loser and I lost cash, not credit, so I was the kind of punter he liked to encourage. Anyway, we got talking and I told him how I'd put in for this council contract and lost it and couldn't understand why because I'd bid really low.'

'Why'd you tell him that, a man you'd only just met?'

'Because it was bloody important to me. Right then I really needed that contract. And I suppose it was very much on my mind and I was talking a lot because I was a little drunk. Donovan was very sympathetic, very interested because that was a borough in which he had a lot of influence.'

I said, 'Donovan has a lot of influence everywhere.'

'Right. But in this place he was particularly well-connected so he said he'd look into it for me. And what he found out was that mine had been the lowest bid until, a couple of days before the deadline for tenders, someone came in just a touch lower and got the job.'

'And someone in the council offices got just a touch richer?'

He nodded. 'That's about the size of it. So Donovan said this was iniquitous and he'd see justice was done.'

'Good old Donovan. Where would justice be without him? I imagine he fixed things all right.'

'Oh, yes. By this time the building work had already started but suddenly the contractors began to run into all kinds of problems. Fires broke out, walls collapsed, there were a couple of unofficial strikes, the cement mixture turned out to be about as adhesive as a bowl of muesli and anonymous callers started phoning the council and threatening to expose what they called this corruption to the Press.'

'Donovan's good,' I said, admiringly. 'He sets his mind to it, there's nobody better at organising things.'

'So I discovered. The council panicked, fired the original contractors and gave the job to me, as the next lowest bidder, rather than waste time going through the whole tendering business again.' He paused, grinning reminiscently. 'And after that, as they say, I never looked back. My company just got bigger and bigger.'

'Probably,' I said, 'because your new partner had very good contacts.'

'Donovan? Oh, sure. Well, as he said, there was a lot of building going on around London in those days and there was no reason why much of it shouldn't be done by us.'

'You were already "us" then? And you didn't mind?'

'Why should I? Before Donovan came along I had 100 per cent of very little. Afterwards we each had 50 per cent of a great deal.'

I gave this a bit of thought. 'The partnership, I imagine, was unofficial. Nothing on paper, nothing signed, just an understanding that a certain amount of money had to be set aside for greasing palms and that unless you kept Donovan happy you might find fires and strikes and cement like vichyssoise turning up on your sites, too.'

He looked defiant. 'Yes, well, that was acceptable.'

I said, 'You're as crooked as he is, aren't you?'

'Oh, please, spare me the morality. We're talking about business here. You play in the big boys' league, you have to play by the big boys' rules. Do you really believe that anyone ever became seriously rich without cutting the odd corner?'

Well, no, I didn't believe that. I just wondered a bit about what constituted a corner and how large a chunk you had to cut off it if you wanted to be seriously rich.

I said, 'Did you make any enemies back then? Any walking wounded? Shafted rivals who might bear you a grudge?'

'I'm sure we made a lot of enemies.' He leaned back thoughtfully, squinting towards the river. 'But I can't think of . . . Well, there's Jack Klug, I suppose.

Do you know Jack?' When I shook my head he said, 'Another builder. Did very well until the recession. We screwed him very badly once. He still seems friendly enough but who knows?'

'What about women then? Can you think of any seriously pissed-off woman among all those you've screwed and discarded who might — '

Beckway looked genuinely upset. 'You don't understand me at all. I don't hurt women. I make them happy.'

'Yes, but if you've been making one woman happy and then you stop and go off to make another woman happy, the first one might get the bizarre idea that you've dumped her. You know how women are. They tend to take these things personally.'

He grunted impatiently. 'Look, it's not like that with me. OK, nobody can ever tell how a woman's going to react, I grant you that. But I always end things amicably. Always. I love women, all women. All right, yes, I love the pretty ones best, most men do, but it's not just their shape, or their looks, or their age or their race, colour or creed, it's . . .' Suddenly, in the pleasure of talking about what was clearly his favourite

180

subject or, if you want my opinion, his obsession, he seemed to have forgotten his problems. He even gave the impression that he was quivering like some animal, like a dog that had caught the distant whiff of a bitch on heat. 'It's the womanness of them that I can't resist.' He took a deep breath and grinned at me. 'You don't approve of me, do you?'

He was a member of the Government, a man entrusted with running the affairs of the country and his brain was stuck in his testicles and he wanted me to approve of him?

'No, I see you don't,' he said. 'Too bad. We all have our weaknesses and women are mine. But the point is I'm good to them. I serve them. I please them. I don't just love them — I like them and they know that. That's why they're attracted to me.'

He leant back again in his chair and looked up at the summer sky, a deep, friendly blue dotted here and there with slowly moving wisps of cloud as virgin white as a bridal gown. 'What are we going to do, Bobby? About this Irish bastard?'

I shrugged. 'Carry on waiting, I suppose, until he tells you what he wants.

Or until he comes after me. Or just hope the police will nail him for killing Freddie Marcus.'

He shook his head firmly. 'No. I don't want the police to catch him. If they do, everything will come out. I want us to catch him. I want you to catch him — and kill him.'

I looked at him then more carefully than I had ever done before and for the first time I saw on his face the kind of expression that might well cause certain kinds of women to go weak at the knees. He seemed almost to be smiling but there was a recklessness, a coldness, a wolfishness to that smile. No sign of weakness or vulnerability any more. It was easy to see in him now not just a man who played by the big boys' rules but a man who had invented the big boys' rules.

'I don't do that kind of thing,' I said.

'No? Donovan says you do.'

'I did it once. I killed somebody once. But that was for personal reasons.'

'Yes, I know. For a girl. For love.' He waved a hand impatiently. 'If you can do it once, you can do it again. If you can do it for love, you can do it for money. And I promise you, Bobby, that if you can find this Irishman and kill him for me I will give you a very great deal of money.' He looked at his watch and stood up, the icy smile relaxing into something resembling an amiable grin. 'I have to go. Give my love to Birgit.'

'What?'

He said, amused, 'You're taking her to dinner tonight. She told me. She said you were most insistent.'

I didn't remember it quite that way but who was I to call a lady a liar?

'Still a case of *cherchez la femme* is it, as far as you're concerned? First Lacy, now Birgit. Frankly, I think you're barking up the wrong tree. Or do I mean sniffing up the wrong skirt? Either way be careful with Birgit. She has an almost infallible way of getting what she wants.' He flashed the grin again, turned and walked briskly back into the building.

By that time there were a lot of women on the terrace and all of them, young, old or simply in-betweens, watched him as he went. A few minutes later I followed him but I wasn't aware of any women watching me.

THIRTEEN

When I got to Donovan's place just off Park Lane he was up in the Pink Bedroom, stuffing a dead Arab diplomat into a bodybag. Well, to be accurate two other Arabs, dark, inscrutable young men in black suits and white shirts, were doing the actual stuffing. Donovan was just overseeing the operation, frowning pensively, hands thrust into his trouser pockets. Two other men, one about my age only a good deal bigger and the other burly and fiftyish, were chatting quietly together by the window and a slim, pretty brunette in pink knickers and bra was sitting on the pink bed and taking gulps from a glass of brandy.

It wasn't quite the scene I'd expected — not that I'd been expecting anything in particular — which was probably why I nodded towards the diplomat and said, stupidly, 'Dead?'

'He'd better be,' Donovan said. 'We'd hardly be shoving him into a fucking bodybag if he was still alive, would we?

I don't think he'd like it very much.'

The men at the window turned towards us. The fiftyish one nodded and said, 'Good to see you again, Bob.'

'Hello, George.' He was a policeman, a very high-ranking one, and a close associate of Donovan's. Like most policemen who had known Donovan for any length of time he exuded well-being and prosperity, too much of it, perhaps, because the jacket of his Savile Row suit was beginning to strain a little over his paunch.

'You know Shitfer, of course,' Donovan said.

I glanced towards the younger man. He was dressed by Armani and looked hard and fit. 'How's it going, Shitfer?'

'John,' he corrected me, automatically. 'I'm fine, Bobby. You?' There was a time, when we were growing up together in the Street, when everyone called him Shitfer. His surname was Braynes and Shitfer Braynes just had a natural ring to it. Besides, for a while the nickname was appropriate. He was a big, fat, dull kid until puberty hit him, at which time the fat fell away to be replaced gradually by muscle and he began to reveal a quick, streetsmart mind, a remarkable talent for cold, calculated violence and a marked distaste for being called Shitfer. People who had quite forgotten his real first name quickly learned to refresh their memories, especially after he was seen beating up his own father, while yelling, 'My name is John. You gave it to me so you fucking call me by it.' Those who witnessed this scene hurried by murmuring to themselves, 'John, not Shitfer — John.' Nowadays only Donovan, his employer, and I — and I only occasionally and absentmindedly — called him Shitfer. For some reason he had never officially asked me not to. Officially, when he was sorting the matter out all those years ago, had involved holding the offender against a wall and inflicting grievous bodily harm. He had never tried that on me, possibly because as a successful young boxer I was regarded as the other hard man in our age group and possibly because, unlike the rest of his contemporaries, I had never tormented him when he was fat and dull.

'Awkward business this,' George said. The two young Arabs zipped up the bodybag and laid it gently on the bed beside the girl.

'What caused it?' I asked.

'Blowjob,' Donovan said. 'Katie there, old Hoovermouth, she did it. Bloke just went and died on her or, you want the literal truth, came and died on her.'

Katie lowered her eyelashes modestly and took another sip of the brandy. 'That's the second one's died like that. I don't know why it is. Maybe I just throw myself into my work too much.'

'How long's he been dead?'

'Hour or so,' Donovan said. He gave the bodybag an affectionate pat. 'We're going to miss him. One of our regulars, big spender, too.'

George said, 'You don't have to stick around here, Donovan. You've got a business to run. Shitf . . . John and I and these two fellers will do the necessary.'

'Thanks, me old mate.' Donovan put his left arm around the other man's shoulders in a grateful hug and showed more substantial gratitude by slipping an envelope into George's coat pocket with his free hand.

'What friends are for,' George said. 'Don't worry about a thing. You won't hear another word about this.'

Donovan led me out of the room and down the wide, gently curving staircase to the bar. It was a very sumptuous brothel he ran, very discreet, too. Even this early in the evening most of the bedrooms were occupied but not a sound could be heard from behind the heavy doors. The decor was tasteful and expensive and the bar and restaurant would not have been out of place in a five-star hotel. Neither would the girls, all of whom were attractive, well-groomed and as smartly dressed as any other highly-paid young career women.

Originally, the brothel had occupied only one of the big, terraced houses in this upmarket street but then it had expanded to take over the house next door as well. There were no complaints from the neighbours because Donovan was his own neighbour. Indeed, he owned the entire block, which he had converted into his own vision of an entertainment centre consisting of a discreet betting shop and a casino as well as the whorehouse, all of them interconnected.

It was, he often said, like a multiplex cinema only a hell of a lot more fun.

'How did you know I was here?' he asked when we'd settled ourselves in the bar.

'Annie told me. I rang her when I found your message on my machine and she said you'd had to rush over here — bit of an emergency.'

'Bloody right. Could have been very nasty if young Katie hadn't kept her wits about her. 'Course, it helps that she knows the procedure.' He shook his head, wonderingly. 'Can you believe that? Two clients have croaked on her now. Exactly the same circumstances, too. I wonder what it is she does to them. Wouldn't fancy finding out for me, would you, Bobby? On the house, like.'

'No way. I'm too young to die.'

'Even if you went with a big, happy grin on your face like the ambassador? Yeah, maybe you're right.'

'Ambassador? The stiff was an ambassador?'

Donovan nodded. 'Just as well he was. Makes it easier to tidy up the mess. His embassy wants everything kept quiet as much as I do. When it happened Katie called Shitfer, Shitfer called me, I called the ambassador's private secretary and he sent those two goons round with the bodybag. What they'll do is, they'll take the old bugger out the back way, stick him in the boot of his limo, smuggle him into the embassy, tuck him up in bed and find him dead of a heart attack tomorrow morning. Everything neat and tidy and no scandal.'

'What did you need George for?'

'Insurance. Anyone happens to talk out of turn, George will make sure the police don't get involved. He's very good at that, I find.' He munched a handful of cashew nuts and washed them down with a slug of whisky. 'I got that message you left for me last night. What's going on with you and Archie?'

I told him — about last night, about the Irishman's call this morning and about the meeting at the House of Commons.

Donovan smiled reminiscently. 'We made a lot of money together, Archie and I. You mustn't underestimate him, you know. He's very smart, very shrewd, except where sex is concerned, of course. He can be a bloody lunatic with women.' He nibbled at a few more cashews. 'So what do you reckon? Jack Klug? Interesting thought. He can be a right nasty bastard that Jack. Or one of Archie's old girlfriends?'

I said, 'Donovan, I don't reckon any-thing. I'm out of my depth here. And frankly I'm not a bit happy about that Irishman knowing what he does about me. I've said this before and I expect I'll say it again — we should let the police take over.'

'Yes, well, you know the answer to that — no police. Once they got involved the Prime Minister would have to let Archie go. He couldn't afford to have another minister mixed up in a sex scandal.'

'All right, tough — Archie goes. So what? He's got a thriving business, more money than he could ever spend. If he resigns and walks away he's only turning his back on a pretty low grade job. He could sit on the back benches for a few years, he's young enough, and then make a comeback.'

'Make a comeback? How? Those pho-tographs won't go away in a few years. He'd be vulnerable forever.' Donovan thought for a moment. 'See what you have to remember about Archie, he's ambitious. You're right, he doesn't need any more money but he's developed a strong taste for power and influence. This job he's got now is nothing much, he knows that. But he also knows his mate, the PM, is grooming him for something bigger. He can't afford to let anyone, other than us, know he's likely to be blackmailed. Archie wants a seat in the Cabinet and he'll probably get it next time around. After that . . .' He shrugged. 'After that, who knows? Chancellor? Foreign Secretary? Prime Minister?'

I choked on my drink. 'Prime Mini . . . ? Archie?'

'He's got time on his side. He keeps out of any scandals, he can afford to wait, climb the ladder rung by rung.'

'God Almighty, Donovan. Archie Beckway — Prime Minister. What's happened to this country? There used to be giants in the land.'

'When? There hasn't been a giant since old Churchill during the war. Clement Attlee maybe. But the rest? Pygmies, all of them. And if we're talking pygmies, Archie's no smaller than anyone else.'

We sat for a moment in moody silence. What Donovan was thinking about I couldn't say but I was contemplating a country run by Archie Beckway, a country in which — to adapt an old joke

— the Prime Minister couldn't care less who was in his Cabinet so long as she had big tits. 'Is that what his wife wants, too? For Archie to be Prime Minister?'

Donovan reached for the cashews again, then stayed his hand regretfully. 'Too many calories in these bastards. Annie's nagging me about the weight I'm putting on. Must be getting soft in my old age, letting a woman nag me.' He pushed the bowl of nuts away from him. 'Archie's wife? I don't know what she wants. I don't even know that she wants Archie all that much. But what I want is Archie right where he is and climbing. So you carry on. Do what you can — and keep in touch.'

'OK.' I finished my drink, got up and walked away but when I'd gone a few paces I stopped and turned back. 'By the way, if we find out who this Irishman is, Archie wants me to kill him.'

Donovan nodded thoughtfully. 'And will you?'

'No.'

He nodded some more. 'Well, that's all right. You find out who he is and I'll get Shitfer to kill him.'

FOURTEEN

I went back to my flat to shower and change and get ready to meet Birgit Cassidy for dinner. There was another message on the answering machine . . .

'Hi, Bobby, this is Linda. I left some stuff in your apartment and, ah, well, Rex will be in London in the next few days and I asked him to call round and collect it. Is that OK? Don't bother to pack it. Just throw it in a couple of dustbin liners or something.' A silence, then . . . 'Dammit, I'm so sorry the way things worked out. I really cared about you but . . . We all screw up, right? We all make mistakes and I've made mine.' And that was it. Thanks, Linda. Terrific. Was I the mistake or did you screw up later? You might at least have told me. You could still tell me. I mean, what's wrong with a letter? Spain does have a postal service, you know. It might take a little time but the mail gets from there to here in the end and . . . Oh, what the hell.

I'd met Linda Kelly in California the

previous summer. She was an actress and like most actresses in Hollywood she spent less time acting than she did filling in between roles. When I came across her she was working as a private detective. She was in her late twenties with the long legs that came from her American genes and the black hair and startling blue eyes that she had inherited from her Irish forebears.

We were good together pretty well from the start, so good that a few months later she gave up the detective business, which wasn't much of a sacrifice, and came to live with me in London.

We were good together there, too. Linda had never been out of America before so we did all the tourist things — art galleries, theatres, Stratford-on-Avon, Edinburgh, the Lake District; we travelled to Rome, Venice, Paris, the West of Ireland where her family had come from and we were happy. The only thing that bothered her was that she couldn't work; as a foreigner she wasn't allowed to seek jobs as an actress. But even that problem would have vanished once we were married and, yes, we talked about that, too.

195

And then Rex appeared. We were having supper at the Caprice one Saturday night when this great, blond, superannuated all-American boy loomed up at our table, all jeans and leather jacket, ruffled shirt open to the nipples, gold chain around the neck, teeth gleaming like a neon sign.

He said, 'Hey, there' and Linda looked up and squealed and then they were in each other's arms, hugging and kissing like, well, like lovers reunited. Which, in a way, is what they were.

Finally they sat down and I was introduced to Rex Poorboy. Honestly, that's his name and if you go to the cinema much you'll probably recognise it. He and Linda had worked together off-off-Broadway, had lived together for a while and then broken up — she to try her luck in Hollywood and he to direct penny-ante movies in New York. A few months back he had scored a tremendous hit with a low-budget road picture which had been pretentious enough to impress the critics and violent enough to please a mass audience.

So then Hollywood had waved fat cheques at him and now he was on his way to Spain with a massive budget to

196

direct some kind of historical epic. You probably saw it; most people did — a blood and guts adventure story about a hunk of an American journalist and two beautiful American tourists caught up in the Spanish Civil War. It didn't make a lot of sense but, what the hell, the body count was terrific.

I didn't like Rex. You may have gathered that. First sight I didn't like him. I didn't like his mop of blond hair. I didn't like his teeth or his suntanned chest.

'Lennox,' he said, helping himself to wine and jabbing a thick index finger at me. 'A boxer, right?'

'I was, yes.'

'Willie Slate slaughtered you in a title fight. Jesus, he was good. Linda, hey, whatta you doing here in London with this bum?' The neon teeth flashed at me. I don't know, maybe he had a hidden switch in his pocket. 'Just kidding, OK?'

That said he seemed to think the social niceties were now dispensed with as far as I was concerned because thereafter he ignored me and talked only to Linda. It was a very long evening.

On the way home she said, 'You didn't like Rex, did you?'

'Not as much as he likes himself but sure, yes, I loved him.'

'Yeah, well, thing of it is he wants me to have dinner with him.'

'You want to go?'

'Yes, I do.' She stroked my cheek gently. 'Don't be jealous. It's not like that. It's just that we go back a long way and there's so much to catch up on. But . . . If you're not happy about it, I won't go.'

I wasn't happy, of course I wasn't, but I said I was — what else could I say? — and she went and after that I heard a lot about Rex. He was in London for a few weeks, working with his script writer, casting some of the supporting roles and rehearsing with the male and female leads. Once or twice we made up a foursome — Linda and me, Rex and Laura Leslie, his leading lady, another mutual friend from off-off-Broadway. The three of them had a lot to talk about, much of it on the theme of what a shame it was that Linda wasn't acting any more.

'Bobby, you should have seen her. She was so good, so versatile.' Laura, the leading lady, was either a better actress than I had suspected or she genuinely meant it. 'All she ever needed was a break.'

Another favourite topic was what a total bitch the second female lead was. Rex hadn't wanted her in the movie but she had come as part of the deal, an executive vice-president at the studio having promised her the role by way of a kiss-off.

'Can you believe that?' Rex ran his hand agitatedly through his blond mane to show how deeply his artist's soul was offended. 'She's a whore. The only time she acts is when she's on her back with her knees up. And the guy gives her an important role in a major movie. Jesus, what kind of integrity does he have?' The two women murmured their sympathy.

I said, mildly, 'Well, I don't suppose she's the first whore who ever made it into the movies and I don't suppose he's the first studio boss who ever paid off his mistress with a co-starring role and I don't suppose you're the first director who ever had to swallow his principles and work with whores and pimps. I imagine it's the nature of the business.'

There was a long, startled silence. Then Rex leaned across the table towards me, tight-lipped, a muscle working in his cheek to denote anger barely restrained. He had probably learned how to do that at drama school. 'You want to run that past me again, friend? Because somewhere in there you sure as hell insulted me.'

I thought about it. 'No,' I said, 'it was quite a long sentence and I don't think I could bear to go through it twice. But if you were offended, Rex, well, just kidding, OK?'

Touché, I thought, but this kindergarten triumph didn't do me a lot of good, not in the long run nor, come to that, immediately because even Linda was at best coolly polite to me for the rest of the evening. By then, in any event, it had become clear that the company of these two, and especially the ever-attentive Rex, was making her think wistfully, regretfully of the show-business career she had been forced to abandon.

One night Rex turned up unannounced at the flat while Linda and I were watching *Casablanca* on video. I let him in and we nodded curtly at each other. Linda greeted him with a big kiss.

'Great movie,' he said, extricating him-self from her and nodding towards the TV screen. 'Mind if I turn it off?' He turned it off without waiting for an answer.

Linda said, 'Rex, it's lovely to see you but what are you doing here?'

'I got good news and I got great news,' he said. 'I think we all better sit down and, hey, I could use a drink.' Linda got the drink — bourbon and water, no ice. He hadn't asked for that but she seemed to know it was what he wanted.

'The good news,' he said, drinking then wiping his lips on the back of his hand, 'is the whore is outta the movie. She got smashed in the Polo Lounge and totalled her car, which is a tragedy because it was a beautiful Corniche. But it's not all bad because she also broke her leg.' He beamed at Linda and swallowed some more bourbon.

'And what's the great news?' I asked.

Rex put his glass down, sank back in his chair and smacked his hands to-gether. 'Are you ready for this? Are you really ready for this? The great news is that I want Linda to take her place and the studio's given the OK.'

'What?' said Linda.

He leaned forward, big hands on big knees. 'Honey, you'd be terrific. Believe me, this could be the break you never had. Lissena me, will you? You and Laura would be perfect together. She's tall and blonde, you're tall and dark, you complement each other. Plus, you like each other. Laura's crazy about the idea. She hated the whore, everybody hates the whore, but she loves you. You and Laura, you'd be a sensation and I'll tell you something even she doesn't know. The part I'm offering you is better than hers. OK, you don't get to kiss the guy in the final close-up? Who cares? You're the one everybody will remember, trust me.' He reached for the glass again and stared at her anxiously.

Through all this I'd been watching Linda. She had listened to Rex with increasing excitement, her lips slightly parted, her eyes growing wider and wider. But now she glanced across at me and the animation left her.

'Rex,' she said, 'Rex, I . . .' She looked at me again. 'I just don't know.'

'What's not to know? I want you, the studio . . . Well, OK, the studio didn't actually *want* you but that's because they don't know you. I do and I pitched it to them strong and they agreed because they believe in me. Listen,' and here pretty much for the first time he shot a look at me, 'somebody was once talking about directors and principles. Well, maybe I mislaid mine for a while but now I got them back. I'm all through with the whores and the pimps. You're my choice, my genuine choice, so don't say no to me, Linda.'

Shit, I thought, he's really doing this rather well. Linda looked at me doubtfully and I held her gaze for a moment. She didn't have to ask for my permission or approval, of course she didn't. She was a free agent and we both knew that. But my permission and my approval were what she wanted, so I took a deep breath and nodded. The dazzling smile of gratitude she gave me was not, as it turned out, much of a reward but it was all she left me to cling on to.

'OK,' she said.

Rex leapt up, she leapt up, they kissed again and he swung her around. When he had put her down he said, 'I knew you'd say yes, I just knew it, so I brought a script with me. We don't have a lot of time, you see. We start shooting in Madrid in two, three weeks so what say you read for me now and I can explain what I want and . . .'

Now they both stared at me. I got up, took *Casablanca* out of the video machine and made for the door. 'Go ahead,' I said. 'If you want us Ingrid Bergman and I will be in the bedroom. Oh, by the way, Linda — congratulations.' I went over to kiss her and, smiling happily, she raised her face to me. But she didn't offer her lips.

As I slipped *Casablanca* into the bedroom video I thought, My God, life does imitate art: Ilsa is going off with fucking Victor Laszlo again. And that was the way it worked out.

I didn't see a lot of Linda after that. Along with Rex, Laura Leslie and the leading man she moved into a hotel near Pinewood Studios where the rehearsals were taking place. These rehearsals were Rex's idea, a way of saving expensive time later when the whole unit was assembled on location, and they seemed to go on throughout the day and into the night.

'It's business,' Linda said, 'that's all. It's nothing personal.'

'You mean aside from the fact that

Rex used to be your lover and wants his old job back?'

She flushed. 'Bobby, please, don't give me a hard time. This is my big chance. You can see that, can't you?'

Oh yes, I could see that. I could see it was Rex's big chance, too, and he took it. Linda and I spent one more weekend together but it wasn't the same. Even while we were making love I had the impression that mentally she was reciting her lines to herself, learning her part. I'm not at all sure she didn't lie there thinking of blond hair, neon teeth and a suntanned chest.

One evening she came to the flat and started packing her clothes. 'They've brought the departure date forward,' she said. 'We fly to Madrid day after tomorrow.' She seemed to be throwing just about everything into her suitcases, stuff she couldn't possibly need in Spain. 'There's a farewell dinner tomorrow night. You'll come, won't you?'

'Are you sure you want me there? I mean, this is pretty short notice, isn't it?' More kindergarten stuff. Petulance this time.

'Bobby, I don't have time for this. But, yes, I want you there.'

So I went. The dinner was in a private room at a West End hotel and the guests were greeted by Rex and Linda, he in a white tuxedo, she in a tight black sheath that emphasised every line and curve in her body. It was a dress I'd never seen before. But . . . He was tall and blond, she was tall and dark and I had to admit they complemented each other.

They were standing there with their arms around each other's waist. As I walked towards them Linda tried to pull away but Rex hugged her to him. 'Glad you could make it,' Rex said. 'Isn't that right, honey?' He was smirking at me.

'You're looking very lovely tonight, Linda,' I said and she mumbled something but she didn't look at me.

Rex said, 'Catch you later, Bobby. We saved you a place on our table. But right now, you know how it is, we have to play host.' He drew Linda away to greet a couple of new arrivals.

It was another thirty minutes before I was able to get her on her own. By then the other guests were beginning to move into the dining-room.

'So,' I said, 'Rex did get his old job back.'

Squirming is something people usually do when they're sitting down but somehow Linda managed to squirm standing up. 'Bobby . . .' She spread her hands helplessly. 'I don't know what to say to you. I didn't want this to . . . It just happened. Rex and I — '

'Go back a long way. Yes, I know. Just tell me this: can I come and see you in Spain?'

She hesitated. 'Well, not for a while. We're going to be very busy. I . . . I'll call you.'

'Right. I'll sit by the phone. Good luck.' I stood there for a moment, absorbing the vision she presented: the glossy black hair, the astonishing blue eyes, the flawless skin, the sleek beauty of her body. And then I left.

Before I reached the door I heard her call my name but I didn't look back. Maybe I should have done; maybe it would have made a difference. Who can tell? But I was proud so I just walked on. And that was the last time I saw her, the last time I heard from her until the message that night on my answering machine.

FIFTEEN

'Archie's in some kind of trouble, isn't he?' Birgit said.

I took a sip of wine, put the glass down carefully beside my plate. 'What makes you say that?'

'He's worried, he's secretive, he doesn't confide in me any more. I know him very well, you see, and I've never known him like this before.' She grinned, briefly. 'I imagine it's a woman. This new girlfriend perhaps?'

'How would I know? I only met him a few days ago.'

She nodded, taking no notice of my denial. 'If you're wondering how I know he has a new girlfriend it's because I recognise the signs. The only thing is, I can't work out how a woman could cause him really serious problems. Archie should know how to deal with women. God knows he's had enough experience. So I'm wondering,' and now it was her turn to sip some wine, looking at me over the rim of the glass, 'whether he's done something utterly stupid and fallen in love with her.'

'I thought he fell in love with all of them,' I said. 'I thought that was his excuse for charging around like a stallion at stud.'

Another nod. 'Well, he does, of course, or at least he convinces himself that he loves them — but only up to a certain point. And that point falls well short of doing anything silly or inconvenient for him, like leaving Felicity and the children. But . . . Well, he's at a dangerous age and I've no doubt the new girl is young and pretty, so I was wondering if this time he really was thinking of doing something drastic.' She stopped, looking at me inquiringly but I wasn't going to swallow that bait.

'Did he love you?' I asked. 'When you were his girlfriend of the moment did he love you as much as the others?'

'Yes,' she said gravely. 'More than most, I think. And you're not going to tell me anything, are you?'

I shrugged. 'What do I know?'

We carried on eating, she giving the poached salmon a seeing to, me attacking the sweetbreads. Langan's was full as usual, the long, narrow dining-room thrumming with noise and activity. Birgit had got us a very good table by the window looking out into Stratton Street and up at the front where the well-known faces normally sat. Archie's influence, I imagined, because they usually tucked me away at the back.

Birgit finished the last of her salmon, put her knife and fork neatly together in the middle of her plate and dabbed her lips with her napkin. 'Of course, you realise that at first I thought *you* were Archie's problem.' She filled my glass and smiled. She had a very pretty smile. 'I couldn't understand what on earth he would want with you. So I checked you out and I still don't understand.' Another smile, a slightly different one this time — the sort of smile that invites a confidence.

'And what did you discover?'

'Well, it was rather interesting. A retired boxer who, people say, came along at the wrong time and would probably be champion of the world if he were fighting now. A university graduate and not a bad university at that. A businessman who has become quite rich, unmarried and never been married, though certainly not gay.' She frowned and nibbled delicately on her lower lip.

'And — which is most interesting of all — one of the few people Donovan trusts.'

'Ah,' I said.

'Yes. You see, what is very curious is that Archie has had no real connection with Donovan for some years but now, all of a sudden, here you are.'

'Strange, isn't it?' I said.

'Yes. And what I want to know is why.'

'Better ask Archie.' The waiter cleared away our plates and we spent a few minutes deciding on dessert. 'Where did you get all your information about me?'

She cocked her head on one side, a gesture which somehow made her look terribly young, and gazed up at the ceiling. 'Archie and I have built up rather a good intelligence service. We built it up together because, well, he's come to rely on me.' She looked down, rearranging her napkin on her lap. 'You see, I joined his firm when I came down from university. He interviewed me for the job of his private secretary on Day One, I accepted his offer on Day Two, started work on Day Three and by Day Five, or rather Night Five, I was in his bed.'

I nodded approvingly. 'Always like a

girl who plays hard to get. I bet you had him guessing on Day Four.'

She gave me yet another smile, a thin one this time. 'Archie told me you were very sarcastic. It's all right, I don't mind. With us, with Archie and me, it was sex and business combined. We're very good at both of those things.' She watched me carefully to see how I was reacting to all this. Rather to my surprise I felt a twinge of jealousy. I reckon I'm pretty good at sex and business, too, but as far as I know attractive women don't go around advertising the fact on my behalf.

The desserts arrived and for a few moments she applied herself to the crème brûlée with single-minded determination. When she had polished it off she said, 'I was Archie's mistress for, oh, three or four years, starting towards the end of the time when he was in partnership with Donovan. It didn't last, of course. My being his mistress, I mean. Well, I never thought it would. There were other women even when he was half living with me.'

'You didn't mind? About the other women?'

'No. Well, not much anyway. There

was a bit of wounded pride when he moved on to another number one girl-friend but by then I was his personal assistant, I had a valuable chunk of shares in his business, a fair bit of money in the bank and my own flat in Knightsbridge. And what's more we both knew that he needed me more than I needed him, not physically any more but in a business sense. So when he got this ministerial job he took me with him. I'm not a civil servant, you understand. It's Archie who pays me, not the ministry. Other people take care of his government work, I just look after Archie.'

I thought it over. 'So what you're saying is that you know where the bodies are buried.'

'If you want to put it that way.'

For a moment I was tempted to confide in her because it seemed to me that if someone from Beckway's past was responsible for his current problems Birgit would probably know better than anyone who it might be.

But the moment passed when she said, 'And it's because I know where the bodies are buried that I'm worried about you, and therefore Donovan, cropping up once more in Archie's life. Archie's got a chance of going right to the top and I want to go with him. He'd be crazy to get involved with someone like Donovan again.'

'He's crazy to get involved with another woman,' I said.

She nodded. 'I know but I can deal with that. Donovan is something else. He's dangerous and that makes you dangerous, too.'

'What did you mean when you said you could deal with it?'

She finished her coffee, dabbed at her lips again and said, 'I think you should get the bill now.'

'You mean that's it?' I was disappointed. Birgit was the first woman I had taken out since Linda left me and sitting there opposite her, our legs occasionally brushing under the table, I had begun to feel some of those wicked old masculine stirrings again. 'That's the end of the evening, the end of our date?'

She put her elbows on the table, cupped her hands under her chin and leaned towards me. Since I was doing much the same thing our noses were only an inch or two apart. 'Well, let's say it's the end of the first part of our date. I thought we might continue this conversation somewhere more private.'

I cleared my throat. 'Right,' I said, somewhat hoarsely. 'Good think . . .'

And then a bottle of champagne arrived. Not on its own, of course — a waiter brought it. 'Compliments of Mr Kale,' he said, nodding towards the bar where Roger Kale was waving and walking towards us. He had a young woman with him.

'What on earth . . .' said Birgit.

'Oh, shit,' I said but before I could say more Kale and his companion were with us. He said, 'Hope you don't mind but it was such a coincidence bumping into you yet again that I thought we might share a bottle together.' He paused, looking just a touch embarrassed. 'Oh God, we're not interrupting anything, are we?'

'Of course not. Please, sit down.' Birgit didn't look at all pleased but what else could I do? A waiter brought chairs and champagne glasses and Kale and I did the introductions. The girl with him, a tall, striking brunette, turned out to be Carly Shawn, Kale's co-star in the cops and robbers TV series.

'How do you two guys know each other?' she asked. She had a good voice, deep and husky.

Kale said, 'Well, we kind of met at the TV Centre and then this morning we were at the gym together and Bobby showed me how to hit the speedball. He used to be a hell of a boxer, you know.' We raised our glasses and toasted each other. 'I never did ask you, Bobby, but what were you doing at the TV centre?'

'Watching Kevin Rycroft's show.'

'You know Kevin, do you?'

'No, but I know the floor manager, Lacy Jones.'

'Ah.' He looked at me thoughtfully, appreciatively. 'I don't know her but I've seen her around, heard a lot about her. Quite a girl, Lacy. Isn't she, Carly?'

'Oh, yes,' Shawn said, dryly. 'Everyone knows Lacy. *Quite* a girl.'

Birgit was looking at me, too, though not as appreciatively as Kale. I had the impression that the name Lacy Jones was not entirely unknown to her. I also had the impression that she was surprised to find that it wasn't unknown to me either. Maybe this was something else Beckway hadn't told her.

'And how about you?' Kale said, turning to Birgit. 'What do you do? No, don't tell me, let me guess. You're an actress, right?'

The intended flattery left her unimpressed. 'I work for a politician,' she said. 'Archie Beckway. I'm his personal assistant.'

'Beckway?' Kale frowned. 'Isn't he in the news at the moment? Or . . . No, not him, someone involved with him. Marcus, was it? PR man or something, who was murdered the other day?'

Birgit nodded.

'Wow,' Kale said. His eyes brightened. 'What's the latest — you know, the inside information?'

'There isn't any,' I said.

'How do you know?' Carly Shawn asked. I had already decided that I didn't like her very much. There was something cold about her, an apparent indifference to anyone else's opinion that seemed to have its roots in arrogance. It was as if she had studied her beauty, which was considerable, in a mirror and decided that that was enough, the only contribution she had to make to the world; she had no need to bother with charm or any of the other social graces.

'I asked Birgit,' I said.

'And how do you happen to know Birgit?' Shawn asked.

'I . . . er . . . I'm associated with Archie Beckway, too,' I said. There didn't seem any point in keeping it secret. Even the Prime Minister knew.

'What as?' Shawn said. 'A sort of minder or something?'

'Hey, chill out,' Kale said, busily topping up the glasses. 'What is this — some kind of third degree?'

'I must say, Mr Lennox,' Shawn said, apparently refusing to chill out, 'you seem to have a lot of very pretty girl friends. Birgit here and Lacy Jones. I wonder how you do it.'

'Forgot to tell you,' Kale said, in a slightly desperate attempt to lighten the conversation, 'I've invited Bobby to come and watch the show being recorded. Good idea, eh?'

'Hmm,' Shawn said and gave me a long, cool look.

We all left soon after that but by then the earlier mood, the nose to nose mood between Birgit and me, had been pretty well destroyed. As we made for the door, the two women walking slightly ahead, I was wondering how it could be resuscitated.

'I think Carly fancies you,' Kale said.

'What? You're mad. She did nothing but niggle at me.'

'Yes, well, that's her way. You come and watch the show and, I promise, it's Buckingham Palace to a pinch of shit that the pair of you end up going off together. Hey, hang on.' He grabbed hold of me and then of Birgit. 'Look, the papparazzi are out there waiting to get shots of Carly and me. If you don't want any awkward publicity you'd better let us go out first.'

Birgit, who had been looking increasingly disgruntled ever since Kale and Shawn first appeared, said, 'Oh, the hell with it. This is too much.' And then she was gone, past everybody and into the street. I tried to follow her but I was hemmed in behind Kale and Shawn.

Shawn said, 'Come on Roger, we might as well face the jackals,' and the pair of them went out, too, to be greeted with a barrage of flashbulbs and shouts of 'This way, Roger, this way, Carly.'

By the time I was able to follow them Birgit was about fifty yards down the street, getting into a taxi. 'Goodnight, Mr Lennox,' she called to me. 'Such a delightful evening. Thank you so much.'

'No, wait,' I said. 'I'll give you a li . . .' But it was too late. She was in the cab and moving away.

Roger Kale, having shaken off the photographers, came over to me. 'I'm really sorry about all that,' he said. 'I have a nasty feeling that Carly and I have screwed your evening.'

I sighed. 'Look on the bright side,' I said. 'At least something got screwed.'

SIXTEEN

It was the sound of the sitting-room window breaking that woke me. Not that breaking comes close to describing it. It was as if the damn thing had just exploded. There was a hell of a noise — glass splintering and crashing, preceded or, it seemed, accompanied by something else, a deeper, sharper sound.

I leapt out of bed and had reached the sitting-room door when the deeper, sharper sound was repeated and a second bullet came through the space where the window had been and buried itself, alongside the first, in the plaster on the back wall.

There was glass everywhere, great shards of it and tiny, deadly little splinters of it all over the carpet. I picked my way gingerly around the potentially lacerating mess and took a quick, careful look out at the Embankment. It was barely dawn on an already bright, warm day but there was nobody to be seen.

I don't know what it was — fear,

221

shock, both? — but I was shaking. My hands were shaking, my head was shaking, my legs were shaking. I stood for a moment, leaning against the wall, taking deep breaths. And then the phone rang.

An Irish voice said, 'Did you like my message, Mr Lennox? Woke you up, I shouldn't be at all surprised, on this fine morning. Of course, I could have put those bullets not just through your window but right through you. You do understand that, don't you?'

I took one more breath. 'The thought had occurred,' I said. 'Just trying to tell me something, were you?'

He chuckled. 'That's right, Mr Lennox. Got it first time, smart fellow that you are. What I'm trying to tell you, and I do hope for your own sake that it's sunk in, is that I don't want you interfering in my business any more. What's between me and Archie Beckway is strictly private. Let's all keep it that way. One poor soul is dead already because Archie was foolish enough to go seeking outside help. Now it's time for the help to back out before I have to take it out. Be sensible, Mr Lennox. We don't want a simple little financial transaction turning into a bloodbath, do we?'

I tried to think of something smart to say but it wouldn't have mattered if I had because he'd gone.

I dressed, cleared up as much of the debris as I could, summoned glaziers and plasterers to come and repair the damage, left my cleaning woman to take care of everything else and drove to the Ministry to see Beckway.

Birgit was polite but cool. 'Thank you again for a *lovely* evening,' she said. 'And how nice of you to invite your little friends in to meet me. Such a thoughtful touch.'

'Look,' I said, 'that was none of my doing and I'm very sorry about it. But I don't have time to go down on bended knees and beg your pardon because I have to see Archie. Now.'

'Well, I'm afraid that's quite imposs— '

'Now.'

Her eyes widened. 'Ooh, the forceful type. Very well.' She got on the phone, speaking softly but urgently. I heard an exasperated yelp from Beckway but in a couple of minutes his office door opened, a pair of civil servants came out and I went in.

Beckway was behind his desk, glaring at me. 'What the devil do you mean by this? You can't come barging in here any time you — '

'Shut up and listen,' I said and told him what had happened that morning.

He took it pretty well, all things considered. He just turned white around the mouth and said, 'Good God. Oh, dear God.'

Then he said, 'Do you think he meant it? Would he really kill you?'

'I don't see why not. He killed Freddie Marcus, after all.'

'But why? Why you?'

'I don't know. Maybe he thinks I know more than I do. Maybe your telling him that I know he killed Marcus had something to do with it. Since he now realises that I was the anonymous messenger who found the body he might think I found something else as well, something that might identify him.'

Beckway said, 'Jesus, what a mess.' He got up and prowled around the office a bit. 'Look, if you want to walk away from all this I quite understand, you know. It's bad enough having Freddie's death on my conscience. I don't want yours as well.'

I'd thought about that. I'd thought about it a lot. 'No,' I said. 'I'll stick with it. I might be a bit more careful than usual. I won't walk down dark alleys or take sweets from strangers but I'll stick with it.'

'You're quite sure?'

'Yeah, well, a man's gotta do what a man's gotta do. What I really want is to find that Irishman, stick his rifle up his arse and pull the trigger. He's really annoyed me.'

'It was a rifle then?'

I nodded. 'Judging by the bullets I gouged out of my wall a $\cdot22$, I think.'

'I'll pay for the repairs to your flat, of course.'

'Damn right,' I said.

He grinned suddenly. 'I really am grateful, you know. In the end there may be nothing either of us can do but it's rather comforting not to be alone in this.' He paused. 'Since you are still with me, will you come to dinner at my house tonight? The place in Hertfordshire. There'll be one or two people there I'd like you to meet.'

'Such as?'

'Well, my wife for one. Also Jack Klug — Sir Jack Klug. You remember?'

I nodded. 'Yes, one of the people who might bear you a grudge. And now he's coming to dinner. Is that just a coincidence or did you arrange it?'

'Neither really. Felicity invited him. I've hardly had any dealings with him for ages but I suppose I mentioned him to you because the fact that he was coming to my house meant that he was on my mind.'

'If you have nothing much to do with him, why would your wife ask him to a meal?'

'Oddly enough I think she rather likes him. More than I do, anyway, and besides she says we owe him hospitality from way back. It's one of those occasions when you pay off old debts. You know?'

'Yes. House full of people you don't really like and would rather never see again. Sounds thrilling. I can hardly wait.'

He said, 'I'm sorry about that but if Jack Klug has any idea how seriously Donovan and I shafted him he could be a very nasty enemy. I'd like you to meet him in any case, tell me what you make of him.' He hesitated. 'I think you should meet Felicity, too.'

'Why? You don't seriously think she might be involved in all this, do you?'

'Bobby, I don't know what to think. Quite frankly, I have no idea what her feelings are towards me.'

'Yes, but you'd know if she was the woman in the Minnie Mouse mask, wouldn't you? You know what your own wife's body looks like, feels like, smells like.'

'Yes, of course, only . . .' He slumped down again in his chair behind the desk. 'The Minnie Mouse woman was wearing some kind of scent that I'd never smelt before and — God, this is an embarrassing thing to have to say — it's been so long since I last saw Felicity naked that I can't honestly say that I would recognise her body any more.'

'Funny old game marriage, isn't it?' I said. 'What time do you want me there tonight?'

'About 7.30. Black tie. Bring a partner if you like and it's probably best that you stay the night. And, Bobby, thanks again.'

On the way out I said to Birgit, 'You want to have another shot at dinner tonight? Archie's place in Hertford-shire? Bring a nightie.'

She gave a little gasp of surprise. 'Are you quite mad? Felicity hates me. If you turned up with me on your arm she'd throw us both out. You'd better take somebody else.'

But there lay a problem — I couldn't think of anyone else to ask so I'd have to go to Archie's alone. Once again it struck me what a drab, celibate existence I'd been leading since Linda walked out.

I called Donovan from a phone box (I've not used my carphone for sensitive messages since Princess Squidgie and her boyfriend got caught out a few years ago) to tell him about the shooting incident. He was sympathetic with me and indignant with the Irishman, though I thought he could have been a little more fulsome in his praise of the bravery I was showing in carrying on. But all he said was, 'That's another one we owe the bastard. Find him for me, Bobby.'

After that I went home, got rid of the workmen in late afternoon, showered, packed an overnight bag, put on the dinner jacket and was just about to start out for Hertfordshire when Annie called. She gave good phone — flirtatious stuff that was innocent and mildly exciting at the same time — and we chatted like this for two or three minutes before she said, 'Listen, this is all very thrilling but it's not getting us anywhere. I have a message for you. Donovan's giving a party tomorrow night. The house in Mayfair. He wants you there.'

'Well, I don't know,' I said. 'This is all a bit sudden. I'm not sure I'm free tomorrow — '

'No, you don't understand. It's not a matter of whether you're free or not. He *wants* you there, okay? That means you've got to be there and if you have a previous appointment at Buckingham Palace to be knighted by the Queen, tough tit, you'd better cancel it. Am I getting through to you, Bobby?'

'I think so,' I said. 'The old brain doesn't work so fast these days but I'm picking up a message that this is kind of important.'

'It is. He wants you there and, as a matter of fact, I want you there, too. I'll tell him to expect you then.'

'What happens if I don't turn up?'

'He'll probably have you shot. So you'll be there, right?'

'I suppose so,' I said. 'You wouldn't like to tell me what this is all about, would you?'

She chuckled. 'No. It's a big surprise and Donovan wants to spring it himself. I look forward to seeing you, gorgeous.' Then she blew me a great, plonking kiss and was gone.

Two minutes later the phone rang again. This time it was Beckway.

'There's been a change of plan,' he said. 'I won't be there tonight after all. I still want you to go but I won't be able to make it. Something's come up.'

'Parliament? Are you actually turning up for once?' He hesitated just a fraction too long and I knew it had nothing to do with Parliament. 'What is it? It's not a woman, is it?'

'Please, Bobby, I don't want to talk about it.' His voice was tense, strained.

'Goddammit, it *is* a woman. You're missing your own dinner party to get your leg over somewhere else. Who is it — Lacy?'

'It's not like you think. This is not something I want . . . I'm sorry but I really can't talk about it. I have to go.' And that was that.

A few minutes later I set off on my

own for a house I'd never seen before to spend the evening and the night with a bunch of people I'd never met before, one or more of whom might possibly have had something to do with an Irishman firing bullets through my window. I just knew I was in for a great time . . .

SEVENTEEN

Beckway's — or rather the Hon. Felicity's — house was about an hour's drive from central London, not far from Hertford. It lay well back from a country road, surrounded first by farmland then, as you bumped over a long, pitted drive, a semicircle of oaks followed by paddocks and lawns. The house itself was small as manor houses went but, the cost of upkeep being what it is these days, that was probably an advantage. It sprawled comfortably, warmly among its lawns and terraces and flower beds, exuding the confidence that comes with age and money. A butler let me in, not a very impressive butler. He seemed too young, too short and too thin for the job and he hadn't yet acquired the right degree of disdain. He took my bag and told me I would be in the Blue Room.

'That's on the first floor, sir, directly opposite the stairs.'

From the way he said it I knew I'd drawn the short straw. I'd get the lumpy single bed, the washbasin if I was lucky, the worst view in the house and the bathroom would be a day's trek down the corridor. All these grand old houses have at a least one bedroom like that.

From a room at the far end of the square panelled hallway came the hum of conversation, but the butler didn't take me that far. He stopped just short of it at the entrance to what was obviously a study. This, too, was panelled although one wall consisted entirely of leather-bound books. A woman was sitting at a desk, putting a letter into an envelope.

'Mr Lennox, madam,' said the butler.

Without looking up she said, 'Thank you.' She licked a stamp and put it on the envelope. 'Yes, thank you, ah,' she made a little clucking sound. 'What was your name again?'

'Lennox,' I said.

She clucked again, impatiently this time. 'Not you — him.'

'Charles, madam,' said the butler.

'Right. Charles, of course. Thank you, Charles. That will be all for the moment.' The butler went away and now the woman got up and came towards me. Tall and slim, late thirties, a mop of dark auburn hair. Grey-green eyes, good cheekbones and jawline. A fine straight nose and a full mouth. Diamonds at her neck and wrists. She wore a long, black evening gown cut so simply that it must have cost about as much as a decent family car.

'In case you're wondering,' she said, 'he's not actually ours. He comes from Rent-a-Butler and I've never seen him before today.' She shook hands. 'I'm Felicity Beckway and you, of course, are the mysterious new man in my husband's life.' She stepped back the better to appraise me. 'You're not at all what I expected, Mr Lennox. I thought you'd be older and fatter.'

'Give me time,' I said.

She smiled a little. 'What precisely do you do for my husband, Mr Lennox.'

'I think you'd better ask him.'

'Yes, well, I would only he's not here. But I expect you knew that already.'

I nodded. 'I gather he's working late at the House.'

'Mmm. That's what he told me. I don't believe him naturally and I'm sure you don't either. God knows where the little shit really is, though I expect it's in some woman's bed. You wouldn't happen to know, just as a matter of curiosity, which woman's?'

'He told me he was working.'

'Of course. What else could you possibly say? A question of loyalty, isn't it, all chaps together, mustn't tell tales out of school. Have you known my husband long, Mr Lennox?' I took a deep breath. 'Long enough to think he's a bloody fool.'

She blinked, startled. 'I beg your pardon.'

'I don't know where Archie is right now, Mrs Beckway. But whatever he's up to he's a bloody fool not to be here with you. If he had any sense at all he'd make sure he was home nights.'

She blushed with, I think, genuine pleasure and looked me over again, slowly, thoughtfully. For the first time there was a sparkle of interest in those grey-green eyes. She said, 'I think we'd better join the others, don't you, Mr Lennox?'

There were ten of us altogether, the others including a couple of middle-aged backbench MPs and their wives and a local landowner, a tall, skinny individual with receding mousy hair and a habit of talking to you with his head thrown back and his eyes half-closed as if he found your aftershave offensive. His wife, who was equally skinny and nearly as tall, had exactly the same habit and a built-in sneer to go with it.

They were the kind of people you forget even as you're being introduced to them but the last two guests were more impressive — or at least he was. Sir Jack Klug, chief shareholder and chief executive of Klug Construction, a building company that had flourished in the boom years but had struggled badly in the recession of the 1990s. There had been rumours lately that it was about to go belly-up and its shares were plummeting.

Klug, a thick-set, balding man in his mid-sixties, was with his wife, who could have been one of Donovan's hand-me-downs, a platinum blonde with the face of a china doll and a body designed for sin. She looked about 25 and seemed to have an IQ to match.

Klug said, 'Bobby Lennox. So you're Donovan's boy, eh?'

'No.'

Felicity said, 'Actually he's Archie's boy now.'

'Wrong again,' I said. 'I'm nobody's

boy.' Another flicker of interest in the grey-green eyes.

'Saw you fight once,' Klug said. 'Donovan took me along. A European title bout against some Eyetie. You knocked him out. You were very good.'

'Not quite good enough,' I said. 'There was a guy called Willie Slate who — '

'Ah, well, no disrespect, son, but nobody was as good as Willie Slate.' One of the MPs drifted up and took Klug to one side and Felicity said, 'Is that right? You were a boxer, a prizefighter? Archie didn't tell me that.'

'I imagine there's quite a lot Archie hasn't told you about me.'

Once again she gave me that long, reflective look. 'I think,' she said, 'that it's time we filled in the gaps in my knowledge.'

The butler loomed up in the doorway to announce that dinner was served and our hostess slipped her arm through mine and said, 'Since we're both unaccompanied I think you'd better escort me in, don't you?' So I did and when we'd made it to the dining-room where a long mahogany table gleamed with silver and crystal any hopes I might have had of cosying up to Jack Klug were scuppered because Felicity said, 'I'm going to change the table plan a little. Jack, would you sit at that end and pretend you're Archie? And you, Mr Lennox, can sit on my right, if you will.'

On the whole dinner was a dull affair. Oh, the food and wine were excellent, no complaints there, but the conversation never took off. The MPs complained about the state of their shares; the MPs' wives complained about the cost of private education; the landowner complained about the anti-blood sports lobby and its determination to deny the fox the sheer pleasure of being hunted; his wife sneered her agreement; and the curvaceous Lady Klug, having just been informed that I was an ex-boxer, said she was ever so surprised to hear that because she'd always thought fighters ended up punch-drunk. She had the kind of shrill voice that killed all conversation around her, probably for about half a mile in every direction, and in the pause that followed her statement I said she was quite right. I said we all finished our careers incapable even of pulling on our own socks but I had been more fortunate than most in that I'd been able to have a brain transplant.

I might have got away with it as a joke if the airhead had laughed but she didn't. She believed me and because she believed me her husband got mad, not at her but at me. He said nothing but the scowl he aimed down the table still had icicles on it when it reached me. And any plan I might have had to retrieve the situation when, as would be traditional in a house like this, the ladies left the gentlemen to their port, cigars and dirty jokes was foiled because Felicity rapped on the table with a spoon and said, 'I know this is the time when the girls are supposed to go off and pee and complain about their husbands but, sod it, I'm quite comfortable where I am so why don't we all stay here?'

I don't know how the others felt but I was happy enough. I'd spent most of the meal with Felicity's leg pressed lightly against mine. When she leaned across to talk to me she rested her fingers on the back of my hand; when I dropped a piece of buttered roll on the table, she picked it up and fed it into my mouth. And all the time there was that sparkle about her. Once or twice I caught Jack Klug watching us thoughtfully but I wasn't in much of a mood to worry about him.

The MPs and the landowner gathered up their wives and departed soon after eleven. The Klugs who, like me, were staying the night hung around for a nightcap and then went to bed. 'Stay where you are, Flicka,' Klug said. 'We can find our way.' We all said goodnight and Lady Klug blew me a kiss and allowed herself to be led by the hand up the stairs.

'Flicka?' I said when they'd gone.

'Don't you dare,' Felicity said. 'I hate it. It's Archie's name for me and only he and his friends use it. But, of course, if you're a friend of Archie's . . .'

'Felicity,' I said. 'Felicity, do I look like a friend of Archie's?'

She laughed, stretched cat-like and said, 'I'll show you to your room.'

'Don't bother. I know where it is. Upstairs opposite the — '

'No,' she said slowly, 'not any more. You've been moved. Come along.' She led me up to the first landing where she paused and pointed to the right. 'The Klugs are down there at the far end.

You're along here in the Rose Room.'
She took me to the left, opened a door
and ushered me in. Rose Room was
right: the carpet, the wallpaper, the
cover on the four-poster bed were all in
a shade of old rose. There was even a
private bathroom.

'I thought you might prefer this to the
Blue Room,' she said. 'Much more comfortable. Will it do?'

'Oh, yes,' I said. 'It'll do fine.'

'Good,' she said. Then she closed the
door gently behind her and took off her
dress.

EIGHTEEN

As she lay on the bed watching me, her hands cupped over her breasts, her long legs primly together, her hips sweetly rounded, I wondered again why Beckway couldn't be content with what he had. This was more than enough woman for most men but then where sex is concerned there's no point in looking for logic, still less fidelity. I mean, dammit, what kind of logic was inspiring me as I kicked off my shoes, ripped off my shirt and let my clothes lie where they fell? I didn't love this woman; I didn't even know her. I was in love with someone else but Felicity was there and Linda wasn't; Felicity wanted me and Linda didn't. As somebody once said, a woman needs a reason to make love; a man just needs a place. Well, only Felicity knew what her reasons were but they were urgent enough for her to provide the place and I was no stronger, no more noble than any other man offered seduction by a beautiful woman. I just wanted to use the place and not bother myself with the reasons and in that I was on a par with Beckway, except that he was married and I was not. And in that moment of heated special pleading, when the hormones were doing more thinking than the brain cells, the fact that Felicity was married, and married, what's more, to Beckway, was quite unimportant.

I got into bed and she pounced on me as if somebody had just rung the bell for the first round, as if she were desperate for every kind of attention I could possibly pay to every part of her, as if she had made out a shopping list of all the things she had ever enjoyed, wanted, lacked, been deprived of, heard about, read about, dreamed about and fantasised about and had decided to grab them all in one lightning swoop on what she seemed to regard as the supermarket of my body.

When, I don't know maybe hours later, we finally came up for air I said, 'What was all that about?'

She nibbled my earlobe and snuggled herself closer. We were both warmly sleek with sweat. 'That was called fucking.'

I put my arm around her shoulders.

'Was it indeed? Well, then, why don't we patent it? I think it would catch on. We could make a fortune.' I pulled the sheet over us. 'The only thing is, were you simply fucking me or were you fucking me to fuck Archie?'

She ran her finger gently down my chest. 'Probably a bit of both. There could have been a touch of the woman scorned in there. But why should you worry? You were the one who had all the fun, not Archie.'

'Fun?' I said. 'What makes you think I had fun? I just lay there, closed my eyes and thought of England.'

'Did you?' she said, easing herself on top of me. 'Oh, did you? Well, you don't get away that easily, my lad. We're not just England any more, we're not even just Britain, we're part of Europe now. So lie back and close your eyes again. You've got an awful lot of other countries to think about before I'm finished with you.'

She went to her own room just before daybreak. As she stood at the door, naked except for her shoes, her dress casually draped over one shoulder, her stockings and underwear in her hand, she said, 'Do you think Archie had as good a time tonight as we did?'

I shook my head. 'He couldn't be that lucky.'

She grinned smugly. 'That's what I'm hoping. See you at breakfast. 8.30 all right for you?'

When she'd gone I fell asleep, my last conscious thought being to wonder whether what I had been up to in the last few hours made me any better than Archie Beckway. My subconscious obviously thought not because in the dream from which I awoke around eight o'clock I *was* Archie Beckway.

At breakfast Felicity and I were formal, Lady Klug complained of pre-menstrual tension and her husband was overtly suspicious. Had I slept well? Yes, like a log. Had Felicity slept well? Out like a light, as she always was after dinner parties. Had either of us heard anyone walking along the landing at, oh, around five? What, us — Felicity and me? No way. He must have dreamt it. He still looked suspicious though when he drove away.

I left soon afterwards. Felicity asked if I'd be seeing Archie that day because there were some letters for him and, since she had no idea when he might be coming home, she wondered if . . .

'Sure,' I said. 'I'll take them in to him at the Ministry, no problem.'

We were in her study off the hall, still being a little formal and distant with each other. I was beginning to wonder whether I'd just been a bit of rough trade, useful to slake her lust on but now to be dismissed with a handshake, when she put her arms around my neck and kissed me with all the fervour she had shown a few hours earlier.

'Pity you have to go,' she murmured. We groped around for a bit like a couple of teenagers and then she pulled away and said, 'Oh, this is ridiculous. Get out before I rape you.'

She walked me to my car and as, for the benefit of any watching servants, I kissed her chastely on the cheek I said, 'If you know so well what Archie's like, why do you stay with him? Because of the children?'

She shook her head. 'They're old enough now to cope with a separation or a divorce. If you really want to know why I stay it's because of this house.' We both turned and looked at it. It was particularly handsome in the morning sunshine. 'I love it. It's my home. It's my family's home and I couldn't begin to afford it without Archie's money.' She brushed a faint smudge of lipstick from my cheek. 'So I suppose that makes me a whore but then perhaps marriage is always a form of whoring anyway.'

I said, 'I thought, or somebody told me, that you stayed with him because you hoped he might be Prime Minister one day.'

She laughed with genuine mirth. 'Archie? Prime Minister? God, I'd emigrate. Anyone with any sense would emigrate.' She stepped back from me. 'Thank you for last night. Now get out of here and this time I mean it.'

So I got out taking Archie's letters with me. I didn't mind acting the messenger because, by way of fair exchange, I'd left my address and telephone number on his wife's desk.

NINETEEN

Birgit was surprised to see me at the Ministry. 'I don't think Archie's expecting you,' she said. 'And anyway he's got somebody with him.'

'I'll wait.' She poured me coffee and I pulled up a chair to sit across from her at her desk.

'I can smell perfume,' she said.

I drew back a little. 'Aftershave, I expect.'

'You wear "Joy" as aftershave?'

'Ah, well . . . Oh, I know what it must be. I kissed Mrs Beckway on the cheek when I left so I imagine it's her scent you can smell.'

She studied me reflectively. 'You kissed her, did you? What did you think of her?'

'Very nice.'

Her eyes widened. 'Very nice? The woman's a famous beauty and all you can say is that she's very nice?'

'Is she beautiful?' I said. 'I really didn't notice.'

The door of Beckway's office opened

and the fat PPS came out. He smiled at Birgit and scowled at me and I ducked past him into the inner sanctum. Beckway, in shirtsleeves, was standing by the window. He looked tired and smudgy-eyed.

'I've brought your mail,' I said and threw the letters Felicity had given me onto his desk.

He made a somewhat listless gesture of acknowledgement. 'Very kind of you. Not necessary but . . . How did you get on last night? Sleep well?'

'Eventually.'

He nodded. 'Which room did Felicity put you in?'

'The Rose Room.'

He smiled reminiscently, maybe even a little sadly. 'Did she? Did she? Lovely room that. Do you know, when we were first married she and I made a point of screwing in every bedroom in the house, starting with that one for some reason.'

'Oddly enough she didn't tell me that,' I said.

'No, I suppose not. What did you make of Jack Klug?'

'Didn't get much chance to talk to him. Your other guests kind of monopolised the conversation, such as it was.'

He murmured sympathetically. 'Gruesome bunch, aren't they? Sorry to inflict them on you. I must say I'm rather glad I wasn't there to suffer them.'

'So where were you?'

He dropped into one of the armchairs while I perched myself on the edge of his desk. 'Where you thought. With Lacy.' He stared at me defiantly.

I said, again noting the weariness, the listlessness. 'You don't seem to have enjoyed it very much.'

'No.' He looked past me towards some point on the far wall. 'I really didn't want to be there. Believe it or not I wanted to be in Hertfordshire. But . . . she rather insisted.' He was silent, brooding, for a moment or two. 'She's a very nice girl, don't get me wrong, but she's becoming somewhat possessive.'

'Difficult,' I said, though not with much sympathy.

'Yes. It happens sometimes and it's always awkward when it does. Sooner rather than later I'm going to have to break things off but that's going to be a very delicate thing to do. You never know how a woman scorned might react.'

'You'd better believe it,' I said.

He didn't respond to that. Probably just as well. 'What did Felicity say about my absence?'

'She said you were a shit.'

He nodded sadly and that touch of weakness, of self-doubt, around his eyes and mouth was more pronounced than ever. 'Do you think she hates me?'

'I've no idea. The question didn't crop up during conversation over the dinner table.' I moved from the desk to the chair in front of it. 'What's with you and Jack Klug?'

He shrugged. 'A building contract. In those days there was a group of companies, a kind of cartel. We'd split the jobs up among ourselves, take it in turns to put in the lowest estimate. Sometimes I would win, sometimes Jack, sometimes somebody else. It was all nicely organised. This particular contract was very, very lucrative and it was Jack's turn to win. But I was overstretched at the time and I needed it more than Jack did, more than anybody did. So Donovan and I underbid him. Oh, we apologised, told him it had been a terrible mistake, let him have the next job that should have been ours. But we'd snatched the really big one from him and I think he knew it. He knew we'd screwed him.'

'He didn't do anything though?'

'Not then, no. But now, well, his company's in big financial trouble.'

'And you think he might be calling in an old debt by setting you up for black-mail?'

Beckway grinned, a wry sort of grin. 'When people are desperate enough they can do desperate things, Bobby. Jack created that business from nothing. He's not going to sit back and just watch it go down the toilet, believe me. He'd do anything to save it and build it up again.'

I thought about this. 'Yeah, but . . . Blackmail? Murder?'

'They're just words. They happen. When you're talking about saving or losing millions, and I mean lots of millions, blackmail's no big deal.' He grunted. 'Murder's a bit extreme, I'll grant you that, but it would take a very naive man to believe it's never been committed in the interests of big business.'

Jack Klug, cornered, ratlike, doing whatever he thought he had to do to protect himself and his company. Could I buy that? Yes. For the moment. I said, 'But what about your wife? What did you expect me to make of her?'

'I don't really know.' He shook his head, either in exasperation at himself or merely to clear it. 'I'm very confused. Felicity and I are neither in love nor do we love each other any more. At least, I'm pretty damn sure she doesn't love me. We haven't slept together for, oh God ages. We hardly even talk any more. What she does for sex or whether she just does without it, I've simply no idea. If I discovered she was being un-faithful, I think I'd . . .' He squeezed his hands together as if he was trying to crush something loathsome. 'I'm being frank with you, you see. We're still together because of the girls and be-cause a divorce would be politically embarrassing to me at the moment. Those are my reasons for keeping the marriage going; she has a different one. She loves that house but can't afford it without my money. If we divorced I'd obviously have to make a settlement on her but it probably wouldn't be enough to let her keep the house. So, yes, it did cross my mind that either alone, or with others or at someone else's instigation she might not be entirely averse to a little blackmail. Set herself up with a nest-egg and then go for the divorce and the settlement. It could solve all her problems.' He eyed me quizzically, his head slightly to one side. 'Now you've met her. So what do you think?'

I said, 'She called you a shit and I think she was right.'

He smiled. 'Probably. But I'm a successful shit and you don't get to be successful unless you consider all the options. Felicity is an option that I'm considering and I think you should, too.'

I was studying this man, this rich, powerful, upwardly mobile government minister and thinking what a complicated mess his life really was, what with all the people he'd screwed either literally or figuratively, when the phone rang. The private phone.

Beckway picked it up, said 'Hello' and then his eyes widened in dismay and he mouthed, 'It's him.'

TWENTY

There was no extension on this line so I went and stood close beside Beckway and he held the receiver a little from his ear so that we could both hear.

The Irishman was saying, '. . . be in suspense any longer, Minister. At last you're going to find out what it is we want. Isn't that a relief to you now?' The voice was the one I'd heard the previous day, Northern Irish but lacking the brutal harshness of an Ian Paisley for the lilt of the South was in it, too.

Beckway said, 'Go on.'

'It's about that new prison complex in Yorkshire.'

'The what?'

The Irishman sighed patiently. 'Pull yourself together, Minister. You know very well what I'm talking about unless you've finally managed to screw your brains out altogether. The new prison you'll be building in Yorkshire, the biggest prison in the whole of Europe. That prison. Have I got through to you yet? God knows you're proud enough of it, you and your friends in the Government. Haven't you been boasting about it for months, how you're building it in the name of law and order? Or do I mean Laura Norder, another of your little tarts? So anyway what we want are the bids.'

Beckway frowned. 'The what?'

Another sigh, a little less patient this time. 'The bids, the tenders. The people who want the contract to build the godforsaken place, we want to know how much they're bidding.'

Beckway said, appalled, 'I can't tell you that!'

'Sure you can, because isn't it your ministry that's in charge of the whole dreadful business?'

'Yes, but these things, these tenders, estimates, they're private. Even I don't know what they are.'

'Of course you don't. You're only the Minister, the fucking mouthpiece, for Chrissake. But your Permanent Secretary has the information and you can get it from him. I don't want all the details, you understand. I just want the bottom line — the lowest bid you've had.'

Beckway glanced up at me. He looked

white and scared. I could think of nothing to say or do that might help him so I just shrugged hopelessly. He said, 'I can't do this. I won't do it.'

The Irishman laughed, though not very humorously. 'So be it, Minister. But if that's your final decision I'd advise you to start clearing your desk now because the Prime Minister and about half a dozen newspapers are going to get some saucy little pictures in the post tomorrow morning.'

Beckway said, 'Wait.' He put his hand over the mouthpiece and said to me, 'What shall I do?'

I gave him another of my hopeless shrugs. 'It's up to you.'

He sat for a moment or two staring into space. Then he took a deep breath and said into the phone, 'All right. But it's going to take some time.'

'Sure it is, Minister.' There was a note of triumph in the Irishman's voice. 'It's going to take two hours because that's all the time you've got. So be quiet now and listen. It's, what, twelve o'clock right now. At two o'clock I want you standing by a telephone at King's Cross station. In the main concourse there's a big arrivals and departures board and behind that a whole bank of phones. Now take careful note of this: you're facing the departure board, okay? So go round the left of it and one of the first four telephones you come to will ring at two or just after that. Be there and have the information with you.' Then he hung up.

Beckway put the receiver down. He looked sick.

'Well, well,' I said, 'the biter bit.'

'What?'

'This is the way you used to do business, remember — steal a march by getting the inside information. So now Mickey Mouse is using your own methods against you.'

Beckway shook his head, the dazed, bewildered gesture of a man who has just taken a hefty right hook to the jaw, which I suppose metaphorically speaking he had. 'What am I to do?'

'What he told you, I imagine. In the short term you don't seem to have much choice. How easily can you get the figures he wants?'

'In a way it's no problem. All I have to do is ask but Harvey's going to think it's very odd.'

'Harvey?'

'Harvey Knox. Sir Harvey Knox. He's the Permanent Secretary. The bids are handled by him at this stage and they're highly confidential. He's not really supposed to disclose them to anyone.'

'But he'll tell you because you're the Minister?'

He nodded unhappily. 'Well, yes, he can hardly refuse. But he won't like it. It's very unusual for a minister to get involved in things like that.'

I said, 'Hey, you're the Minister, right? You're all gung-ho and eager beaver, you just want to keep on top of things, make sure your finger's on the pulse and all that, er —'

'Bullshit?'

'That's the word.'

'That's what I thought.' He took a deep breath. 'Jesus, oh Jesus, I don't want to do this. If anyone ever found out . . .' He looked at me beseechingly but I had nothing to offer him.

'I can't help you,' I said. 'I'm sorry, Archie.'

'No. No, of course not.' For a moment he sat there, drumming his fingers on his knees, then reluctantly he reached for the phone and dialled an extension. 'Harvey? Archie. Fine, thank you, just fine. The reason I'm calling . . . No, it's not about the meeting tomorrow. It's, well, the new prison complex in Yorkshire . . .'

From what I could gather of Harvey's end of the conversation the Permanent Secretary was more than a little surprised at Beckway's request. Words like 'somewhat irregular, Minister' and 'highly confidential matter, you understand' drifted through to me but Beckway was convincingly gung-ho, giving a good enough impression of a Minister determined to keep abreast of everything that was going on to allay any doubts or suspicions Harvey might have entertained.

Of course, how the Permanent Secretary might feel if a new, lower tender suddenly came through was something else again. But that could wait till another day.

TWENTY-ONE

We got to King's Cross at ten to two. All the first four phones on the left were in use. Beckway said, 'Oh, Christ, what shall we do?'

'Nothing. Just wait. He'll get through.'

Just after two one of the phones became free and twenty seconds later it rang. Beckway snatched it up, said, 'Yes, it's me' and then listened. The call lasted only a few moments and when he turned back to me he looked whiter, more shaken and more haggard than ever. 'He wants us to go to the Langham Hotel. He's going to call us there. Oh, God, I don't even know where the Langham Hotel is.'

'I do,' I said. So we went there. And from there the Irishman sent us to the Inter-Continental and from there to Grosvenor House and on to the Dorchester and that's where the trail ended. I watched as once again Beckway picked up the ringing phone and identified himself. This time the conversation lasted a little longer — not much, just long enough for Beckway to take a sheet of paper from his pocket and read out the details written on it.

When the call ended he stood for a few seconds, his forehead pressed against the wall above the phone. After a while he shook himself and walked slowly back to where I was waiting. 'What have I done?' he said. 'In God's name what have I done?'

'Not a lot,' I said dryly. 'Just committed a whopping criminal offence, that's all. Come on, I'll buy you a drink.'

I led him to the bar and fed him a large brandy. 'The bad news,' I said, 'is that now you're doubly in the shit. But the good news is that at last we know what the Irishman wants and that gives us something to grab hold of. He's coming out of the shadows. With any luck the way he uses the information you've just given him could lead us to him.'

'Yes? And then what?' he said bitterly.

'Well, then we get the pictures back.'

'Not enough. I want him dead.'

'Don't keep telling me that. I don't want to know. I'll find him for you but what happens afterwards is down to you.'

He took in a deep gulp of brandy.

'What was all that about? All that chasing around? I could have told him what he wanted to know over the phone in my office.'

'He was being careful, like they do in the movies. What if you'd cracked and called in the police? There'd have been a trace on the office phones, people listening in. Not healthy for our Irish friend. But the way he worked it he was probably sitting at home with his feet up knowing that none of the calls could be traced back to him. And then, too, it was probably some kind of power play. Keep you rushing about, doing whatever he told you, never sure what he might command you to do next. He wanted you to know who was in charge.' I sipped my diet cola. 'Tell me something, Archie: what's your Ministry doing building prisons? I thought that kind of thing was handled by the Home Office.'

He nodded. 'In the past it would have been. In a way it still is, since I have to answer to the Home Secretary. But these days a lot of government building is done directly through my department. It's the PM's idea. Focus on industry, give it a high profile, show people that after all the years of neglect this government really cares about it.'

'And do you?'

He turned slowly, bitterly, towards me. 'Please. Not the famous Lennox cynicism, not now. Haven't I got enough problems without that?'

'Says a lot for our society, doesn't it,' I said, 'that in this apparently enlightened age the Government's planning to build the biggest bloody prison in the world? Dear old Laura Norder's really done her stuff, hasn't she?'

He made a resigned gesture. 'What can we do? The crime rate keeps going up and all our existing prisons are so out of date and overcrowded that they're getting us into trouble with the European Court of Justice. Comes to something, doesn't it, when even rapists are thinking of suing the government because of the state of the gaols? It's happening, you know, so we needed more prisons. Simple as that. This one in Yorkshire's going to be an enormous complex — maximum security, compounds for juveniles, compounds for women, real state of the art.'

To be fair to him he didn't sound happy about it but on the other hand the brandy seemed to revive him a little and when he'd finished it I poured him into a taxi and told the driver to take him to the House of Commons. Then I walked round the corner to Donovan's casino. He was in his office on the top floor and Annie was with him.

'Hello, handsome,' she said and gave me a smacking great kiss.

'Less of that,' Donovan said, 'or I'll send people round to his home to make sure he's not handsome any more.'

Annie went over to where he sat behind his leather-topped desk, took his big head in her hands and kissed him, too. 'Ah, is my Teddy Bear jealous then? Hmm? Is he? Is the big old Teddy Bear jealous?'

'Get off,' he said, struggling out of her grasp. 'Hop it. And don't spend too much money.'

'Where are you going?' I asked as she passed me on her way to the door.

'To buy a dress. But if that mean old Teddy Bear thinks I'm going to buy it at Marks and bloody Spencer or the British Home Stores he'd better start thinking again.' She turned back towards Donovan and blew him a long, lewd kiss, leaning forward, eyes half-closed, rump wriggling from side to side. Then she went out. A moment later the door opened again. 'Don't worry,' she said, 'I won't spend *too* much.' And then she was gone.

Donovan wiped lipstick off his face and gestured to me to sit down.

'Well, well,' I said, 'so you're just a big old Teddy Bear, are you?'

He shook a thick forefinger at me. 'Not a word, you hear me? One fucking whisper of that gets outside this room and you're a dead man.' He scowled to make sure I knew he meant it. 'So what do you want?'

I filled him in with the events of the last twenty-four hours, starting with the call from the Irishman and its aftermath and working back to last night's dinner. I didn't tell him what had happened after dinner because there are some things a gentleman doesn't reveal about his relationship with a lady. Or so I'm informed. Not laying any claim to being a gentleman I wouldn't really know but I kept the after-dinner activities to myself anyway.

Donovan listened in silence and when I'd finished he said, 'Archie could be right about Jack Klug. Last time I saw him, lunch about a month ago, all he could talk about was the trouble he was in. And the other business, that time Archie and me put one over on him, yeah, that probably did get right up his nose. But as for Felicity . . .' He shook his head. 'I can't see her being involved in all this. If it was just straight blackmail, possibly, but it's getting a lot more complicated than that, isn't it?'

'Yes, it is, and that puzzles me. I mean, why is it so complicated?'

Donovan gave the question due consideration. 'Maybe it's like the Irishman said. Archie's very rich, yes, but that doesn't mean he's got a lot of money lying around. Very few rich people have. So to raise anything substantial he'd have to sell things, shares, whatever. All right, that's not the Irishman's problem. If all he was after was money, he'd just have to wait a few days for it. But with that kind of blackmail the danger point comes when somebody has to collect the cash. Now, OK, like the Irishman said, Archie might pay once, he might pay twice. But maybe by the third time he'd be getting seriously pissed off and that time whoever goes to pick up the money could find the police waiting for him. But this way . . .' He paused. 'You know something, Bob, I'm beginning to get some respect for that Irish villain. This way no money changes hands, there's no meeting, no pick-up point, just a few phone calls maybe two or three times a year. And the only one who runs any risk is Archie, because if anyone finds out he's giving away insider information he's in as much trouble as a politician can be.'

'True,' I said, 'but none of that explains what's in it for the Irishman. How does he make a profit?'

Donovan shrugged. 'For that we'll still have to wait and see.'

So we were back to waiting again. What the hell, I was getting used to it. A little later when I got up to go Donovan said, 'Don't forget the party tonight. My place, 7.30.'

'I'll be there but what's it in aid of? Annie was very secretive about it.'

'Never you mind,' he said. 'Just be there.'

TWENTY-TWO

Shitfer opened the door to me when I got to Donovan's house just after eight. I know Donovan had said 7.30 but I got there after eight. I'm independent; nobody tells me what to do.

Shitfer was too big, too tough, too casual in another of his Armani suits to have satisfied Rent-a-Butler but I shouldn't have liked to be the gate-crasher who tried to get past him. 'Upstairs, Bob,' he said, with a jerk of the head. 'You been here before, you know the way.'

There was a lot of noise from upstairs, laughter, conversation, a big party going on. 'What's this all about?' I said.

He grinned. 'Can't tell you. I mean, I don't even know. Nobody does. It's a big surprise.'

'What do you think? Donovan's been made a duke? Governor of the Bank of England — some little job like that?'

'Maybe he's bought Buckingham Palace as his town house,' Shitfer said. 'With Donovan anything's possible.'

The party may have been laid on at short notice but Donovan obviously had social clout because there must have been forty people in the big first-floor sitting room, among them a couple of cabinet ministers, a few front bench spokesmen from the Opposition, a sprinkling of industrialists and the like, a clutch of peers and an assortment of MPs. Apparently nothing of great importance — except maybe to the voters and who cared about them? — was going on in Parliament tonight. Some of the politicians and businessmen were accompanied by younger women who were almost certainly not their wives but in this freemasonry of the rich and powerful indiscretions and infidelities would be safe enough. None of these men would tell on the others and the tabloid press and its informers wouldn't stand a chance of getting in with Shitfer on the door. Jack Klug was there with his animated Sindy Doll and, slightly to my surprise, Archie Beckway had turned up with Felicity. Also present was a handful of Donovan's more socially acceptable employees, probably to make sure none of the other guests stole anything.

I stood for a moment in the doorway, taking in the scene, and then Annie came across with a big, joyous 'Hello' and an even bigger kiss, smack on the lips. Over her shoulder I saw Donovan frowning at me so I pulled away fast, though not so fast as to kill the pleasure. I was beginning to find this Annie very disturbing and I didn't think it would be too healthy for me if Donovan realised that — at least not while she was still his live-in bimbo. After they'd parted he would probably be delighted for me to take her on.

She was dressed, though only just, in something short and flowing and silk and she smelt, felt and tasted delicious.

'Like the dress?' she asked, twirling so that the skirt flew up high around her thighs. 'It's the one I bought this afternoon.'

I examined it deadpan to hide my appreciation of the vision she presented. 'There's so little of it,' I said, 'that it must have cost a fortune.'

She put a finger to my lips. 'Don't say things like that. Donovan would go mad. He hasn't any idea how much I paid, thank God.'

At which point Donovan joined us,

slipping a powerful arm around Annie's waist. 'Good to see you, Bob. What do you think of my girl then?'

'Fantastic. She looks like you could eat her with a spoon.'

'Ooh!' Annie's mouth and eyes made circles of wicked delight. 'Sounds lovely. No need to bother with the spoon, though.'

Donovan slapped her rump. 'Get out of here, you saucy mare. Go and talk to our guests.' She squealed at the impact of his palm, rubbed her left buttock, said, 'Yes, master, right away, master', winked at me and plunged into the crowd. Donovan watched her with a proprietorial air.

'You fancy that, Bob?' he asked.

'Be a strange man who didn't.'

He nodded. 'Yeah. Don't fancy her too much though, will you?' We stared solemnly at each other for a moment and then I grinned and so did he. 'Pity your mum's not here,' he said. My mother was in Spain, on holiday with a couple of friends. 'Enjoy this, she would.' He paused, thoughtfully, then grinned again. 'Well, give her a good laugh anyway.'

'All right, Donovan,' I said. 'Enough of

the mystery. What's going on?'

He looked at his watch. 'All in good time, my son, all in good time. Lots of people here you ought to meet so go and mingle.' He slapped me affectionately, dismissively, on the shoulder so I went and mingled.

There'd been a message from Birgit on my answerphone that evening suggesting we might meet for dinner and for a moment I'd been tempted to invite her along to Donovan's. But, I don't know, I wasn't as flattered as I might have been at her apparent eagerness to see me. Of course, I could have put it down to my overwhelming masculine charm and indeed I wanted to; but somehow I had this nagging suspicion that she was less interested in the carnal delights I might offer than the opportunity to interrogate me again about Archie and what exactly was going on in his life. So I left a message on her answerphone expressing heartbroken regrets and promising to be in touch. I was developing a great fondness for answering machines and the facility they offered for passing on information people didn't want to hear when they weren't around to hear it. The next thing I would do, I thought, was buy a fax machine and communicate only on electronically transmitted bits of paper. That way you could send veritable toilet rolls of excuses and never have to explain yourself any more than you wanted to at the outset of the message.

In any event, now as I wandered across to where Beckway and Felicity were standing by the window I was particularly glad that I hadn't brought Birgit with me to Donovan's. Her presence there, along with that of the Hon. Mrs Beckway, would have been just too embarrassing — not only for Archie, whose discomfort I could have suffered with no pain, but also for me. I had a sudden, disconcerting, realisation that I wouldn't want Felicity to see me with another woman and especially one who had once been her husband's mistress.

The Beckways didn't seem too happy in each other's company and indeed they appeared to be in the middle of a murmured but nevertheless heated row. They broke it off as I approached and Felicity gave me a warm smile and a kiss on the cheek. Archie merely grunted. He looked tired and worried.

'Hard day?' I asked.

Before he could answer Felicity said with pointedly mock sympathy, 'Oh yes, the poor darling has been working his fingers to the bone. Well, perhaps not his fingers exactly but he's been so busy for days and days that he didn't even have time to tell his own wife where he was. And now just look at him — he's simply worn himself out. I keep telling him he mustn't work so hard or he'll end up on his back. You didn't end up on your back, did you, darling?' From a distance the smile she bestowed upon him might have looked connubial but close up it was savage.

Beckway said, 'Shut up, Felicity.'

She turned to me. 'There. You see? He's been so hard at it, whatever it was, that he's got himself into a nasty old temper.' She gave me a quick, dazzling smile. 'But how about you, Mr Lennox? You look absolutely splendid. You really must tell Archie how you manage it. An exciting sex life perhaps? Has your sex life been exciting lately, Mr Lennox?'

I said, somewhat taken aback, 'Well, yes, one doesn't like to talk of these things but as a matter of fact it's been marvell— '

'Oh, good, I'm so glad.' She darted a

swift look around the room. 'Ah, there's Caroline. I simply must go and talk to her. You will excuse me, won't you?'

When she'd gone Beckway said, 'Bitch.'

'You've upset her,' I said. 'I have very delicate antennae. I can sense these things. She knows about Lacy, right?'

'Well, not actually Lacy but she knows there's somebody.' He knocked back a glass of Krug in one long swallow. 'I've had the most godawful day I can ever remember. Lacy called me at the House, insisted on seeing me, wanted to come here . . . I couldn't get away in time to meet Felicity so we had to arrive separately and she's been in that sort of brittle mood ever since.'

I said, 'Why doesn't this touching story of yours break my heart?'

He was glaring at me, searching for a sharp answer, when the bloated shape of the Chancellor of the Exchequer loomed up alongside us, pointing its paunch at Beckway. 'Archie, dear boy, a word in your ear if you don't mind . . .' He put his arm around Beckway's shoulders and drew him firmly away. He didn't bother to apologise to me for the intrusion.

I took some champagne from a passing waiter and surveyed the scene. In the adjoining dining-room a cold buffet had been laid out on tables along three walls. Not your conventional rubber chicken and limp lettuce buffet either but great bowls of caviar, lobsters, crabs, whole salmon and God knows what else besides. A waiter stood in the doorway politely refusing entrance to the more dedicated freeloaders until Donovan or Annie should announce that it was time to come under starter's orders. More waiters bustled about dispensing champagne and anything else a thirsty drinker might require.

Beckway and the Chancellor had gone out onto the landing in search of privacy. Felicity was talking animatedly to a trio of other well-groomed women. Annie was surrounded by a group of assorted MPs and businessmen, one of whom, flushed with drink and younger than the others, reached across and pinched her bottom. Annie's vivacious smile didn't falter for a moment as she subtly shifted position, stepped back a pace and brought a stiletto heel down hard on the offender's instep. He gave a sharp yelp and spilt his champagne down his tie. Annie was very solicitous.

I grinned and looked away to where Donovan was holding forth to a bunch of elderly, prosperous-looking coves, at least two of whom I recognised as chief executives of multinational conglomerates. These were powerful men, although in his own way Donovan was even more powerful. Chief executives, after all, were to some extent constrained by the law; Donovan didn't suffer any such handicap.

Jack Klug broke away from his Sindy Doll and the couple they had been talking to and drifted over to me. 'So,' he said, 'how was she then?' He said it with a smile but not a friendly one.

'Pardon?'

'Flicka. How was she? Must say I envy you. Wouldn't mind getting across that myself.' His voice was just a little slurred.

'Fuck you,' I said.

He waved a hand and champagne slopped from his glass onto the carpet. 'Watch it, son. Be careful how you talk to — '

At that moment Donovan clapped his hands loudly together and shouted, 'My lords, ladies and gentlemen, your attention, please.' Gradually the laughter stopped and the conversation died down. Well, Donovan was the host and it was his booze everyone was knocking back. The least we could do was listen to him.

He stood, his arm around Annie's waist, in the middle of the room.

'Won't keep you a minute,' he said. 'I know you're all hungry and there's plenty of grub laid out in the other room but I've got just one little announcement to make.' He pulled Annie even closer to him, grinned like a kid and said, 'Annie here has done me the great honour of agreeing to be my wife.' And from his jacket pocket he pulled out a platinum ring bearing a diamond about the size of an overweight walnut and slipped it onto the third finger of her left hand.

There was a moment of silence and if there had been a competition to find the most astonished person in the room I'd have won by a street. Marriage? Donovan? I couldn't believe . . . It simply wasn't . . . Not Donovan, not after all these years . . . Then Annie put her arms around his neck and kissed him and the whole company burst into applause. I was slow joining in, not because I disapproved — at that moment I didn't know what I felt — but because astonishment slows your reflexes.

Beside me a voice muttered, 'That little tart's done herself a bit of good.' It was the flushed bloke on whose instep Annie had trodden. Apart from the bright red of his cheeks and the flushed pink of his eyeballs he was a rhapsody in blue — navy suit and knitted silk tie, pale blue shirt and bright blue silk handkerchief dangling from his breast pocket.

I said quietly, 'I wouldn't let Donovan hear you say that.'

He turned to me, sneering, his breath sour on my face. 'I'm not afraid of Donovan. I'm a Member of Parliament.'

'Is that right? And Members of Parliament have unbreakable legs, do they? Even if someone like him,' I nodded towards Shitfer, who was leaning hugely, impassively against the wall by the door, a glass of orange juice in his hand, 'even if someone like him came after you with a baseball bat?'

'What are you talking about? Who the hell are you anyway?'

'Oh, I'm nobody much — just a concerned bystander who wouldn't like to see a parliamentary career, even a total arsehole's parliamentary career, ruined on account of a stupid, flapping mouth.'

'How dare — '

'Ah, shut up.' I left him and joined the throng of well-wishers gathered around Donovan and Annie, shaking their hands, kissing them, offering congratulations. When it came to my turn I said, 'OK, this is supposed to be a surprise party. So what's the surprise?'

Donovan laughed and hugged me. 'What do you think your mum would say?'

'Probably much the same as me — congratulations to you and commiserations to Annie. It's, I don't know, it's the most amazing piece of news I've had in years and I'm delighted for you. Both of you.' I stepped back to study them. Annie was glowing like Cinderella when she found the shoe was a perfect fit and Donovan couldn't have looked happier on the day he pulled off his first armed robbery. 'When's the wedding?'

'Haven't decided yet. Soon, anyway. Oh, and I've got another surprise for you, my son — you're going to be best man.'

'Me? Donovan, I don't know what to say. I'd have thought you'd get the Prime Minister at least.'

'Fuck the Prime Minister. Day like that I want my real mates about me. You'll do it, won't you? You'll stand up for me?'

'I'd like to see somebody try and stop me.' So then we went into a big emotional bearhug and after that I gave Annie a bearhug, too, and she kissed me again but on the cheek this time as a chaste, newly-engaged young woman should.

Donovan watched approvingly. 'That's much better. You've had your last big wet kiss from Annie. Or you have if you both know what's good for you.' But he smiled when he said it.

I didn't stay too long after that. I got myself a plate of food and ate it standing up while making desultory conversation with a group of people whose names I didn't catch. But the people I might have wanted to talk to — Donovan and Annie, Beckway and Felicity — were all too busy with their own agendas.

So when I'd finished eating I said quick goodbyes, paused a while to exchange a few words with Shitfer and stepped out alone into the street to grab a cab home.

That was a mistake.

TWENTY-THREE

They grabbed me as I was strolling down towards Berkeley Square.

It wasn't that late and it wasn't that dark but there was nobody about except me and they timed their attack perfectly, darting out from the entrance to a little mews, a hand clamped over my mouth, my arms pinioned behind me.

Three of them — Mickey Mouse, Goofy and Pluto, well-built men, my height or taller, in dark sweatshirts and jeans and the Disney masks.

Goofy and Pluto had me by the arms and one of them had his fist jammed into my mouth so I couldn't cry out. Mickey stood in front of me, a short metal bar in his hand. The street was empty and any sign of life in the little mews houses was hidden by the drawn curtains.

'Well now,' said Mickey Mouse in the Irish accent I was beginning to know so well, 'isn't it the little busybody you turned out to be?'

I said nothing. The way they were holding me I couldn't do anything but mumble through the fist but he seemed to take my silence for dumb insolence because he hit me across the stomach with the metal bar. I saw the blow coming and prepared for it as best I could but it still hurt like hell. I doubled up, groaning, and heard Pluto say, 'Hey, Mickey, come on, there's no need for this.' Pluto had a well-modulated, Home Counties sort of voice, no trace of an Irish accent.

'Yes, there fuckin' is,' Mickey said and slammed the metal bar across my left shoulder. There was more excruciating pain and the arm went numb. I just hung there, sagging, supported by Pluto and Goofy.

Mickey said, 'I have to hand it to you, friend. You're a bigger nuisance than I ever thought you'd be, trailing around after Beckway all afternoon like his fucking gundog. Wasn't two bullets through your window a strong enough hint for you? What else do I have to do to persuade you to keep your nose out of my business?' Another swipe with the bar, this time across the ribs. Nothing broke but again there was worse pain than anything I had ever suffered in the ring.

Goofy said, 'For God's sake, stop it, Mickey. Let the bastard stand up. It's breaking our arms holding him like this.' Goofy wasn't Irish either; West Country maybe but not Irish. He and Pluto hauled me to my feet as Mickey took a step backwards.

'Have you got the message now?' Mickey said to me. 'Punch-drunk as I'm sure you are do you have enough brain cells left to understand what I'm saying to you? I don't want you interfering any more.' He punctuated the last six or seven words by ramming the bar repeatedly, savagely, into my stomach and again I doubled up, moaning with the pain.

Pluto and Goofy yanked me upright again but as they did so the pressure of the hand against my mouth relaxed a little and I sank my teeth deep into the fleshy part of the thumb. Goofy screamed and let go of my arm and instinctively I pulled away from him, swung round and hammered the back of my fist against his face. With a morbid satisfaction I heard his nose break and then Mickey shouted, 'You bastard!' and leapt at me, raining blows on me with his metal bar. I caught one on the chest, another across the right thigh, a third scraped down the side of my face bringing blood from a long cut on my temple. Goofy was leaning against a wall, moaning, his hands to his face; Pluto wasn't sure what to do.

He was still holding on to my numb left arm but he was also trying to interpose himself between me and my assailant believing, as I did, that Mickey Mouse was trying to kill me. He was yelling, 'Mickey, for God's sake stop. We were just going to warn him. We don't need murder.' And I, well, I was just yelling as loud as I could to attract attention, anyone's attention.

Another blow across the chest wrenched me free from Pluto's grip and I fell backwards onto the pavement, hurting everywhere, half-blinded by the blood streaming from the wound on my head, with Mickey standing over me, the metal club raised above his shoulder for a blow that would certainly have cracked my skull.

And then a startled voice from behind Mickey and Pluto shouted, 'Hey, what the devil's going on there?' Mickey whirled and looked back, then he muttered, 'Christ! Let's get out of here,' and he and Pluto grabbed hold of Goofy and dragged him away round the corner, out of the mews and into the street.

I heard footsteps running past me and then, as I sat up and brushed the blood from my eyes, I saw two middle-aged men and a young woman staring anxiously down at me. One of the men said, 'Are you all right?' I nodded and took a deep breath through ribs and chest that ached abominably. In a moment the people around me were joined by a younger man, who said, 'They got into a car. I couldn't see the number.'

Gently, carefully, they helped me to my feet and one of the older men said, 'What was that about?'

I mumbled, 'Muggers. They wanted my wallet. I . . . I resisted. Stupid of me.'

With great tenderness the four of them helped me to a mews house about twenty yards away where the young woman washed the blood away and put a Band-Aid over the jagged tear on my forehead. They wanted to call the police but I told them not to bother; nothing was broken, nothing was stolen, no permanent harm was done and with reluctance they agreed that I was probably right.

The younger man said, 'What can the police do anyway? They'll never catch the swine. This sort of thing's going on all over the country, even in a neighbourhood like this, and nobody seems able to do anything about it. God knows what this bloody country's coming to.'

I stayed with them while they fed me hot, sweet tea and after a while I could think clearly again, though my whole body hurt and my head throbbed as if someone inside it was trying to break out with a steam hammer. When they were sure I was OK to go out on my own they phoned a taxi for me and I thanked them for their help and with the four of them watching me solicitously I hobbled into the cab and went home.

I took great care going into my building but there was no further sign of Mickey Mouse and his friends.

TWENTY-FOUR

The doctor told me what I already knew — nothing broken, no internal damage but a mild case of concussion. He wanted me to go to hospital for observation but we agreed on a compromise; I said I'd stay in bed for twenty-four hours and he said he'd come and see me again that evening. Staying in bed wasn't difficult; I didn't feel like doing anything else.

When the doctor had gone I made a couple of calls, first to Donovan to tell him about the events of last night and how I'd been beaten up by half of Disneyland. He listened intently and said, 'That's good. That's very good, Bob. We're smoking them out.'

I was pleased that he was pleased but since it was my head and my shoulder and my stomach and my ribs that hurt I couldn't quite see where the 'we' came into it — nor, come to that, what was so good about it.

Then I spoke to Beckway, who at least had the decency to sound more appalled and sympathetic than Donovan had done and asked me again if I was sure I wanted to carry on with this business.

'More than ever,' I said grimly. 'When I get my hands on Mickey Mouse I'm not just going to shove his rifle up his arse, I'm going to shove his metal bar up there, too.'

But then Beckway rather spoilt all the concern he'd been showing by saying, not reproachfully perhaps but wistfully anyway, 'Pity you couldn't have just hung on to one of them.'

'I'm not Jean-Claude Van Bloody Damme, you know. I'm not master of the martial arts. If those people hadn't turned up when they did I'd be a hospital case now, or worse.'

Ten minutes later Birgit rang me. Beckway obviously hadn't told her anything because she didn't ask after my health, just said she wanted to see me. She was quite coquettish about it at first. 'I think we have some unfinished business, don't you? Until your friends turned up the other night I was going to ask you back to my flat for coffee and . . .' a seductive pause, '. . . whatever. So why don't we do that tonight? Come and have dinner.'

'I'm ill,' I said, wimpishly. Well, I hurt all over and the very thought of a spot of whatever, even with somebody built like Birgit, and the inevitable thrashing about that it would entail sent little arrows of pain all over my body. 'I think I've got the 'flu.'

She didn't believe me because now she turned sulky. 'Well, of course, if you find me that repulsive we could always meet in a more public place and — '

'No, I'm ill. Honestly I am. I'm in bed now feeling terri— '

'Are you deliberately trying to humiliate me?' By this time she'd moved on to anger. 'Do you think I come on like this to every man I meet? Do you think I need to?'

No, I didn't think that but I did still wonder why she was coming on to me. I'd gone well past believing it was down to my blue eyes and noble profile. I said, 'Birgit, believe me, the last thing I want is to humiliate you and any other time I'd cancel anything to have dinner with you but right now I'm genuinely unwell. Perhaps in a day or two . . .'

She was silent for a while and then, much more reasonably, she said, 'A day or two might be too late. I want to talk to you about Archie. I'm very worried about him. He looks ill and worried and this new girl of his, Lacy whats'ername, has taken to phoning him at the office.'

So that's what it was about. Definitely not the blue eyes and noble profile. I wasn't altogether surprised; disappointed maybe but not surprised. 'Oh dear,' I said.

'It's her, isn't it? She's the one behind all this trouble he seems to be in. Why won't you talk to me about it? I could help, you know. I've helped Archie get rid of troublesome women before.'

'Really? He told me he always leaves them happy.'

'That's what he thinks! Archie Beckway, the great lover. He ought to know about women but he doesn't really. He doesn't know a thing about how to deal with them when they become a nuisance.'

I was beginning to feel tired now, the painkillers kicking in. 'There's nothing I can tell you. If Archie won't talk to you about it, I certainly can't.'

'Damn you,' she said and slammed the phone down.

The last call I had was from Rachel Grant. A surprise this because she was actually following up on all our loose talk about having lunch together. Why didn't we do it on Tuesday — her treat, second floor restaurant at the Television Centre? I was touched because, I remembered, this was typical of Rachel; she was the only person I knew who would take a casual remark like 'Let's do lunch sometime' seriously. I told her I'd be there.

The next morning I felt a lot better. My body was still sore and stiff but my head no longer hurt and a long, hot bath and a few gentle muscle-loosening exercises continued the improvement.

Donovan and Annie brought me lunch, a takeaway from an expensive Chinese restaurant that didn't normally do takeaways. We ate it together around my dining-room table, Annie carefully monitoring Donovan's intake.

'I've made him lose eight pounds,' she said, 'and I want at least another ten off him before we're married. I'm not kneeling at the altar alongside a hippopotamus in a morning suit.'

Donovan accepted this with surprising meekness. None of his previous girls would have dared even to criticise him, still less insult him, but from Annie he took it with pleasure. He was in love, it was as simple as that and, to my own incredulity, I found myself hoping he wasn't going to get hurt. Donovan hurt? It was an entirely novel concept. Donovan didn't get hurt; Donovan gave hurt. I watched and listened carefully, wondering whether in Annie he had at last met his match, a young woman who could manipulate and exploit him as he was used to manipulating others. But there seemed no sign of that; on the contrary, despite the huge difference in their ages, she seemed genuinely very fond of him.

Annie was concerned about my injuries, the bruising and the sticking plaster on my head and the way I winced occasionally when I made a sharp movement. Donovan had told her I'd been mugged and I was content to let her believe it. Engaged and in love or not there were clearly things about his business that he didn't want her to know.

We talked a little about the wedding and in which fashionable London church it might be held and we discussed the engagement party. This had ended some time after one o'clock and in the latter stages had been notable for an unpleasant incident in which Jack Klug had said something to Felicity Beckway which caused her to slap his face. Fortunately only a few people had witnessed this and Beckway had not been among them.

Nobody had heard Klug's remark either but . . .

'He was well out of order, that Jack,' Donovan said. 'Pissed, of course. I had to get Shitfer to ask him to leave, him and that little tart of his. She was almost as pissed as he was.'

'Jack probably refers to me as your little tart,' Annie said, calmly.

'He'd better fucking not.' Donovan leant across and kissed her tenderly on the cheek. 'He was in a strange mood though, Jack, all night. I think Archie could be right — I think Jack could be brooding over what we did to him that time.'

'And what was that?' Annie asked.

'Never you mind, my girl. The less you know the better.'

Annie looked at me with an exasperated smile. 'Hasn't this daft old idiot ever heard of women's lib?'

'He's heard of it,' I said, 'but he doesn't

like it and he's rejected it. As far as he's concerned it never happened.'

'Bloody right,' Donovan said.

Annie left us after the coffee, pottering about in the kitchen cleaning up the debris of the meal. It was a tactful withdrawal, gracefully done. Donovan said, 'All right, come on, what do you think? Am I just being a bloody old fool?'

I had wondered about that but now, having seen them together . . .

'No,' I said, 'I really don't think so. She seems as happy as you are. It's just, well, the suddenness of it. When did all this happen?'

'Few days ago. See, Annie knows a couple of the girls who've lived with me before so she knows the pattern. And she's been with me quite a while now, longer than most, so she figured it was bound to end soon and because she's got her pride she wanted to be the one who ended it. So, right out of the blue, she said she was thinking of going abroad. Oh, she'd miss me and all that but the time had come to move on, that kind of thing. Well, it was a real shaker, I can tell you, because I suddenly realised I didn't want her to go.' He shook his head wonderingly. 'So I asked her to marry me.'

I waited a moment. 'And when she'd stopped laughing . . . ?'

'Cheeky bugger. No, that was the funny thing. She just sort of looked at me, all wide-eyed. I mean, she was totally astonished. Then she burst into tears and hugged me. It was the last thing she'd expected — that I'd want to marry her. Last thing I expected, too.'

I thought it over. 'What was she going to do when she went abroad? What was she going to live on? It takes money to do something like that.'

'She's got money. Not just money I've given her either. A few years back her granny died, left her a house in Islington. Not much of a house by all accounts but it was in a street that had come up in the world and she got a good price for it, a hundred grand, maybe more. And she was shrewd with it, invested it. So if you're thinking she's a gold digger she's already a lot better off than most gold diggers.'

'No,' I said slowly. I had been thinking that but I was thinking something else, too, something none too easy to say to a man besotted with a woman young enough to be his daughter. But I had no need to mention it because he had guessed already.

'What you're wondering, young Bob, is what a girl like that can possibly see in a man like me, apart from money. I wondered that, too, so I asked her and as far as I can make out she sees me as a sort of cross between Santa Claus, a lover and the father she never knew. He died when she was a baby, her mother died when Annie was four and she was brought up by this old granny and a couple of aunts, first in one place, then in another. Never had any roots. You wouldn't think it to look at her, but basically she's a very insecure girl.'

An insecure girl looking for a daddy figure. Well, there were probably worse bases for marriage, especially if the daddy figure knew the score and was happy.

I said, 'Will that be enough for her, just being Mrs Donovan? She doesn't want to go back to acting?'

He shook his head. 'No. She was never much of an actress anyway. A dancer mostly. Did a couple of West End shows in the chorus, a few walk-on parts. That's how I met her — I told you. And she did some modelling, no Page Three tits, nothing like that, worked quite a lot in cabaret, night clubs and that. She talks about the old days sometimes but she doesn't want to go back to them.'

At first I had thought he was trying to convince himself as much as me but now I could see I was wrong. He was perfectly confident about this woman he was going to marry. Besides, he wouldn't have deigned to explain either himself or her to anyone but me and probably my mother. In a curious way he looked upon us as his family and, almost alone among the people he knew or employed or dealt with or owned, our good opinion was important to him.

I went to refill his glass but he pushed the bottle away, presumably in the interests of the low calorie diet Annie had put him on, and when he looked up at me he was the old, hard, tough Donovan again. 'Just remember one thing, Bobby, I know what I'm doing. Anyone thinks I've gone soft or stupid is making a big mistake.'

I believed him. 'I'll put the word around,' I said.

From the kitchen Annie said, 'Have you finished your grown-up talk yet?

Because if you haven't I'm going to clean this oven. It's filthy.'

'Clean the oven,' Donovan said, 'and shut that kitchen door. I don't want you eavesdropping.'

I heard Annie muttering, 'I'm just a skivvy round here, that's all I am — a bloody skivvy.' But she shut the kitchen door and Donovan asked me about Beckway. I repeated what Birgit had told me — about Lacy phoning him at the Ministry — and Donovan took a deep breath and let it out with a long, soft, puffing sound. 'Bloody fool,' he said. 'How he could get involved with some little tart with this other business going on . . . He could blow it all.'

'You have plans for Archie, do you?'

'Once he gets in the Cabinet, yeah. Poxy job he's got now there's not a lot of good he can do me but in the Cabinet . . .' He shook his head regretfully.

Annie came back. 'All right, you two, you've talked about me long enough.' She looked at me very seriously. 'So what's the verdict? Do I pass muster? Or am I just a cunning little bitch who's after Donovan's money?'

'You're OK,' I said. 'As a matter of fact, and I'm only telling you this as a friend,

I think he's marrying you for *your* money. And when he's robbed you of every penny you've got and you can't stand it any more, you know where you can find a good home.'

She laughed delightedly. 'Oh, isn't that sweet. Donovan, can I kiss him? One last time?'

Donovan said, 'Well, all right, but just once and remember I'm watching you.'

So she kissed me and he watched. It was a very nice kiss but it might have been even nicer if he had looked the other way.

TWENTY-FIVE

It was Monday before we discovered what the Irishman wanted but before that I had Rex to deal with. And after Rex . . . Well, he was enough to be going on with.

Sunday morning, feeling better, looser, less pain around the ribs and abdomen, though my left arm was still heavy and dead. A butterfly plaster on my head wound, a brown and purple bruise around it. Altogether, not too bad.

And then the doorbell rang and Rex Poorboy stood in the corridor, flashing his neon teeth, his sun-bleached hair and his deep, Iberian tan.

'I've come for Linda's stuff,' he said. No hello, no how's-it-going, nothing.

I asked him in and went away to get Linda's belongings. When I came back with them, making three trips in all with three suitcases because I couldn't yet trust my left hand to hold anything heavy, he was in the middle of the sitting-room, looking around him with a neon-lit sneer. By London standards mine's a very nice flat; by Beverly Hills standards it's probably nothing much and that's how Rex seemed to regard it. The few good pictures and pieces of furniture I've acquired are good in an understated English way; they don't scream 'Louis Quinze!' at you; they're not ornate or elaborately gilded; they're just good. But Rex was obviously an ornate, gilded, Louis Quinze man and he had only mild contempt for my things.

'You seem to have done pretty good for a fighter,' he said patronisingly. 'Get the place furnished properly it won't look bad. They tell me this is a pretty nice address. For London.'

'It's OK,' I said, dumping the last suitcase at his feet.

'Yeah.' He took another look round the comfortable sunlit room. 'Even so, I still don't see how you ever thought you could keep a girl like Linda in a place like this.'

'I wasn't keeping her,' I said. 'I don't know what your relationship with her is like but I never thought of her as a kept woman. She was here because she wanted to be, because we were partners, because we were lovers.' The use of the past tense still hurt.

'That so?' He threw another gleaming sneer at me. He was cockier than I'd ever seen him, probably because Linda was now with him and not with me. 'Partners, huh? You mean she hadda pay her way? Like help with the rent and stuff?'

'No.' Gently I massaged my left arm, trying to make the strength return a little faster. 'Why don't you just take her things and go? I don't think we've got a lot to say to each other, do you?'

'There's three cases here. You gonna help me down with them or what?'

I nodded. 'If you can manage two I'll bring the other.'

He stared at me, grinning. 'You look pretty rough, old buddy. Cut on your head, bad arm. Whaddya do — pick a fight with the paper boy and lose?'

'Something like that.' I picked up the biggest of the suitcases in my right hand. 'If you're ready — '

'Hey now, hold on.' He stood before me, big, blond, bulging with that particular Hollywood kind of designer muscle that looks good but is never used for anything more strenuous than lifting cheques. 'Now I got you here there's a couple things I wanna tell you. Like, first, I don't want you sniffing around Linda any more. You know what I'm saying to you?'

'Yes,' I said wearily. 'Unless I'm missing a hidden message somewhere you don't want me sniffing around Linda any more.'

The neon grin vanished. Lips were drawn thin and tight to go with the tough-guy glare from the narrowed eyes. It was probably the kind of look that scared the shit out of nineteen-year-old third assistant directors. 'Don't be a smart ass or I might be forced to bounce you around a little.'

I was tired of this: tired, angry, irritable and resentful that Linda seemed to prefer this overgrown college boy to me. But right then the last thing I wanted was to get into another brawl. So, as mildly as possible and controlling my temper, I said, 'You've got what you came for, you've got Linda's things. Why don't you just leave? We don't have to get into a pissing contest here.'

'Why?' The big, sneering grin was back. 'Scared you'd lose, champ? Huh?' He punched me playfully, but playful like a vicious little boy, on my left bicep. The pain shot up to my shoulder and neck and made me grunt. 'Hey, that hurt, right? That paper boy sure must have given you a going over.'

'Don't do that,' I said. 'Please. Just don't do that.'

'Why not? It's kinda fun.' He gave me another thump on the injured arm. Again I grunted and winced. 'You wanna know why it's fun? Because I want to make sure you don't even think about coming back into Linda's life. She still talks about you, you believe that? I don't like it but she does. Well, OK, time will take care of that but it'll take care of it a lot faster if you butt out — and I mean now and for ever. You got that?' He hit my arm a third time. 'Am I making myself clear?'

I put the suitcase down and rubbed my arm. 'Yes. So let me make myself clear, too. You touch me one more time and I'm going to hurt you, very badly.' I still didn't want a brawl but sometimes, try as you might, you just get drawn into these dumb macho situations.

He looked at me — smaller than him, lighter than him and with one dead arm

— and gave me the full neon grin. 'Gutsy bastard, aren't you?' he said and punched my arm again.

So I hit him. Hit him first in the stomach — a right uppercut that started at hip level and had everything behind it. And then, as he doubled over, I hit him in the mouth, again with the right because there wasn't a lot I could do with my left. Blood spurted from his lips to his chin and down onto his shirt and he swung at me, a big, wild left, followed by an equally wild right. I ducked inside both punches, brought my knee up into his groin and hit him in the stomach again, once, twice, three times. As he moaned and started to fall I hooked him to the jaw and he dropped to his knees, sobbing, one hand to his face, the other clutching his balls.

I grabbed him by the hair and lifted his head so that he was looking up into my face. 'Here's what happens next,' I said. 'You're going to pick up two of those cases and take them down to the street and I'll follow you with the third. Alternatively, if you don't like that and want to carry on pretending you're Rocky Balboa I'm going to hammer your face to pulp.' Both his lips were steadily leaking blood and a lump was already coming up on his left cheek. He nodded, dumbly. 'Right,' I said.

So then we went downstairs, in the order I'd outlined, to the chauffeur-driven limo awaiting him in the street. The driver, a small, elderly man, got out looking concerned.

'Mr Poorboy, what on earth — '

'Nothing to worry about,' I said soothingly. 'Mr Poorboy slipped and hurt himself on the stairs. It looks worse than it is.'

The chauffeur put the cases in the boot and watched Rex hobble into the back seat of the car, still tenderly clutching his groin.

'Vicious stairs, you've got,' he said. 'Kicked him in the balls as he fell, did they?' He went round to the driver's door and I leaned in through the open back window to talk to Rex. 'I have a message for Linda,' I said. 'Give her my love and tell her she's welcome to call me as soon as she's come to her senses.'

Then I shut the door and watched the car drive away. When it had turned the corner and disappeared I went slowly back upstairs. My left arm was hurting more than ever and my head was beginning to ache again.

In my sitting-room I picked up one of Rex's front teeth and flushed it down the lavatory. After that I washed his blood off the carpet with very cold water and as I was doing so an amazing thought occurred to me, a thought that would have been inconceivable only an hour ago: I'd got over Linda. I hadn't stopped loving her but I'd stopped needing her, yearning for her. I knew that if she called and said, 'It's all been a mistake. Can we start again?' I would tell her to hurry over. Of course, it wasn't likely to happen and I'd always realised that — but what I also realised now was that it didn't matter any more: I could live without her. So why didn't I feel happy and open champagne by way of celebration? You tell me. Yes, sure, a burden had been lifted, a door had closed, a chapter had ended — all that crap. But I just felt sadder and a little older and in no way wiser. Something had gone from my life, something I had treasured, and though I didn't treasure it any more I still felt the poorer for its loss.

And then Lacy turned up. Not immediately, a few hours later. I'd gone out to read the Sunday papers over lunch in a brasserie in Chelsea and when I got back I found her sitting on the stairs outside my flat, sobbing, all the horizontal lines of her face drooping downwards in grief, smudges of damp mascara under her eyes. She looked like some ultra-cute animated cartoon character, the heartbroken imprisoned Beauty, perhaps, before she discovered that the Beast was really all mush inside and not such a bad guy after all.

I looked down at her and she looked up at me, snorting back her tears. 'Archie?' I said.

She snuffled, gulped, nodded. I sighed. 'You'd better come in.'

She followed me in and I sat her down in an armchair and brought her the traditional British panacea — hot, sweet tea. She sipped at it, holding the cup in trembling hands.

'What's he done now?' I said.

More gulping and sniffling, then . . . 'It's over. He's finished with me. He doesn't want to see me any more.' The cup clattered in the saucer and I took the whole lot away from her before she spilt it on the carpet. It's not that I'm particularly houseproud, just that I'd done as much carpet scrubbing as I fancied that day.

'He said that, did he? He said, "It's over, get out, never darken my doorstep again", words to that effect?'

'Yes. Well, no . . . Well, sort of.' A sniff, a swallow, some nose-blowing. She looked somehow small, vulnerable, waiflike, all tucked up in the big armchair — not a bit like the confident, rather abrasive young woman of our previous encounters. 'He hasn't said anything really except . . . except not to call him at his office any more. He said he'd call me but he hasn't. I keep trying the Dolphin Square number but there's no reply.'

'Well, it's the weekend. Maybe his daughters are home from school and he's spending time with them in the country. Maybe he . . .' I gave up thinking of excuses for him and patted the bowed, blonde head in a brotherly sort of way. 'Thing is, Lacy, Archie's having a bad time right now. He's got a lot of problems.'

She gave her nose a rough wipe with her handkerchief. Her nostrils had gone all pink. 'I know and I want to help.'

I said, sharply, 'What do you mean —
you know? How do you know? Has he
talked to you about it?'

'No. He hasn't said anything but I can
tell. A woman always can, you know,
when the man she loves is in trouble.'

I thought, Oh God, she's been at the
Mills & Boon again, and that was a
surprise because I'd have marked her
down as someone who went in for
rather ballsier reading. 'Look,' I said,
'I've known him just about as long as
you have and the only reason I know
he's in trouble is because he told me
so. But he hasn't said anything to you
so how come you suddenly realise
there's something wrong?'

She looked up at me, the whites of
her eyes now as pink as her nostrils.
'Because I love him and I thought he
loved me. But he . . . he doesn't want
to see me any more and I think there's
another woman and I think . . . I think
she's the problem. Is there . . .' the pink
and blue eyes gazed at me beseechingly,
'is there another woman?'

Well, in a way there was, I suppose
— there was Minnie Mouse but I didn't
think this was the time to mention her.
I shook my head. 'Not to my knowledge.

It's a different kind of problem Archie's got. Listen to me,' I took her face in my hands, her skin a little damp but still smooth and silky to my touch, and stared into her eyes to attract her full attention, 'I don't know whether Archie's in love with you. He doesn't confide in me about that sort of thing. But let's for a moment assume the worst, that he's gone off you and found somebody else. What are you going to do? Are you going to blow the whistle on him? Are you going to sell your story to the newspapers?'

She wrenched herself away from me, her eyes big with indignation. 'Of course not! What kind of a person do you think I . . . Haven't you been listening to me? Didn't you hear anything? I love him. I want him. I'd do anything for him and I know we can work things out, I just know we can. All I ask is the chance to see him, to talk to him.'

I did some more patting — on her hand this time. 'OK. I can't promise anything, you understand, but if you like I'll speak to him, I'll tell him what you've said and ask him to call you.' We gazed solemnly at each other and I thought, Dammit, I've got to stop this;

I'm playing the pimp again, only this time I'm trying to procure him for her.

After a bit more sobbing she calmed down, smiled tremulously at me and went to the bathroom to wash her face and repair the tear-stained wreckage of her make-up. And after that I walked her to her car and then I phoned Beckway.

But there was no reply from any of his numbers, just answering machines with their false, cheerful promises to get back to you.

TWENTY-SIX

And so to Monday morning and the desperate, frantic call from Beckway. 'Bobby, I'm at the office. Get over here as fast as you can.' He sounded strung-out. I could almost hear his nerves twanging. 'It's happened.'

'What's happened?'

'I can't tell you on the phone. Just get here.'

Birgit was on guard in Beckway's outer office, dressed in something creamy and giving an Oscar-worthy impersonation of an ice maiden. 'I'm afraid you'll have to wait, Mr Lennox. The Minister has Sir Harvey with him.'

Mr Lennox? So we were back to that, were we?

I said, 'Birgit, please — '

'I'm rather busy at the moment. Do forgive me.' She started clattering away at her computer keys as if I weren't there. With her blonde hair and that dress she looked as if she had been concocted out of dairy ice-cream and I found myself wondering wistfully what might have happened the other night if bloody Roger Kale hadn't turned up.

'Give me a break,' I said. 'I can explain — '

'I'm so glad to see you've recovered from your 'flu', she said without taking her eyes from the computer screen.

The door to Beckway's office opened and a small, bald bloke came out wearing gold-rimmed glasses and a deep frown. From behind him I heard Beckway said, 'Harvey, I can only repeat what I've already told you. I knew nothing about this, nothing at all.'

'Of course, Minister. I hear what you're saying.' The bald bloke nodded curtly at Birgit and bustled out with the look of a man who may have heard what the Minister was saying but reserved the right not to believe it.

Birgit said, 'You may go in now, Mr Lennox.'

Beckway was at his desk. He looked awful, hair all mussed as if he had been tugging at it, heavy eyes, deep lines in his face, his whole posture exuding worry and anxiety. He didn't bother with any greetings, just said, 'We've had another tender for that prison complex, appreciably lower than any of the others.' He paused. 'It came from Jack Klug. Then, just before you got here the Irishman called. All he said was, "We like Klug's bid. You'd better like it too." '

'Surprise, surprise. Is Jack in time? I mean, what's the deadline for submitting tenders?'

'End of this week. Oh, he's in time all right. And if he can justify his figures he'll almost certainly get the contract. All the others came in at much the same total, give or take. Jack has undercut the lot.' He ran both hands through his hair in a distracted sort of way. 'Christ, what a mess.'

'I saw your Permanent Secretary — whats'isname, Sir Harvey — on his way out. He didn't look happy.'

'Can you wonder at it? Thursday, out of the blue, I ask him what the estimates are and today we get this bid from Klug. Harvey doesn't like it. I told him it was a coincidence but I'm not sure he's going to buy that. Would you?'

'Very possibly not but if I was Harvey what would I do?'

'Oh God.' He shook his head despairingly. 'He'll talk to his counterpart in the Prime Minister's office, who in turn will talk to the PM and he'll want to talk to me. Then what do I do?'

I said irritably, 'Oh, for heaven's sake, you do what politicians are good at — you lie. You stick to your story. Who's going to deny it? Klug? The Irishman? Coincidence does happen, you know. Your mates in high office might not like it but if you keep your nerve they can't prove anything against you. In the end they'll probably be quite happy, they'll be saving money. This is a government project, isn't it? And that means the cheaper the better.'

'Yes? And what about the next time Klug or the Irishman want something from me?'

'We'll worry about that when it happens. At least we know now who's behind all this, so that's a plus for our side.'

Beckway rubbed his hands over his face. 'I can't believe what's happening to me, Bobby. There's all this business and . . . and then there's Lacy. She's becoming a real problem. How could I have been such a fool? Why did I ever get involved with her? I wish to God I'd never met her.'

I had a shrewd idea he wasn't the first man to have said that about a woman but this was no time to get into a philosophical discussion on that topic. I said, 'That reminds me. She turned up at my flat last night.' I told him what had happened and he groaned some more and cursed a bit and somehow gave the impression that it was all my fault. The usual fate, I suppose, of the messenger who bears bad news.

'It just gets worse,' he said eventually.

'Oh come on, pull yourself together. Give the girl a ring. Murmur sweet, sexy things to her. How hard can that be for a man like you? You probably do it in your sleep. The important thing, particularly now, is to keep her happy. We don't want her going around making waves.'

He made a sort of hollow laughing noise. 'Happy? Do you know what she wants to make her happy? She wants me to marry her, that's all.'

That was, I had to admit, a bit of a shaker but I rallied well. 'You must have faced that kind of problem before,' I said.

'Yes, but not with anyone like Lacy. She's not quite what she seems, you know. She's very . . . volatile. Unpredictable.'

'Why not have a word with Birgit? She tells me she's helped you get rid of bothersome women before.' I got up to go.

He said on a panicky note, 'Don't leave me. Not now. Where are you going?'

'To see a man about a contract,' I said.

The head office of Klug Construction was in Borehamwood, just off the A I. A three-storey building on a small industrial estate, Klug had moved there from a place in the City because property was cheaper in Borehamwood during the recession of the late 1980s and early 90s.

I turned up just before lunch and talked my way as far as the office where Klug's private secretary sat protecting him from intruders. A smart, middle-aged woman with neat grey hair, round spectacles and a general air that suggested, in the most genteel possible way, that she wasn't about to take any bullshit from anybody. I told her who I was and that my business with her boss was personal and confidential.

She wasn't impressed, said Klug never saw anybody without an appointment and beside he wasn't in. I told her he damn well was in because I'd just walked past his Roller with the personalised number plate, though God alone knew why anyone should need a personalised number plate to remind him who he was, and the bonnet was still warm.

She asked me, icily, not to swear at her. I said, 'Oh damn, I hadn't realised I was swearing and now can I go in?' She said certainly not; not only did I have no appointment but she had never heard of me and had no idea who I was. I said I'd just told her who I was but she said that wasn't enough.

I said, 'Look, please, I'm trying to be nice here.'

She said, 'I'm very sorry.' She didn't strike me as being sorry at all. Obviously this was a woman impervious to nice.

'OK then,' I said, 'try this one. Tell him I want to talk to him about a tender he's just submitted. Tell him that if he doesn't see me within ten minutes I'm going to the police and if I do that he won't be building the new prison in Yorkshire, he'll be its first inmate.'

She was shocked. 'How dare you threaten Sir Jack. Kindly leave this office — '

'Madam,' I said, 'that wasn't a threat,

that was a guarantee. So get yourself in there and give him the message.'

She didn't like it but I had her worried. She huffed and puffed for a while but in the end, after locking her desk with great deliberation, she went into Klug's inner office. Two minutes later she came out again, her manner both peeved and bewildered.

'Sir Jack has kindly agreed to see you,' she muttered, her voice all sulky.

Sir Jack didn't look kind, nor did he look pleased to see me. He looked furious, a short, stocky, shirtsleeved figure glowering aggressively from behind a big oak desk. 'Fuck do you think you're playing at?' he asked. 'And what's all this crap about the police?'

I ignored the hard upright chair on my side of the desk and instead sat in one of the black leather armchairs that were clustered together in a kind of lounge area near the window. The desk and the authority it lent him were no longer between us because Klug had to swivel sideways to look at me. It disconcerted him a little.

'Where did you find the Irishman?' I asked.

'What?'

'The Irishman. And the other two men and the girl. Where did you find them?'

'What is all this? I don't know what you're talking about.'

I sighed and settled back in my chair to show him that I was a patient man prepared to wait.

He said, 'You've got five minutes, then I'm going to have you thrown out.'

'No, you're not because that would be a very silly thing to do. I've got as long as I need. We both know that.' He glowered some more and I carried on looking calm and patient. After a while I said, 'All right, let's talk about this new prison complex. Bit late bidding for the job, weren't you?'

'What?' He seemed genuinely bewildered. 'You know perfectly well why . . . Hang on, hang on. You are still working for Archie, are you?'

I nodded.

'Then what are you asking me these damn fool questions for? Archie tipped me the wink. That's why I put my bid in. He told me what the lowest tender was.'

'Archie did?'

'Yes. Well, I assume it was Archie. I got a note delivered here last Thursday afternoon. Some kind of dispatch rider handed it in. Wasn't signed, of course. Just the bottom line figure and the words "Go for it".'

'What makes you think Archie sent it?'

'Who else? I took a nasty bath a few years back because of him and Donovan and I thought this was Archie's way of making amends.'

I gave him my most disbelieving sneer. 'You really think that Archie, in his position, would put himself on the line by sending you that kind of inside information?'

Klug returned my sneer with a nonchalant shrug. 'Why not? He owed me. Look, I'll be honest with you. If I hadn't known what the target bid was I wouldn't have put in for this job. A few years ago, sure, I wouldn't have hesitated, but things haven't been so good lately. They've not been good for anyone in the building trade but my company has suffered more than most and I knew any bid I made would have to be far and away the most competitive or I wouldn't be taken seriously.'

'But when the little note turned up, you didn't think twice?'

'Of course not. I knew all the specifications — I applied for those when the job was first advertised. I tell you, I worked like a bastard this weekend to get the numbers right because even at the price I submitted there's a fortune to be made. OK, it's a hell of a big job but I can handle it. I get this contract and I'm right back on top again. That'll put paid to all the nonsense about a takeover.'

'What takeover?'

'I don't know — nothing, just a bunch of rumours been going around lately. This is a good firm I've got but it's a bit shaky financially right now, so it's not surprising there were rumours.' He leaned back more comfortably in his chair. 'Not any more, though, not when I've landed this one.'

'You're sure you'll land it, are you?'

He looked at me thoughtfully, head on one side. 'Maybe not quite as sure as I was before you pitched up but pretty sure nevertheless. Fact that you're here tells me two things — one, that bit of paper didn't come from Archie but, two, the information is accurate otherwise you wouldn't be getting your knickers in such a twist. Now that's a puzzle, I'll grant you, but it's not one I'm going to spend a lot of time worrying about.' He had talked himself out of any concern he might have felt earlier and had returned to being his usual, cocky unlikeable self. 'Matter of fact, it tells me a couple of other things as well, like first, Archie's in some kind of trouble or he wouldn't have got Donovan to lend you to him. And, secondly, for whatever reason you haven't the slightest intention of going to the police.'

Right on all counts. I said, 'We're talking at least insider trading here and it doesn't faze you a bit. You really are a crook, aren't you?'

He laughed: a short, sharp barking sound. 'What fucking planet are you from? Listen, you may have fought under the Marquess of Queensberry rules but I got news for you: they don't apply in business. Business is who you know and what you know and how to find the short cuts. You call that crooked? I call it reality. Frankly, I don't give a shit where that information came from so long as it's kosher.' He looked at his watch. 'Now if that covers everything piss off out of my office.'

I said, 'What did you say to Felicity

Beckway to make her slap your face?'

His lips curled upwards in a malicious little grin. 'Asked her what you were like in bed.' He stroked his cheek reflectively. 'That was quite a wallop the bitch gave me. What I should have done, of course, was go straight to Archie and ask him what she'd said about you.' Suddenly he sprang up and came out from behind his desk, doing his best to loom menacingly in front of me which is never an easy thing for a short person to do. 'And if you give me any more aggro I might try that.'

I stood up fast, deliberately fast, and it shook him enough to make him take a nervous step backwards. He had to look up to meet my gaze, the cold hard gaze that I'm famous for. 'What do you think you're playing at,' I said, all dead macho, 'standing there, towering under me, with your stupid threats? You try stirring things up with Archie and I swear to you, Jacko, your life won't be worth living.' All very childish but it worked pretty well as an exit line, causing old Jack to scuttle back behind his desk where he felt big and safe.

As I opened the door he said, 'If Archie didn't send me that information, where did it come from? And what was all that stuff about an Irishman? What's that got to do with me?'

I just ignored him. Best thing to do really, especially as I didn't have any answers to give him.

TWENTY-SEVEN

Beckway was at the House of Commons. Some big debate going on about the Government's latest plans to screw up the National Health Service. I didn't leave a message for him; I reckoned he probably had enough problems to be going on with right where he was. I called Donovan instead and filled him in with the story so far.

'Interesting,' he said. 'If Jack Klug's not behind all this, who the hell is?'

'You tell me. And while you're about it you might tell me why the Irishman should have picked on loveable old Jack as the beneficiary.'

'Good point. Got any ideas?'

Not ideas, nothing as definite as that. Just a few vague, worrying thoughts, which I wasn't going to pass on to Donovan. Not then. Not till I'd checked them out. 'I'm working on something,' I said. 'I'll let you know what turns up.'

'What? Don't be so fucking secretive. Tell me, for Chrissake. What's the matter with you?'

'Nothing. I've got some stuff to do, that's all.'

But I wasn't able to do it, not right away, because various things happened to waylay me.

First there was Felicity Beckway. I'd just put the phone down on Donovan when my doorbell rang and there she was, managing to look simultaneously stunning and agitated. She was in the flat almost before I could say 'Hello' and she was in my arms, sobbing, even as the door closed behind her. I could feel her tears soaking through my shirt and lying damp on my neck. I led her gently into the sitting-room, sat her down, handed her a box of tissues and, swiftly summing up the situation like the sophisticated man of the world I am, went to mix her a stiff drink, wondering what it was about me that had all these women weeping at me and what role I was expected to play this time. Pimp again? I did hope not.

By the time I got back, bearing whisky and soda for both of us, she had controlled the tears. All her make-up had gone, transferred to the wet, crumpled tissues on the table in front of her, but she was one of those women who don't really need make-up. There was natural colour in her lips and cheeks; the long, thickly curling lashes were all her own and the few faint lines around her eyes enhanced her beauty rather than detracted from it.

We sat in silence while we knocked back half our drinks and then I said, 'All right, what's happened?'

For a moment I thought she was going to start crying again but instead she shook her head impatiently and took something from her handbag. 'This,' she said. 'I got it in the post this morning. Just this, nothing else.'

She handed it across to me. It was a photograph of her husband getting a blow job from Minnie Mouse. Beckway had shown me one exactly like it at the flat in Dolphin Square. Felicity watched me carefully as I looked at it.

'You know about it, don't you?' she said. 'You're not surprised or shocked or . . . or horrified or anything. You've seen it before.'

I nodded. 'That's why I'm working with Archie now. It's because of this and other pictures like it that he's in trouble. He's being blackmailed.'

'By that little tart?' Tart is not an easy

word to hiss but Felicity managed it.

'And by the men who were with her and took the photos.'

'Dear God. Oh, dear sweet God.' She finished her drink and held the glass out for a refill but before I could get up and oblige she said bitterly, 'If you're telling me the truth, it serves him right. He deserves to be black-mailed. How could he, how could he do something like that . . .' The tears — of grief, anger, I don't know — were on their way back.

'It's not like that,' I said. 'This wasn't some orgy that he willingly took part in. There were three men who forced him to pose for the pictures.' I told her then what Beckway had told me about that evening at the Television Centre and she listened in silence, watching me all the time.

When I had finished she said, 'And you believe him? You believe that grubby bastard?'

I looked again at the picture. There was nothing in it to indicate where it had been taken or under what circum-stances — just Beckway and Minnie Mouse with her mouth full and a plain white wall as a backdrop. 'Yes, I think so. I can't see any reason why I shouldn't.'

'You don't know him as well as I do. You don't know what he's like with women.' Her shoulders began to heave and I moved to the sofa beside her and took her in my arms. She clung to me and let the tears flow as I stroked her head and made what I hoped were soothing noises.

When she had recovered I said, 'There was no letter? Just the picture?'

She nodded, gulping. 'It was posted on Saturday in the West End. Why would anyone do that, why would anyone send me something as vile as this?'

Interesting question, I thought, and one to which I couldn't begin to find an answer because the situation didn't make sense. The hold Mickey Mouse had on Beckway was the threat to show the pictures to the Prime Minister and/or Felicity — but the whole point about blackmail was that the incriminating evidence should be a secret shared only by the blackmailer and his victim. Beckway's main concern was to save his political career, a trick that would be made a lot harder if he were involved in a messy divorce. And he would only be useful to the Irishman if that career were to continue. How then could it be in the Irishman's interests to send the picture to Felicity? Or was it someone else who had sent it?

I said, 'Have you told Archie that you've got this photo?'

She shook her head. 'I was going to. I even started to phone him but then I felt so horribly alone. I . . . I just had to talk to somebody. You can't imagine how awful it was to open that envelope and find this . . . this disgusting . . .'

I stroked her hair some more, very gently. 'Why me?'

'I don't know. I couldn't tell any of my girlfriends. It would be too humiliating.' She uttered a quick, bitter laugh. 'God, the kind of man Archie is, that bitch in the photo could even be one of my girlfriends for all I know. So I thought of you, I suppose, because . . . because after that night I thought you were my friend.' She drew away from me. 'Oh, God, am I making the most awful bloody fool of myself?'

I pulled her back into my arms. 'No. I'm your friend. You can rely on that. But what happens now?'

'I'll divorce him. I was an idiot — I

should have done it ages ago. I was going to until he got this government job and stopped playing around. But I couldn't possibly stay with him any longer — not after this.'

'Even though he was forced to pose for that photograph?'

'That's what he says. You can believe him if you like but I don't. I'll never believe him.'

I disengaged myself from her and went to refill our glasses. When I came back I didn't rejoin her on the sofa but plonked myself down, very business-like, in an armchair opposite her. 'I think you should at least talk to him first. He's in very big trouble already. I don't think he could handle a divorce right now, not on top of everything else.'

She snorted disbelievingly. 'What trouble?'

'I told you — he's being blackmailed because of that photo and a lot of others like it. I can't tell you what the black-mailer wants — '

'Why not? Good old male bonding again, is it? Keep the little woman in the dark?'

'No. As far as anything between you and Archie is concerned, I'm on your side. You must believe that. But in this other business, the blackmail, I'm working for Archie and I have to keep his confidence. All I can tell you is that if things go wrong . . .' I didn't like to think about what might happen if things went wrong. 'Well, at the very least he'd be finished in politics and he might even end up in gaol. So I think, before you do anything else, you should talk to him, listen to what he says. Will you do that?'

She considered it for quite a long time. Then she sighed and said, 'All right. Tomorrow. I'll talk to him tomorrow.'

I took a sip of my drink. 'And in the meantime?'

'The meantime? Oh yes, the meantime.' She leaned back and gazed up at the ceiling for a moment. 'In the meantime can I stay here with you? I need a friend. I need comfort.'

I got up and joined her on the sofa. I mean, come on — what are friends for if not to provide comfort? 'Yes, you can stay here.'

A little after that, because we were hungry, we made omelettes. And then we made love and at one point while we were making love she did to me what

Minnie Mouse was doing to Beckway in the photograph. I don't think she did it for me; I think she was taking revenge. I think it was a case of sauce for the gander . . .

I didn't catch the news the next morning. Didn't turn on the radio or the TV, didn't even glance at the paper. I didn't get around to the stuff I'd told Donovan I was planning to do either. I'd intended to do it in the morning but it was after nine before Felicity and I woke up and everything else was postponed because I had to put in a little more comforting before she felt able to phone her husband.

I didn't hear any of that conversation because I was tactfully having a shower at the time but she arranged to meet him at their home in Mayfair and she left me around eleven, the Minnie Mouse photograph in her bag.

'Wish me luck,' she said.

I studied the cold, angry look in her eyes, the determined set of her chin. 'Maybe I ought to wish him luck.'

'Don't you dare.' She opened the front door, hesitated a moment, closed it again, leaned her back against it and held out her arms. 'I don't want to go. I don't want to confront him. Come here, give me courage.'

So I went there and delayed her departure for a good ten minutes. When finally I stepped back I said, 'That's all the courage you need. Let me know what happens.'

I pottered around the flat for an hour or so after she had left, clearing things up, and I was about to set off for the City to do all that stuff I'd mentioned to Donovan when the nagging little worry that had been lurking around in the back of my mind popped out into the open and I suddenly remembered that I was supposed to be meeting Rachel Grant for lunch at the Television Centre.

It was already noon and too late to cancel. I thought, The hell with it, the City will still be there this afternoon, and headed for Shepherd's Bush. Traffic was heavy on the Westway and I was late arriving at the Centre. The woman on reception said that Rachel was already upstairs waiting for me in the restaurant, and I was about to pile into the lift when Lacy stepped out of it.

She looked tired and drawn and there

were dark semicircles under her eyes, as if she hadn't slept for some time. She had her head down and I think she would have walked past without recognising me if I hadn't grabbed her arm.

She was not pleased to see me. 'Liar,' she said. 'You didn't talk to him, did you?'

'Yes, I did. I told him what you said and he promised to call you.'

'Well, he didn't. I've waited and waited by the phone and there wasn't any call. And I've tried a dozen times to call him but all I get is his answering machine.'

There was a febrile quality about her, a constant nervous movement of the hands and eyes that I found disturbing. I said, 'I know he was at the House last night. Big debate, three-line whip, real heavy stuff. They probably didn't rise till after midnight.'

'I called him after midnight, at Dolphin Square and his house in Mayfair. I called him at three o'clock and again at six o'clock. He wasn't there, was he? He wasn't at either place. Where was he? Who was he with?' She stared at me, her face scrunched up, her mouth quivering.

I said, 'Maybe he was at his house in

Hertfordshire. Or, OK, maybe he was at one of his London places and was just too tired to take calls. From anybody.'

'He ought to take calls from me. He *has* to take calls from me. We're going to be married. I don't know how he could treat me like this. I don't . . . I don't . . .' She let out a soft, heartbroken wail and ran away towards the ladies' loo. Perhaps I should have hung around till she came out, made sure she was all right, but I doubt if it would have done any good. In the neurotic state she was in she probably blamed me as much as if not more than Beckway. She clearly wasn't in the mood to trust me or believe anything I said, and besides, what could I say about this fantasy she had concocted that Beckway was going to marry her? So I chickened out, arguing to myself that I was already keeping another woman waiting upstairs.

But at that moment I did have the choice — I could stay and try to reason with her and placate her, or I could leave — and I chose to leave. Maybe it would have made a difference if I'd stayed. I don't think so but maybe . . .

Rachel had got us a table for two at

the far end of the restaurant. She had also ordered a bottle of chablis and was well into it by the time I joined her. She looked pale and worried and her eyes were pink as if she had been crying. I didn't seem to be encountering any happy women that day.

I kissed her on the cheek, sat down, took the glass of wine she poured for me and said, 'What's up?'

She shook her head as if contemplating something almost unbelievable. 'You haven't heard? It's all over the news. One of our stars was murdered at the weekend.'

'What? Who?'

'Roger Kale. He played the CID inspector and — '

'I know. I've met Roger Kale. Good God. What happened?'

'It's all here.' She passed me a copy of one of the tabloid papers. The story occupied the entire front page. It didn't matter that Britain's economy was in its usual dire state, that dreadful things were happening in Eastern Europe, that scores of thousands were starving to death in Africa — the murder of a small-time TV star was the big news of the day, pretty nearly the only news of the day, as far as this paper was concerned.

Kale's body had been discovered late the previous afternoon by a friend, another member of the cast named Alex Twill, who had been expecting to meet him for lunch. Twill and somebody called Ray Richards had turned up at the appointed restaurant at the appointed hour but there had been no sign of Kale. They had tried to phone him several times but without getting a reply and in the end Twill had been concerned enough to go to Kale's flat in Bayswater to see if anything was wrong. There was — as he swiftly gathered from the small pool of now dried blood that had seeped under the front door and into the hallway.

Twill had called the police who had found Kale lying just inside his flat with the back of his head smashed in. He had been dead at least twenty-four hours, maybe longer. According to the paper there was no apparent motive for the killing. The contents of the flat seemed undisturbed and there was no obvious suspect.

'How did you know Roger?' Rachel asked.

'I met him here, in this building, last week. Then he turned up at my gym and then at a restaurant I was at. Coincidence really.'

I read on. Kale was 34, a bachelor noted for putting himself liberally about among good-looking young women but recently 'linked romantically' — as the paper put it — 'with his co-star Carly Shawn'. There was a picture of the two of them looking romantic and a smaller picture of Twill taken the previous evening. He was 35, though he looked older, rugged rather than handsome, with fair hair receding fast from the temples. There were quotes from him, Rachel and various other people connected with the show expressing shock, horror, grief and the other emotions people claim when confronted with the sudden, violent death of somebody they know. There was no quote from Carly Shawn, however. She, apparently, was 'unavailable for comment'.

'I didn't know him at all well,' I said. 'What was he like?'

'Bit conceited because women threw themselves at him but quite sweet really. Not a bad actor either, although not as good as this rag says he was. If you believed all this rubbish,' she rapped the newspaper with the back of her hand, 'you'd think he could have given lessons to Depardieu, De Niro and Anthony Hopkins.'

We ordered food and I said, 'Didn't you miss him yesterday? I mean, this is your recording day, right? So surely there'd have been rehearsals yesterday.'

Rachel shook her head. 'Obvious you don't watch the show. It's set in some Metropolitan police division and we do alternating stories — CID one week, with Roger and Carly as a leggy chief inspector, uniformed branch the next week. This is a uniformed week and that doesn't involve either Roger or Carly.'

'Just as well.'

'Yes. God knows what we'll do next week though. I suppose we'll have to rewrite everything for Carly until we can find a replacement for Roger.' The already pink eyes began to moisten. 'I can't believe this has happened. Why on earth would anyone want to kill him?'

The food arrived and we ate for a while. Then Rachel said, 'Funny, isn't it, how sometimes you think you've got a problem and then something else happens and you realise that what you'd been worrying about earlier simply wasn't worth the bother.'

'How d'you mean?'

'Well, in the show Roger had two side-kicks — Alex Twill, who played his sergeant, and Ray Richards as the young, eager detective constable.'

'Usual stereotypes,' I said, nodding.

'Of course they're stereotypes. What do you expect? This is a sort of weekly soap, it's not supposed to be bloody Shakespeare. Audiences like to know where they are with the characters. Anyway, all I was worried about last night was whether Ray would recover in time to do next week's show. I wish that was the only problem I had now.'

'Sick, is he?' I asked, delicately picking a fishbone out of my front teeth.

'No, smashed his nose. End of last week, Thursday night I think. Had to see a plastic surgeon apparently. He said he fell down some stairs but if you ask me I reckon he had a fight with Alex. They live together, you see. Oh, absolutely devoted but I gather they're inclined to get a bit rough with each other when they're carried away.'

I paused with a forkful of chips half-way to my mouth. 'Was Kale gay, too?'

'Good God, no. He couldn't keep his hands off women, though just for sex really. Treated them like tissues — use them once and throw them away. Even this alleged romantic attachment to Carly was more publicity than anything else. Certainly they screwed but they'd been screwing on and off for years and I'm damn sure there was nothing serious between them.'

I chewed the chips and a bit more fish. 'Was Roger big mates with Twill and Richards?'

'With Alex mainly. They'd been in repertory together ages ago, then they did a few TV shows before we signed them both for *Shoot to Kill.* Ray just tagged along, really. He does pretty well what Alex tells him. But, yes, Roger and Alex were good friends.'

'Were they all here on Tuesday night two weeks ago?'

She scratched her head, thinking back. 'No, I don't belie . . . Oh, yes, they were. Just for an hour or two. We were doing a uniformed episode that night but Roger and the others — not Carly, though — were in a couple of the early scenes. It happens like that sometimes. Why do you ask?'

'Just curious.' Coincidence. I'd gone all my life without even knowing of the existence of Roger Kale and then suddenly, briefly, he was all over the place. Coincidence. I'd shattered Goofy's nose and now suddenly one of Kale's side-kicks had a broken nose, too. 'Was Roger Kale Irish?'

'No. A Londoner. He could do an Irish accent though. He could do any kind of accent. He was very good at that.'

I mulled this over for a bit, this further coincidence. Then I said, 'You couldn't let me have an address for Alex Twill and Ray Richards, could you?'

TWENTY-EIGHT

I didn't get to the City that afternoon either because Rachel found me the address I had asked for and gave me the name of Roger Kale's agent as well, even though I wouldn't tell her why I wanted this information. She was puzzled and exasperated and I was evasive, saying only that it was important, trust me. In the end she did what I asked because, well, it's not just Oxbridge that operates an Old Boy (or Girl) network; redbrick universities do it, too.

Twill and Richards shared a third-floor flat in a 1930s block in Maida Vale, the smarter part of the Edgware Road, and they were both at home that day. I rang the bell and Twill opened the door. He was barefoot and wearing baggy linen trousers, a loose, white shirt and a polite but questioning look which became a little less polite and a lot more troubled when he saw me standing on his welcome mat.

'Now you,' I said, 'you were Pluto. Am I right?'

He didn't turn pale beneath his tan; he just went a bit red. 'Are you mad?' he said and tried to close the door. But I was ready for that. I gave him a hefty shove in the chest and I was inside the flat with the door shut behind me before he had fully recovered his balance.

'What the devil do you think you're doing?' he said. 'I'll call the police.'

'No, you won't.' I gave him a second shove and then another and, because like most people who are generally unused to violence he was confused by it, he simply staggered backwards, unresisting, down the short hallway and into a fair-sized living-room A tall, slim young man had sprung up from an armchair beside the window and was watching us with big, startled eyes. He, too, was barefoot and wearing jeans and a shirt — a blue one — and he had a mop of auburn curls and a whole mess of plasters over his nose.

'Don't tell me,' I said. 'You must be Ray.' He nodded, involuntarily. 'And, of course, you were also Goofy. How's the nose coming along?' I made a playful little jab in its direction and he stepped back, hands up to his face.

Twill said, recovering fast and trying

to sound menacing, 'Whatever you want it had better be important or I'll throw you out.' From the look of the muscles under his shirt it was a reasonable bet that he did some weight training; most actors do these days. I think Stallone and Schwarzenegger started it, this idea that if you can't emote much you might as well look tough. Let the muscles do the acting. But there is a difference between looking tough and being tough, between being strong and being a fighter. I didn't think Twill was a fighter; in fact I was rather banking on him not being a fighter.

'I don't think you'll do that either,' I said.

He sneered at me. 'There's only one of you and there are two of us.'

I nodded to show that I took the point. 'True. But the last time you set on me there were three of you and I still managed to do a fair bit of damage.' I gestured towards Richards' injured nose and again his hands went up to his face. He shot a worried, frightened, look towards Twill, who frowned at him and shook his head slightly.

It was a nicely furnished room, a touch over-furnished perhaps, and every table and shelf was liberally supplied with little china and porcelain knick-knacks, expensive-looking objects most of them.

Twill said, 'The hell with this. Get the fuck out of our home.' He took a step towards me but I held up both hands in a placatory gesture and he hesitated.

'Before we go any further,' I said, 'let me tell you a joke.'

'A what?' Twill said, scowling.

'A joke. It's about a young Australian sheep shearer who went to the big city for the first time and picked up a prostitute. Well, she took him to her flat, sat him down and said, "I won't be long, darling", or Cobber, or Blue, or whatever Australian prostitutes call their clients, and went into the bathroom. When she came back he'd piled all the furniture up against the wall. She said, "What the hell d'you think you're doing?" and he said, "I've never had a woman before but if it's anything like a kangaroo we're gonna need all the room we can get".'

Twill and Richards stared at me blankly. 'That's not funny,' Twill said.

'I didn't say it was funny, I just said

it was a joke. But there's a moral to it, you see. You can try to throw me out and between the pair of you you might even succeed. But I'll resist and then we'll start bouncing each other off the walls and we'll probably wreck the entire room. In fact I *promise* we'll wreck the entire room. So what I'm saying is, if you're really going to try any rough stuff you'd better get rid of all the ducky little ornaments and start piling the furniture against the walls because we're gonna need all the room we can get.'

Twill looked at Richards and Richards gazed with anguish at the china and porcelain knick-knacks. Then Twill turned back to me, fists clenched, face tight with anger.

'All I want to know,' I said, 'is why you and Roger Kale were blackmailing Archie Beckway. I can't prove you were doing that but I know you were and I want you to tell me why. Simple really.'

Richards said, 'Alex — '

'Shut up! Shut up, Ray, for Christ's sake, I'll deal with this.' And then, apparently careless of the knick-knacks and what might befall them, he rushed me, pushing me back against the bookshelves that lined the wall behind me, his hands reaching for my throat, his right knee thrusting viciously towards my groin. I couldn't get out of the way of his hands but I managed to twist enough to take the knee on my thigh instead of in my crotch. As he started to choke me I took hold of his long, thinning hair in my left hand and yanked his head back. He grunted but didn't relax his grip.

We were so close together there was no room to throw a punch. I tried pummelling his back with both fists but that didn't help. He just kept throttling me until my eyeballs began to pop. So I took the only other option that seemed open to me: I reached down and grabbed his balls in my right hand. I could feel them, soft and squelchy, through the thin material of his slacks and I squeezed, heard him yelp, liked the sound, squeezed again, heard him screech this time, his voice high and thin and full of agony, liked that sound even better and squeezed a third time. He let go of me and fell to his knees, his hands between his legs, face white and clammy, eyes wide with agony, mouth open and drooling a little. I hit him with a hard, downward-chopping left hook on the side of the jaw and he moaned and rolled onto his side.

I staggered away, the winner and still champion, though God knows what the British Boxing Board of Control would have made of my performance, and with relief felt the air wheezing into my lungs.

Richards was pressed up against the opposite wall staring at me with big, scared eyes.

'You want some of that?' I asked in a menacing croak. Twill had really hurt my throat. It felt as though somebody had set fire to it on the inside.

He shook his head rapidly, jerkily. He looked as if he was trying to use the wall to levitate himself up to the safety of the high ceiling.

'What have you done to him?' he asked breathlessly.

I gave the recumbent Twill a prod with my foot. 'Nothing much. His balls will be very sore for a day or two, that's all. So be gentle with him, OK?'

I massaged my thigh where Twill's knee had dug into it, gently stroked my throat and took some more deep breaths. Richards watched me, his hand cupped protectively over his damaged nose.

'Now then,' I said, still croaking. 'This is what we're going to do: we're going to sit down and you're going to tell me all about Archie Beckway and the photographs and why you were blackmailing him.'

He shook his head. 'No.'

'Well, there is an alternative but you might not like it a lot. The alternative is that I'll smash up the rest of your face and then I'll smash his. You probably think that's unreasonable but then, you see, I thought that what you two and Kale did to me the other night was also unreasonable. Are we beginning to understand each other?'

From the floor Twill said, 'Ray, don't listen to him. Don't say anything.'

Richards made a helpless, frightened gesture with his hands. 'He'll hurt me, Alex.'

'Bloody right,' I said. The croak made me sound so menacing I almost scared myself. Twill looked up, tried to get up and then fell back with a little moan of pain. 'Oh, God,' he said, 'what's the use?'

So Richards sat down and started to

talk and after a while Twill joined in, too, because all the fight had left him and I think he just wanted me out of the flat as fast as possible and at whatever cost.

It had been Kale's idea, they said. He had told them it would be easy; it would be safe; nobody would get hurt and it might even be rather fun. Beckway was a slimeball, he had said, a notorious pussyhound and there was no need for anyone to feel sorry for him. And on top of that, if all went well they could make a great deal of money, not once but several times.

'What did you want the money for?' I asked. 'From the look of this place I wouldn't have thought you were hard up.'

Twill said, his voice still full of pain, 'Ray and I like to live well.' When I looked quizzical he added, 'We spend a lot. Clothes, holidays, restaurants. Oh yes, I know — we're on the telly regularly so we must be rich. But it's not like that. The pay's not so hot really, not when you're playing a supporting role in a series. And besides we've got a thumping great mortgage on this flat and we're totally fucked because these days the place isn't worth what we paid for it. So the idea of extra money wasn't exactly unwelcome.'

'How did Kale suggest you were going to make all this loot?'

Richards said, 'He told us to raise every penny we could and buy shares in a company called Klug Construction. So that's what we did. Even took out a second mortgage.'

'Odd way to go about things. Why not simply ask Beckway for, I don't know, fifty, a hundred thousand?'

Richards hesitated. Then, 'Well, Roger said . . .' And what Roger had said was pretty much what he had told Beckway: that the handing over of information was less painful for the blackmailed than the handing over of money.

'Roger said if we left it to him there wouldn't be any danger.' Twill grunted ruefully. 'But he also said there wouldn't be any rough stuff and he was wrong about that, too.'

Kale had not told them why they should buy shares in Klug. He had just said they should do it, that they couldn't fail to double or triple their money and that this would be only the first of many scams they could pull off while Beckway remained in government office. They were to look upon the photographs as an investment that would keep paying off, tax free, and the higher Beckway climbed the more they would make. Beckway, Kale told them, was now theirs; they owned him.

Thinking about it and Twill's and Richards' part in it, I could see that Kale had a point: it did sound comparatively easy, if not exactly fun — not my idea of fun anyway. But then these people were actors and dressing up and playing parts was pretty well what they lived for. Even so, I was surprised that Kale had been able to persuade the others to go along with him so compliantly until a possible explanation occurred to me. 'You've done this before, haven't you?' I said. 'This wasn't your first shot at blackmail.'

Twill hesitated, then nodded. 'It was years ago when Roger and I were in repertory together up in the North. Ray wasn't involved; I didn't even know him then. There was a local businessman, a bigwig, member of the city council, well in line to become mayor, all that shit. A nasty, fat old bastard. Happily married, kids, respected pillar of the community. Only thing was, he couldn't keep his hands off girls and we had quite a few in the company. Anyway, we threw a party one night, Roger and I, in this grotty flat we rented and the businessman pretty well invited himself. There was a lot of booze; somebody brought some coke; everyone got well pissed or stoned or both and the noble city councillor ended up in bed with one of the young actresses.' He grunted, remembering, not much liking the memory. 'It was a girl Roger was knocking off at the time, actually. Well, anyway, I took some pictures of the randy old devil on the job, no reason really, just that photography's always been one of my things and it just seemed like a funny idea. When I developed them I showed them to Roger, for laughs really, but he got mad when he saw who the girl in the bed was and sent them off to the councillor and asked for ten thousand quid. He said he was punishing the bloke for daring to screw his girlfriend.'

'And the man paid up?'

'Yes. That time he did. We had him running around all over the place before we told him where to leave the money and we followed him, just to be sure he was all by himself, hadn't called the police in. It was easy.'

He was silent until I prompted him. 'What happened the second time?'

'Yeah, well, that was different,' he said gloomily. 'That time, everywhere we sent him there was this other bloke tagging along behind. The old sod had been to the police. Surprised us, I can tell you. We didn't think he had the balls. So we cut our losses, didn't go anywhere near the money and burned the photos and the negatives.'

'And learnt a lesson.' I mulled things over for a bit. 'Tell me, who was the girl in the bed?'

'Who can remember? Just a girl starting out to be an actress, played small parts, maids and that sort of thing.' He shrugged. 'Pretty enough but . . . I can't really remember what she looked like, let alone her name.'

I said, 'All right then, why did you send a picture to Beckway's wife?'

Both Twill and Richards looked genuinely astonished. 'We didn't,' Twill said. 'I mean, Ray and I couldn't have done anyway because Roger had all the prints and the negs. But . . . No, you must have got it wrong. It would have been stupid to send pictures to Beckway's wife. Unless . . .'

He stopped and I finished the sentence for him. 'Unless Beckway refused to obey orders. But, you see, he didn't. He did exactly as he was told but his wife still got a sweet little photo through the post.'

Twill said, 'I'm sorry but I don't understand. I really don't. It just doesn't make sense.'

No, it didn't. I said, 'All right, so what happened to Kale? Who killed him?'

'We don't know,' Richards said. 'Alex and I have talked about it and talked about it but we can't even make a guess. It's very frightening. I mean, we could be in danger. Of course, the police say it was an intruder but — '

'But you don't believe that and neither do I. Interesting, isn't it — Roger killed Freddie Marcus and now he — '

'What?' The pair of them were looking at me in total disbelief. 'Marcus — that government PR man? Roger didn't kill him. He can't have done. Why should he?'

'I don't exactly know why but he did. And he didn't tell you two. What a lot of secrets he seems to have kept from you.' I studied them as they sat there, close together, Twill still clutching his testicles. They seemed sincere enough but, come on, they were actors. Any competent actor should be able to play sincere. 'So what about the girl, Minnie Mouse. Who was she?'

'I don't know,' Twill said. Somehow it didn't surprise me. 'I truly don't. She was a friend of Roger's. He had a lot of girlfriends. He never told us her name. She just turned up that night and we never saw her without the mask, did we, Ray?'

'No. And she kept talking in that silly Cockney accent. It was awful. I mean, it wasn't a real Cockney accent, it was amateur night at the village dramatic society.'

I said, 'If she went to those lengths to disguise herself, is it possible she was someone you knew? Or maybe someone Beckway . . . ?'

'God, I don't know. He didn't introduce us and we left it at that. I mean, it wasn't exactly a social event you know.' Twill laughed, then winced. His balls obviously hurt him when he laughed. 'My assumption was that if he hadn't told us who she was, he probably hadn't told her who Ray and I were either. I liked that — the less everybody knew the better. So she could have been almost anyone. What can I tell you? She was Minnie Mouse with a very nice body, long legs and a rotten Cockney accent and that's all.'

Given the disguise a lot of women, including several I knew, could have matched that description.

Richards said, 'Now you know about all this, what will you do?'

'I'm thinking about it,' I said. 'Right now I really don't know what I'm going to do.'

They watched me, puzzled and a touch fearful, as I went to the door and when I had got there I turned back and said, 'I'll give you a bit of advice, though. Hang on to your shares in Klug Construction because Roger was right — I reckon you're going to make a lot of money.'

TWENTY-NINE

Shitfer was lolling in an armchair, reading the *Evening Standard,* in the anteroom that led to Donovan's office at the Mayfair betting shop.

'Is he in?' I asked.

'Yeah. Counting the day's take. He always likes to do that by himself. I wonder why.' He gazed at me expressionlessly.

'Tut, tut,' I said. 'You can't be suggesting that some of the money might stick to his fingers while he's counting it?'

'Perish the thought. Close the door gently, will you, as you go in. He hates it, anybody causes a draught and makes the money fly about all over the room.'

I went in softly and eased the door shut. Donovan looked up, grunted and carried on counting, his lips moving silently. There were piles of banknotes, thousands of pounds worth, laid out neatly on the desk in front of him. He finished counting the wad in his hands, looked at it thoughtfully, shrugged and put it in his jacket pocket.

'Don't move,' I said. 'This is a stick-up.'

He leant back, smiling reminiscently. 'Last time I heard those words I was using them myself. A bank in Finchley, it was, more years ago than I care to remember.'

'Good old days, eh?'

'Were they fuck. These are the good old days. What do you want, Bobby?'

'I've found out who was blackmailing Archie.'

That really grabbed his attention. He leant eagerly towards me, disturbing a couple of piles of money. 'Yeah? Who?'

There was a *Daily Mirror* on the edge of the desk. I passed it across to him, front page upwards. 'Him,' I said, pointing to the picture of Roger Kale.

'A bleedin' actor?' Donovan skimmed quickly through the story. 'And you killed him? Christ, Bob, you done well.'

'Of course I didn't kill him,' I said. 'I didn't even connect him to the blackmail until he was dead.' Donovan's casual assumption that I had meted out summary justice to Kale was not surprising really. I had killed somebody once, a long time ago, as Donovan knew; he was also convinced that I had killed another man, too, my former fight manager, but in that he was wrong.

⁄Once again I filled him in with the events of the day. I was beginning to feel like a middleweight Scheherezade with all the tales I had to bring him. But then that was one reason why he had brought me and Beckway together — so that I could keep him up to date on what was happening.

'And you knew this geezer, this Kale?' Donovan said.

I nodded. 'Looking back on it, I think he sought me out. I think he was sizing me up. But the strange thing is, he knew I was working for Beckway right from the start. Now how did he know that?'

Donovan looked at me blankly. 'Search me.'

'Another question: why did he send a picture to Felicity Beckway? It must have been Kale. He was the only one who could have done it because he had all the pictures and the negs.'

'According to your two poofters,' Donovan said. 'How do we know they weren't lying to you? Maybe you didn't scare them enough, Bobby. Maybe I should send Shitfer round to have a word with them.'

'No, leave them alone. They were just help. The whole thing was Kale's idea — unless there was somebody else, somebody who was working Kale and who then came to the conclusion that he didn't need old Roger any more.'

Donovan tidied up the money on the desk. 'What about the girl? If we could find her — '

'She'd probably know about as much as Twill and Richards did.' I shrugged. 'She may well have been somebody they knew, somebody who worked at the BBC, but the chances are Kale told her no more than he told the two blokes. See, I was assuming that he had set the whole thing up but now he's dead we know there had to be somebody else. Don't we?'

We stared thoughtfully at each other.

'I suppose,' Donovan said. Then he said, 'Know what I'm wondering? I'm wondering where those pictures are now.'

'I imagine they *were* in Kale's flat. Interesting to know whether the police found them. If they did, then maybe Kale really was killed by an intruder and there wasn't anyone else involved in the blackmail.'

Donovan reached for the phone. 'I'll have a word with George. Bayswater's not on his patch but he can talk to the cops in charge of the murder investigation and ask them if they found anything. Least he can do for me. I pay the bugger enough'. He dialled, asked for George and waited. Then . . . 'George? Donovan. Listen, that actor Roger Kale, got himself wasted at the weekend — were any dirty photos found in his flat? Girl in a Minnie Mouse mask giving a blowjob to some bloke, that sort of thing. No, never mind who the bloke was, none of your business. Yeah, I know it's not your case but you can ask somebody, can't you? You can call somebody. Right, so just do it.' He cupped his hand over the mouthpiece. 'He's calling somebody,' he said to me. A few minutes went by while Donovan gazed at the ceiling and I looked at all the money on his desk. Then he said, 'Yeah, still here. You're absolutely sure? OK, thanks, George. I owe you.'

He put the phone down. 'No pictures. So what does that mean?'

'Either that he didn't keep them in his

flat or that someone else has got them, probably whoever killed him.'

'Your Mr Mastermind, you mean,' he said with a touch of scorn. 'I don't really buy that theory.'

He got up and started putting the money into the wall safe.

'All right,' I said, 'what about Archie? As the killer.'

Donovan was startled enough to drop a handful of notes and fell instantly to his knees to pick them up. 'Archie? You've got to be joking.'

'No, think about it. Let's say Kale was my Mr Mastermind all along. What he'd organised was a neat little scam which entailed hardly any danger to himself if he followed it through according to plan. All he wanted was information which, passed on to the right recipient — as it was — means that Jack Klug gets a huge building contract that'll have investors clamouring for his shares — '

'There isn't a fifty quid note under your chair, is there?' Donovan asked, still scrabbling about.

'No, there isn't. Listen to me, will you? Now, we can assume that Kale did what he told Twill and Richards to do — he bought Klug shares when they were at rock bottom knowing he was on a certain winner, the only drawback being that he'd have to wait a while until the shares really climbed. But what if he got impatient, or a little greedy or just needed money immediately? And what if he decided on a spot of private enterprise and, without telling any of the others, tried to hit Archie for some cash? Not impossible. He'd blackmailed someone for money before and got away with it. But what if this time Archie found out who he was and went to his flat and smashed his head in?'

Donovan rose slowly to his feet. 'Archie wouldn't do that,' he said. 'He'd tell me about it so I could send someone else round to smash the bugger's head in.'

'And then what? Kale would be out of the way but you'd have the photos. How does that make Archie any better off?'

Indignantly Donovan said, 'What are you saying — that Archie wouldn't trust me?'

'Would you? In those circumstances and with material like that? I'm not sure I would.'

Donovan looked at me sorrowfully.

'You're a nice sort of friend you are, Bob.'

'I'm right, though, aren't I?' I said and left him to think about it.

Coincidence, a genuine one this time. There was a brief story in the financial pages of the *Evening Standard* saying that shares in Klug Construction were on the rise. Nothing too spectacular but there had been a fair amount of movement lately, thus lending fuel — said the writer — to recent rumours of a possible takeover bid . . .

I read that while I was hanging on the phone, trying to get in touch with Beckway, but I couldn't reach him that night. I called his office number but by then it was late and everyone had gone.

There was no reply from Dolphin Square and only a servant at the Mayfair house so I called Birgit at home. She hadn't seen Beckway since around four in the afternoon when he had left for the House of Commons but . . .

'What the hell is going on?' she said. 'He came in late this morning, looking desperately worried, and wouldn't tell me why. Then he had a couple of calls on his direct line and they upset him even more. Can we meet, you and I? I really must know what this is all about, Bobby.'

Bobby? Well, it was a step up from being Mr Lennox. Maybe the blue eyes and the profile were getting to her after all, though somehow I didn't think so. I told her I was rather busy right now and she reacted to that by injecting frost into her voice and didn't use my first name again during the rest of the conversation, not that it lasted much longer, for she had little more to tell me except that she hadn't heard from Beckway since he went to the House.

I called him there but he had gone. He had been around earlier in the evening but then he had left and nobody seemed to know where he was going.

On an impulse I called Donovan, but he was out, too.

'God knows where,' Annie said. 'Business is what he told me but that's all he ever tells me. He's a secretive old bugger.'

'Yes, well, he operates on a need-to-know basis and what he figures is that nobody but him ever needs to know anything about what he's doing.' Including me, I thought.

A little later Felicity, the undoubted cause of Beckway's desperate worry that morning, phoned me.

'How did it go?' I asked.

'Gruesome.' I could almost hear her shudder. 'God it was really, really awful. He cried when I showed him the picture. I mean, he just broke down and wept. He said he was forced to submit — don't you just love that word, submit? — he said he was forced to submit to the Minnie Mouse woman and when I refused to believe him he cried even more. He said he was being blackmailed and — '

'He was telling the truth.'

'Bobby, I don't even care any more.' She sounded weary, drained of emotion. 'Seeing him there in that picture . . . He had a huge erection . . . I really don't care whether he was doing it from choice or by coercion or what — he was enjoying it! All right, so he's being blackmailed. Tough. All right, so maybe this once, just this once, he was actually forced to have sex with another woman, so what? There've been too many other women, Bobby, far too many and . . . and the worst of it all was that the bastard actually had the nerve to tell me he loved me.' Now there was a quiver in her voice. Anger? Grief? Frustration? I don't know. 'That was the worst thing. That I could show him a picture like that and he could talk about loving me. He had his . . . his . . .'

'All right,' I said. 'All right. I've seen the photograph. I know what was where. The thing is, what are you going to do now?'

She took a deep breath. 'I'm going to divorce him. I told him that. And I told him that . . . that if he made any trouble I'd use the picture to screw him for everything I could get.' The last few words came out as a wail and then she was sobbing. 'Oh, Bobby, I feel such a bitch. I hate him so much and yet I feel like a bitch . . .'

'Do you want to come over here?' I asked gently.

There was a long silence while she forced herself to speak calmly. 'No, I'd love to but I can't. I'm in Hertfordshire. I said I'd wait for him here. I will divorce him, this time I will, but there are so many things still to discuss. He went off in such a state that . . . that I'm not sure he really knows how determined I am. We have to talk about the girls and

. . . and not hurting them more than is absolutely necessary.'

There was more sobbing at the Hertfordshire end of the line. I waited for it to stop before I said, 'Look, calm down, take a deep breath. I can take it, can I, that you're not still in love with Archie, that you really don't want to stay married to him?'

'No.' The answer was fierce, unequivocal. 'I hate him.'

'Then you should be laughing, not crying. You've got him by the short hairs. Anything you ask for he's going to have to give you — the house, maintenance, half his kingdom, you name it. And that photograph is your trump card. It was a real piece of luck, the way it turned up in the post like that.'

'I suppose.' She sniffled for a bit. 'I wish I could come to you. I wish we could be together, so you could hold me and cuddle me.' I thought about holding and cuddling her, remembered what it had been like and got a thick, salty taste at the back of my throat. But before I could say anything, she said, 'Only I must stay here. I must have it out with Archie.'

So we left it at that and soon afterwards I went to bed. It wasn't much past ten o'clock but I'd had a hell of a day.

I fell asleep thinking about Felicity Beckway and wondering how good an actress she had been.

THIRTY

Beckway didn't make it to Hertfordshire that night. He ended up stabbed to death in his car on the Thames Embankment instead.

I heard about it just after six o'clock in the morning. A persistent ringing of the bell and a hammering on the door woke me from a heavy sleep. I got up, cursing, pulled on a dressing gown and went to investigate. My old friends Detective Inspector Mason and Detective Sergeant Clark stood on the threshold, crumpled and unshaven like men who had been up a long time already.

I think they asked me to invite them in. I can't remember but they came in anyway.

'Where were you last night?' Mason asked.

'What? Here, of course. Where else would I be?'

'Can you prove that?'

I shook my head disbelievingly. The questions policemen ask. 'Oh sure. Talk to Kim Basinger, Michelle Pfeiffer, Julia

Roberts, Sharon Stone — they were all here with me. We had quite a party. What is all this?'

'What would you say if I told you someone could swear to seeing you on the Thames Embankment in the early hours of the morning?'

I led the way into the kitchen to put some coffee on. 'I'd say you were telling me lies or someone was lying to you. Which is it?'

They watched as I got the coffee percolating and found the cups, milk, sugar and a packet of biscuits.

Mason said, 'When did you last see Archie Beckway?'

I thought about it. So much had happened lately. 'I don't know. Monday? Something like that. Why?'

'He's dead. Murdered.'

'What?'

Mason nodded. 'Someone stabbed him to death in his car sometime after midnight.'

'On the Embankment?'

Sharply he said, 'Why do you say that?'

'If he'd been killed in Stockton-on-fucking-Tees you'd hardly be asking me if I was on the Embankment this morning, would you? Am I a suspect?'

'Maybe.'

I poured coffee for all of us and we carried it into the sitting-room. The news took a while to sink in and even then it shocked rather than distressed me, angered rather than grieved me. Beckway and I had not been friends and it would have been hypocritical to pretend that we were. But in a way I had been his minder and the fact that, nevertheless, someone had been able to kill him was almost a personal insult.

Clark said, 'Guv, the news ought to be on the telly by now. Want to have a look, see what they're saying?'

Without asking whether I minded or not, Mason switched on the set. The early news programme was dominated by the murder. There were shots of the car in which Beckway had been found, the discreetly anonymous Ford I had seen him driving at Dolphin Square the first time I met him; shots of his homes in Hertfordshire and Mayfair. There were reported, though not yet visual, tributes from the Prime Minister and other politicians. But there was no sign of Felicity, who was generally understood to be overcome by grief and shock. Neither was there a mention of Dolphin Square or of Beckway's reputation as a womaniser; the biographical emphasis being entirely on his business and political careers. Nor, I was happy to hear, was there any mention of Donovan or me or blackmail either. The motive for the killing, the newsreader said, appeared to have been robbery, since Beckway's wallet was missing and his pockets had been emptied.

'So what brings you to me at this hour of the morning?' I asked. 'Scotland Yard baffled, are they?'

Mason dunked a custard cream into his coffee and sucked on it. 'You, Bob? You're the sort of wild card in all this. First Freddie Marcus, now Beckway — someone dies and somehow you turn up. You say — Beckway said — you were going to work in his publishing house and yet you've still never been near it. Thing is, Bobby, everyone else around old Archie fits in but not you, so you know what I think? I think you were pimping for him.' He held out his cup to me. 'Got any more of that coffee?'

'Get it yourself.'

He cocked his head towards his sergeant. 'Clive?' Clive took the cup and went into the kitchen with it. He took his own cup, too, but he didn't offer to refill mine.

'We know all about randy old Archie and his women,' Mason said. 'The bugger lived for pussy and what I think is that you found it for him.'

'Wrong,' I said, although remembering how I had delivered Lacy to Beckway's flat I felt an unpleasant twinge of guilt.

'I don't think so. I don't think he was killed for his wallet either.' He sipped from the cup Clark had given him and grunted appreciatively. 'Good stuff, this. What kind of beans do you use?'

'Fava beans,' I said. 'Get to the point, if there is one.'

'What makes me think you're a pimp is that Archie had been very quiet on the sexual front lately, almost like he'd turned celibate. We knew all about that flat of his in Dolphin Square, how he'd kept it on as a fuck pad but the odd thing is he hadn't been using it lately, not to entertain women. Very unlike him. So then, after we met the other night, I got to wondering about you and suddenly it all began to fit. Archie was getting discreet, now he was in the Government, and you were fixing him up with pussy elsewhere.' Again without asking whether I minded or not he lit a cigarette. 'That assistant of his, that Birgit Cassidy. Was Archie still fucking her?'

'I don't know what you're talking about.' But I watched him with a little more respect, the suspicion creeping up on me that he was cocky because he was good.

He nodded thoughtfully, exhaling smoke from his nostrils. 'Question is, are *you* fucking her? Because if you are we might have a motive here. Jealousy. Always a belter of a motive that.' He flicked ash into his saucer. 'Matter of fact, whether you're screwing the Cassidy woman or not, the jealousy motive still looks pretty good to me. I mean, what was Felicity Beckway — I beg her pardon, the Honourable Felicity Beckway — what was she doing here the other night? Being honourable, was she?'

I was startled and I must have shown it because he said, 'Come on, Bob, you've got neighbours. Nice, law-abiding neighbours only too happy to help the police with their enquiries. Show 'em pictures and, "Oh, yes," they say, "yes, we know her all right. Went into Bobby's flat one night and never came out till morning, looking well-knackered." '

I said, 'Have you been following me?'

'Not you — her. And not following either, just keeping an eye on her. Wife of a government minister and all that. Interesting, though, you have to admit. She spends a night here and then a couple of days later her old man turns up dead. What's a poor, simple-minded policeman supposed to make of that?'

'Are you charging me with anything? Because if you are — '

'Nah, too early for that. Couple of other things to follow up first. But we're thinking of you, Bob, we're thinking of you.' He dropped his cigarette end into his cup and it sizzled briefly in the now lukewarm coffee. 'Come along, Clive. Mustn't take up all of Mr Lennox's morning. Have a nice day, Bob.'

And they left.

I couldn't get through to Felicity or to Birgit. A maid took my call in Hertfordshire, an answering machine in Knightsbridge. Then I stopped using my own telephone because after the visit from the cops paranoia had begun to set in and I was sure the line would be tapped. So when the phone rang and Donovan's voice said, 'Bobby?' I said, 'Don't mention your name. Are you at home?'

'Course I bloody am, this hour of the morning. I've only just got up and heard about Ar . . .'

'Stay put. I'll call you.'

I took a cab to the Connaught Hotel and rang Donovan's home from there. He said. 'What's all the mystery? I want to talk to you about Archie. I saw it on the telly.'

'Yes, well, the police seem to think I killed him.'

'What? Where are you?'

I told him.

'Wait there. I'll be with you in ten minutes.'

I waited fifteen minutes in the foyer and then Shitfer came in. 'He's in the car,' he said. 'Come on.'

I got into the back seat beside Donovan, who said, 'Fuck's going on, Bobby? How could you let this happen to Archie?'

'Me? How could I stop it? I wasn't his baby-sitter.'

He grunted. 'Who did it then? And why do the police think it was you?'

I gave him an edited version of what Mason had said, leaving out all reference to Felicity Beckway, on the grounds that anything between her and me was none of Donovan's business.

'And were you banging her?' he said. 'That Birgit, were you giving her a seeing to?'

'No. Chance would have been a fine thing.'

He considered what I had told him. 'OK, you didn't kill Archie. Only a bloody fool or a copper would think you did. But that brings us back where we started: who did kill him?'

I shrugged. 'Maybe the same person who killed Marcus and Kale. We assumed — I assumed — that the Irishman, Mickey Mouse, Kale whatever, killed Marcus but that was just because of the voice on the answering machine. It didn't have to be Kale who went round there and killed him. But if you're asking me why, God knows.'

I could understand why Marcus had been killed; he had seen something, someone, he shouldn't have seen at the Television Centre that night. But why

Kale? And why, in particular, Beckway? With him dead the blackmail died, too. That nice little earner which could have brought Kale and his associates lucrative inside information for years to come had now ended.

Donovan said, 'What about that pair of queens, worked with Kale. Do you fancy them for the job?'

'What, three murders? No, I really don't think so, Donovan.'

'Well, think harder. Maybe you didn't lean on 'em enough. Maybe it's time I got Shitfer to pay a friendly call on them.'

'No. Not yet. Later perhaps but not yet.' I opened the car door. 'Beckway was important to you, wasn't he?'

'Yeah. Not personally, mind. We were never what you'd call mates but business-wise he could have been a very handy meal ticket. Why?'

I got out of the car, closed the door behind me, leaned in at the open window. 'It's all very puzzling,' I said. 'I can understand why Marcus was killed and I can imagine various scenarios that would lead to Kale having to go but I really can't understand why anyone should kill Beckway.'

THIRTY-ONE

The agency occupied a ground-floor office in a house in Meard Street, an alley that linked Wardour Street and Dean Street in Soho. I walked in, took a business card from my wallet, handed it to the dark-haired receptionist and told her I wanted to see Jenny Bloomingdale. To talk about her late client, Roger Kale.

I was lucky — maybe it was a slow day in the showbiz world — but after doing her stuff on the telephone the receptionist said I could go straight in. I went through a half-glass, half-pine door into an office where Jenny Bloomingdale was sitting, commendably straight-backed, in a leather swivel chair behind a big oak desk. It was a fair-sized, thickly-carpeted office with heavy curtains at the window, a fridge in the corner and comfortable-looking chairs dotted about. Bloomingdale was youngish, fair and perhaps a little plumper than she should have been. Her eyes behind the big, round, gold-rimmed glasses were sharp and intelligent and overall she looked like somebody's aunt — an unmarried aunt who could be either stern or fun depending on how the mood took her.

I gave her my card and she read it and said, 'Davies. Teddy Davies. Why doesn't the name ring a bell?'

I said, 'I'm new to the showbusiness beat. Used to be a sportswriter, as a matter of fact.'

'Well, new or not you're a bit late, aren't you? I've already talked to somebody from the *Daily Journal*.'

'Ah, well, yes . . .' And then I went into my spiel, telling her how I was doing this special in-depth feature about Kale. The idea, I said, was to chronicle a young actor's career from the early struggles to TV fame and perhaps, who knew, the threshold of even bigger things and then to tie in his tragic death with the violence of modern society and the fact that nobody, not even gilded youth, was immune to it.

She said she could see how that might make a powerful piece but — she looked at her watch — the sort of interview I obviously wanted would take quite a bit of time and she —

'What I also wanted to weave into it,' I said, 'was the important part advisers, people like yourself, play in the building of a career like Roger's.'

'Ah, right,' she said. She picked up the phone and told the receptionist that she would be frightfully busy for the next half-hour and didn't want any calls. 'Fire away,' she said to me.

I got out a tiny tape recorder and, for good measure, a notebook and pen as well while she found Kale's personal file and then we both fired away.

For the most part it was fairly run-of-the-mill stuff. Kale had been born in Melbourne of middle-class English parents, now both dead, had come to London in his late teens, gone to drama school, worked in a repertory theatre, appeared in a couple of London plays, then made his breakthrough into telly stardom with the cops and robbers series. I quoted what the tabloid press had said about his glittering promise and enormous talent.

'Well, yes,' she said, 'but . . . Listen, turn that machine off for a minute, will you?' I turned it off. 'Can I talk to you off the record?'

I nodded.

'Right. Well, I don't want to speak ill of the dead, you understand, but I don't want to make a fool of myself either. The fact is that Roger really wasn't all that good. Oh, he had a certain presence and women loved him but in truth he wasn't much of an actor and I think he knew it. Actually, I'm sure he knew it. Deep down all that really interested him about acting was the women and the money. This is off the record, isn't it?'

I assured her it was and put both tape recorder and notebook away to prove it.

She took her glasses off, gave them a quick wipe and replaced them. 'He wasn't the easiest client to handle because he was always urging me to ask for more money than I knew the market could stand.' She fumbled about in her handbag, produced cigarettes and lit one. Then she looked at her watch again, muttered, 'Oh, sod it', went to the fridge and poured two glasses of chilled sherry, one of which she handed to me. 'Thing is, I don't believe Roger would have got much further than he'd got already. His co-star, Carly Shawn, now she's really got something.'

I said, 'Do you represent her, too?'

Bloomingdale shook her head. 'Nearly did. Roger brought her to me, oh two, three years ago. They were in a play together in the West End and she was looking to change her agent. Well, of course I'd seen the play and I knew how good she was, so I was quite interested. But . . .' She sank some sherry and dragged on her cigarette. 'The trouble is she was as bad as Roger as far as money was concerned. Worse even. Greedy little bitch, if you want to know the truth. I couldn't cope with it.' She paused, reflectively, and gave a short, sharp laugh. 'Carly Shawn. What a name. Not her real one, of course. Believe it or not her real name is Thatcher — Margaret Thatcher. You can see why she changed it, can't you? Changed everything, come to that. A proper little mouse she was when she started, nothing like the rather dashing, glamorous creature she is now. Anyway, that's the background and not for publication, OK? What else do you want to know?'

I got the notebook out again, looking through it to stall for time. This interviewing wasn't as easy as I'd thought it would be. I said, 'Some years ago Roger worked for a repertory theatre in the

North. I thought I might look into that. You know — for the real early days stuff.'

She clucked sadly. 'You'll be lucky, dearie. It closed down ages back. So many of those lovely little rep companies did. I don't even know who else was there with him. It was well before my time. I've only been looking after Roger for the last five years or so.'

I looked through my notes again. There was something else she had said that had interested me. What was it? No, it wasn't there. I hadn't written it down because . . .

'Oh yes,' I said, 'that play he was in with Carly Shawn. Can you remember who put it on? And the other West End show, too?'

'The producers, you mean?'

'Well, yes, and the backers, the money people.'

She looked at me quizzically over her sherry glass. 'This is all getting a touch recondite, isn't it?'

I smiled at her as boyishly and disarmingly as I knew how. 'I suppose so but, well, I'd just like to talk to as many people who knew him or might have known him as possible.'

I couldn't tell whether it was the boyish smile or the sherry but something had got her into a nicely helpful mood. 'All right. I imagine I can find out for you but it'll take a couple of calls.' She picked up the telephone. 'Help yourself to another sherry while I'm on the dog and bone. Oh, and you might give me a refill while you're about it . . .'

I called Rachel at the Television Centre. 'Where can I find Carly Shawn?' I asked.

'Hah,' Rachel said bitterly. 'Good question. I'm trying to find her myself. Far as I know she's somewhere in the Loire Valley with a couple of friends. Well, she had some time off due to her. She probably hasn't even heard about Roger's death yet and doesn't realise I want her back, like, yesterday.'

'When did she leave?'

'I don't know. Probably at the weekend some time. What do you want with her?'

'Just a chat,' I said vaguely.

Rachel said, sounding severe, 'Listen to me, my lad: I've already given you a lot of information about people in my show and I can't for the life of me imagine why I did it. You've taken the old pals' act much too far already, d'you hear me? I'm not telling you another thing until I know what you're up to. We may have been friends at university but we weren't that close. Christ, you never even asked me to sleep with you.'

Astonished, I said, 'Did you want me to?'

She hesitated, then laughed, 'Actually, yes. Then, I mean, not now. I'm not built for it now and anyway I'm very happily married. But I wasn't bad-looking in those days and you might at least have made a pass at me. God knows I gave you enough encouragement.'

'I didn't notice,' I said, weakly.

Another laugh, not much humour in it. 'Thanks a lot, Bobby. Look, I've got to go now. As far as Carly's concerned I can't help you. OK?'

I was amazed. Not for a moment, all those years ago, could I remember Rachel showing the slightest sexual interest in me. We'd spent a fair bit of time together, yes, but purely it seemed to me as friends. We'd talked about books, politics, movies, sport, not about *us* as a couple, not about sex. If she'd fancied me, why hadn't she let me know? When a man fancied a woman everybody knew it; lust, love, whatever was stamped all over him. Why did women have to be so subtle, so infinitely devious that a poor bewildered male had not the remotest idea what they really wanted? No doubt now, if I could think back clearly enough, I might be able to remember little hints that Rachel had let fall, but at the time I couldn't even recognise them as cryptic clues.

You might argue that men don't understand women but women don't understand men either. And what women most signally fail to understand is that men, and young men particularly, have no real confidence in their powers of sexual attraction. Oh, they swank and swagger around as if they were direct descendants of Don Juan but deep down they don't believe anything of the sort. They need more than hints — they need help; they need a woman to take control and make it clear that the attraction is mutual.

I thought of Rachel as I had known her at university and felt a pang of regret that she had not realised early enough that, while young women are fully grown-up, young men are just little boys who have merely got a bit bigger and older.

And I thought, too, of calling her back and telling her all those things but I didn't reckon it would get me any closer to finding Carly Shawn.

Ray Richards opened the door this time. His eyes opened wide and his hand went instinctively to his damaged nose when he saw me standing there in the hall.

I raised both hands in a peaceful gesture. 'It's all right. No rough stuff this time, I promise. I just want a word or two with Alex.'

Twill came out of the sitting-room, glaring at me suspiciously. 'I've nothing more to say to you,' he said, 'and I don't care what you do.'

'We'll just go and sit down, shall we?' I said and eased my way past him. 'Make ourselves comfy. Cup of tea would be nice. You wouldn't mind making us a cup of tea, would you, Ray?'

'No.' He glanced at Twill and shrugged helplessly. 'No, not at all. Alex, he did promise no rough stuff. You did, didn't you?'

I nodded and sat down to show I was harmless. Twill leaned against the bookcase, arms folded across his chest, glowering at me. 'What the hell do you want now?'

'More information really.'

He shook his head decisively. 'No. I've said all I have to say to you and so has Ray.'

'I don't want to talk to Ray — I want to talk to you.'

'Tough.'

I sighed and eased myself back into the chair. 'I know a man, a very, very dangerous man — much more dangerous than me —who thinks you and Ray killed Archie Beckway.'

A look of alarm crossed his face at the mention of Beckway's death but he recovered well enough to utter a derisive snort. 'He must be mad.'

'No, not mad. Very angry, yes, but not mad, not in the sense you mean. So far I've managed to persuade him that you're both innocent but if I go away from here unhappy and tell him I was wrong he'll probably come round with an exceedingly big and unpleasant guy who may well beat you both to death.'

He sneered. 'Look at me, I'm quaking.'

'You should be because I'm being very serious here.'

His hand went gently to his groin, reminding himself perhaps of how serious I could be. 'This man, whoever he is, why should he care?'

'Because he had a long-term business interest in Archie Beckway. Not like yours, of course — well, maybe a bit like yours only rather more subtle. Beckway's death has kind of ruined all that, as you can imagine, and he wants revenge — not for Archie, he doesn't really give a shit about Archie, but for himself.'

Twill went and sat in a chair opposite mine, crossing his legs gingerly. 'Ray and I didn't kill Beckway. We couldn't kill anybody. And there's no point in asking us questions because, apart from what we've already told you, we don't know anything about him.'

Richards brought in the tea on a silver tray. When we all had a cup I said, 'I don't want to ask you about Archie. I want to ask you about Roger Kale and in particular about the time you and he were in rep together up North. What I'm going to do is, I'm going to throw some names at you, the names of people who might have been in the company when you and Roger were there and I want you to think very carefully about them.'

Twill sipped his tea. 'All right then. I can't promise anything but I'll do my best.'

'Fair enough,' I said. 'The first name is Margaret Thatcher.'

Twill laughed so hard he spilled his tea down his trousers. 'Margaret Thatcher? That cow!'

THIRTY-TWO

On my way home I stopped to phone Felicity and Birgit again. Still no luck with either of them. I bought an *Evening Standard* but though Beckway's killing filled the front page and two or three inside as well, relegating the murder of Roger Kale to a brief column on page two, it had little more to tell me than I had learned that morning from the television.

The seven o'clock news on TV, however, was much more informative. They hadn't been able to get a comment from Felicity but the Prime Minister cropped up, looking suitably grave, outside Number 10, talking about 'this terrible tragedy' and fulminating about increasing violence in society and how his government was more determined than ever to Do Something About It. The Chancellor and a couple of other ministers were interviewed, too, reminiscing about their late, deeply lamented friend and the way a career of extraordinary promise had been cut off in its prime.

But it wasn't any of this that really interested me. What grabbed my attention was an interview with a taxi driver who had seen somebody throwing something that had glittered, something that might have been a knife, into the Thames at about the time Beckway had been killed and very close to the spot where his body had been found.

The cabby had given a description, both to the police and to the TV reporter. It was a pretty good one, too, and it let me right off the hook because it wasn't a description that came anywhere near fitting me. On the other hand it did, at last, help to make some kind of sense of Beckway's murder.

I found the address I wanted in the telephone book. It was just off Goldhawk Road, near Shepherd's Bush.

I went out again and got into my car. As I drove away a dark blue sedan, parked about a hundred yards down the road, pulled out and followed me. In the evening traffic it fell back to about three cars' lengths behind me. I kept an eye on it but I didn't try to shake it off.

The place I was looking for turned out to be a small, terraced house in a street that must have started out as working-class but had since been yuppified, presumably in the boom years of the eighties when the BBC had moved more of its operations into the Shepherd's Bush area.

The man who opened the door was in his early thirties, fair, medium height and with a bushy moustache and an incipient beer belly. Most of the time, I thought, his face probably wore an amiable, easy-going expression but right now he looked desperately worried.

'My name's Bobby Lennox,' I said. 'I'm a friend of your wife.'

'Was she with you?' he said. 'Last night, was she with you?' That's the sort of question which, asked by a husband of another man, you would usually expect to be accompanied by anger, jealousy, clenched fists and general displays of aggrieved macho indignation. But he merely seemed to be anxious, almost eager, as if above all things he wanted me to say, Yes, she was with me. He said, 'She wasn't here, you see. Well, she wasn't even expecting me. I got home early. Well, actually, I was late. The plane was delayed.'

The sentences were short, staccato.

He was telling me something but telling it almost as if he hoped that I already knew and that when he had finished I would nod reassuringly and say there was no need to worry because I could explain everything.

He said, 'I wasn't supposed to be back until . . . But we finished a couple of days early and . . . I didn't tell her. I thought I'd surprise her. But she . . . she wasn't here. I knew she'd be with a man. I mean, she's done it before. But she was so late and . . . and when she got in I thought there must have been an accident. There was, wasn't there? There must have — '

'She wasn't with me,' I said. 'I think I'd better come in, don't you?'

The brief flicker of hope drained away and he looked more desperate than ever.

It was a three-storey house, probably two rooms on each floor. Here, on the ground level, a passageway led to a kitchen at the end. A door on the left of the passage opened into a small sitting-room and he took me in there.

'Where is she?' I asked.

'Upstairs. She's . . . she's in a very bad way. Just keeps weeping. I can't seem to do anything to help her.'

'There was an accident,' I said. 'Well, a sort of accident. She was with Archie Beckway last night.'

'Oh, Christ,' he said. 'Oh, Christ.' He had slumped against the wall and there was such anguish in his eyes that it seemed an intrusion into grief even to look at him.

Gently, I said, 'I think you'd better call her down here.'

He took a deep, shuddering breath and straightened himself up. 'I'll go and get her.'

As we left the room there was a loud hammering on the front door. I motioned to him to go upstairs and when he had gone I opened the door. DI Mason and DS Clark were waiting on the step and another obvious plain-clothesman loitered on the pavement behind them.

'Well, well,' said Mason, 'fancy seeing you here, Bob. Surprise, surprise.'

'Surprise?' I said. 'I don't see why it should be unless you Keystone Kops are always surprised to find yourselves in the right place at the right time. God knows I made it easy enough for you to follow me.'

'This time you did. Not earlier, though. Out of your flat a bit sharpish this morning, weren't you? Didn't give us time to put a tail on you.'

I moved back, away from the door. 'Well, are you coming in or are you going to stay out there all night?'

Suddenly he looked doubtful. He exchanged glances with Clark and they both hesitated on the threshold.

I said, 'You don't even know what you're here for, do you? You just followed me. Or maybe it wasn't you, maybe it was Inspector Clouseau there.' I nodded towards the third man lurking behind them. 'It was just a knee-jerk reaction, wasn't it? Somebody had to follow me because I'm a kind of suspect. You've no idea what kind of a suspect but you suspect me anyway because suspecting's just about all you're good at, isn't it? I bet you don't even know who lives in this house.'

'Yes, we do,' Clark said. 'We checked it out. The owner's name is — '

'I know what his name is,' I said. 'But I don't think he's going to help you much.' The pair of them stared at me, caught between bafflement and a strong desire to bully somebody. 'Come in,' I said. 'I'm about to do your careers a powerful lot of good and I hope you'll be grateful to me.'

They left the third man outside and followed me into the house. As I shut the door behind us there was a sound on the stairs and we turned to see Lacy coming down, her husband's arm around her. Her face was quite colourless, a white backdrop on which the only expression was one of almost unbearable grief.

'If you're looking for Archie Beckway's killer,' I said to Mason, 'there she is.'

It turned out to be a long night. We were all taken to the police station near the House of Commons and interviewed separately. Well, I was interviewed anyway and so was Lacy's husband, Phil, the TV cameraman who had returned early from his foreign assignment and stumbled into the aftermath of murder. But there was not much he was able to tell them.

From Lacy herself the police got nothing. When Mason stepped forward to caution her in the hallway of her house she let out a wild scream, turned to run back up the stairs and struggled furiously for a few minutes while the policemen and her husband tried to restrain her. Then, suddenly she went limp and silent and after that she didn't utter a sound.

'I dunno,' Clark said much later as he brought me a cup of tea. 'She seems to be in some sort of catatonic trance. Hasn't said a word. They've got her under sedation at the moment.'

He had become quite friendly and chatty, as had Mason now that I'd helped them to a collar that would do wonders for their chances of promotion and had filled in the background for them.

I told them about Beckway's affair with Lacy, about how she had become increasingly possessive and neurotic and how he had grown wary of her and tried to break off the relationship. And I told them to be especially nice to their taxi driver witness because his description had fitted Lacy so accurately.

By the time I had finished my statement Mason and Clark were being congratulated by everyone from the Commissioner downwards for their astute detective work and they were feeling well-disposed towards me, which was why we were drinking tea together and chatting away like old pals.

What Phil, the husband, had told them was that he had got home just after midnight and found the house empty. Lacy had come in around 3 A.M. with blood on her dress and in such a state of distress that he had been unable to get any kind of articulate response from her. He was sure she had been with a man but he had no idea which man and there was certainly no reason why he should have associated her with Beckway. He wasn't even aware that they had ever met. All he knew from her behaviour and the stains on her clothes was that something pretty awful must have happened.

At first, until he undressed her and put her to bed, he thought she was the one who had been hurt. His next guess was that she had been attacked and had defended herself with the knife.

'What knife?' I said.

'The knife old Phil gave her after she was assaulted coming out of the TV Centre one night a few months back,' Mason said. 'Nasty area round there. Lot of people looking for money to buy crack. Big clasp knife, it was. She carried it in her handbag apparently, naughty girl, but there's no sign of it now.'

That morning she still hadn't been talking; instead she was weeping incessantly. Phil had wanted to call a doctor but when he suggested it she screamed and shouted and in the end he gave her a sleeping pill. She had spent the rest of the day alternately sleeping and crying, with her husband fluttering around her, torn between wanting to get help for her and fear of what he might learn if he did.

As for Beckway, he had left the House of Commons the previous evening to go to a private cocktail party and had then had dinner at a restaurant near Westminster with a couple of fellow MPs. They said he had seemed worried and preoccupied but had refused to tell them what, if anything, was bothering him. Around nine they had all returned to the House for a debate and a division and Beckway had stayed there till midnight which was the last time anyone had seen him alive.

Piecing all that together with what I had told them and the fact that the blood on Lacy's dress was the same type as Beckway's, the supposition was that he had agreed to meet her somewhere near the House of Commons. Lacy, they knew, had left the Television Centre about 10.30 after the transmission of *Speaking Out* and the traditional spell in the hospitality room. According to Kevin Rycroft and others Lacy had been quiet and withdrawn for the last couple of days and, after the programme, had sat by herself and drunk at least three, maybe four, glasses of wine, which was very unusual for her. If, after that, she had gone home to get ready for her rendezvous with Beckway she must have left her house shortly before her husband arrived.

What the police believed was that she had driven to Westminster, parked her own car and joined Beckway in his. If he had intended, as I thought likely, to end the relationship he would not have wanted to take her to Dolphin Square where she might well have tried to make him change his mind by getting him into bed. So he had driven down the Embankment, turned into a side street and parked.

And after that . . . well, it was all

guesswork, of course, but the probability seemed to be that they had talked, that Beckway had said his piece, that Lacy had pleaded with him maybe, grown angry with him, that the chat had turned into a hurtful row and that she had whipped out the knife and carved him up.

'It sort of fits,' Mason said. 'I mean, there's no doubt she killed him but when you consider how she behaved afterwards I'm sure she can't have planned it. All right, when she realised what she had done she took his wallet and money to make it look like a robbery, threw everything in the Thames and then walked back to her own car. Probably didn't have far to walk either. Taking the money and stuff, that might look premeditated but I don't think it was. I think it was just panic.'

It was late, very late, by the time I left the nick. As I was going Mason said, 'Look, I'm sorry about, you know, the way we treated you earlier. It wasn't personal.'

'I suppose that should make me feel better,' I said. 'Maybe it will later on.' I stopped and turned back to him. 'When your people were searching Lacy's house they didn't find any dirty pictures, did they?'

'What sort of dirty pictures?' He sounded interested.

'A woman in a Minnie Mouse mask and a half-naked man giving each other a bit of the orals.'

'Tasty,' he said, then shook his head. 'Not to my knowledge but I'll ask around later on if you like. Are you the bloke in the pictures?'

'No. I was just curious. It's not really important.'

He walked me out to my car. 'Those photos,' he said, as I got in, 'would they have any bearing on old Archie's murder?'

I thought it over. 'If you'd found them in Lacy's house,' I said, 'they might have a bearing on a lot of things.'

THIRTY-THREE

I finally got through to Felicity in the morning. She said, 'I really don't know how I feel. Shocked, mostly, I think and sorrowful. But . . . no grief, no real grief. It's strange, isn't it? Maybe that'll come later, maybe not. He wasn't . . . he wasn't a very nice man.'

Some epitaph. 'Here lies Archie Beckway. He wasn't a very nice man.' True enough, though. Like Felicity I, too, felt shock, more now curiously enough than I had when I first heard of his death. I felt pity, as well, and maybe a little sorrow but, again like her, not grief.

'Is there anything I can do?' I asked.

She was silent for a while. 'I don't think so, Bobby. Not at the moment. The girls are here and they need me with them. Everything is so changed now. We need time to . . . to come to terms with it all.'

'You will be in touch, won't you?'

'Oh, yes. Soon. I can't say exactly when but soon. I promise.'

After that I talked to Birgit. She *was* grieving. Curious. The widow just felt shock; the former mistress was broken up, aching with loss. She said, 'What am I going to do? I loved him. I can't think what I'm going to do without him.'

I made consoling noises, promised I would be round to see her as soon as I could and wondered to myself at women's amazing capacity to give their love to the most undeserving men.

Then her mood changed to anger and she was on about Lacy, blaming Lacy, blaming herself. 'I should have done something about it. I shouldn't have waited for Archie to ask. All the signs were there — the neurosis, the obsession — and I ignored them. I should have warned her off. I could have done it, you know, I could have done it. Oh God, that evil little bitch — I'd like to kill her. I'd like her to hang. Why don't we have the death penalty in this stupid country?'

There was about fifteen minutes of this — grief followed by rage, followed by grief, followed by self-pity, followed by grief again. I kept listening and murmuring, sometimes sympathetically, sometimes non-committally — the death penalty, for God's sake! — and in the end she calmed down and I was able to hang up.

The phone rang as I was leaving the flat. I didn't touch it, just stopped and listened as the answerphone kicked in. It was Donovan. 'Bob, are you there?' This was followed by a lot of irate background chuntering, too far away for the machine to pick up. Then, 'Shit, I hate talking to these bloody machines. Come on, I bet you're there, you bastard, pick up the phone.' A pause and more indecipherable mumbling, conducted on a note of subdued fury, that seemed to go on for a long time. And after that, 'I want to know what's going on. I've had George on. He tells me that Lacy's been arrested and you know all about it. So pick up the bleedin' phone and — ' His time ran out. Message ends.

I walked to Sloane Square, took the tube to King's Cross and changed onto the Northern Line. At Old Street I got off, went past the flower shop and the hamburger bar, along the littered concrete tunnel and took the stairs from Exit 4 to City Road.

Companies House was about fifty yards down on the left-hand side, one of those modern, functional buildings that make no attempt to please the eye. 'I'm an office block,' it seemed to be saying with a kind of dour belligerence: 'that's all I was ever meant to be and if you want to make something of it, step outside.'

The security guard checked me through into a light, spacious room with, at the top end, a bank of computer screens. On one of these I looked up the registration number of Klug Construction and armed with this asked at the counter if I could see the list of the company's shareholders. For £3 I could. Indeed, I had a choice. I could look at the list there and then or I could hang about for an hour and wait for a copy to be run off for me to take away. Same price either way.

I said I'd like to see the list right now and was handed a small envelope of dark blue microfiches, which I took to one of the projectors clustered together at the end of the room and so arranged that nobody could see which company anyone else was investigating without standing behind him and peering at the screen.

There were a lot of us earnest seekers

after knowledge, nearly all male, and we went about our business quietly. The atmosphere was like that of a public library.

It took me barely fifteen minutes to discover everything I wanted to know. Predictably, Jack Klug was by far the major shareholder in his company but an awful lot of other people had pieces of the action, too. They were listed alphabetically, which made things easier, along with their addresses and the number and kind of shares they owned.

Roger Kale was a big investor, so were Alex Twill and Ray Richards. I scanned through the list, jotting names and numbers on a notepad, handed back the microfiches and left.

At the station I bought an early edition of the *Evening Standard.* There was only one story on the front page that day — the story of Lacy's arrest. There was a smudged, unflattering picture of her, probably procured from the BBC, alongside a portrait of Beckway, looking debonair and devilishly handsome, and that morning's shot of my friends Mason and Clark, wearing the modest smiles of dedicated law enforcement officers who never ceased in their efforts to keep the public safe from the dastardly actions of homicidal floor managers. There was no mention of my part in the arrest but I didn't mind that.

THIRTY-FOUR

Donovan handed me a glass of white wine. 'Things had turned out different this would have been champagne but . . .' He shrugged. 'I can't honestly say you done well, Bob. Still, least it's over now. Poor old Archie.' He raised his glass in a toast to the recently departed.

Early evening and just the three of us in the first-floor sitting-room in the Mayfair house: Donovan in open-necked shirt and slacks; Annie curled up in a soft white Armani outfit on the sofa; me in leather jacket and jeans lounging in an armchair.

'Maybe I did better than you think,' I said.

'How? Well, yes, I suppose. I mean, you did set the police onto that Lacy woman but you didn't do Archie a whole lot of good, did you, not in the long run?'

He sat down beside Annie, who moulded herself against him, her head resting on his shoulder. He put his arm around her and squeezed her.

'She was in the theatre, wasn't she, one time — this Lacy?' Donovan said.

I nodded. 'In repertory, yes. An ASM.'

'A what?'

Annie grinned and kissed him affectionately on the cheek. 'Assistant stage manager, darling, a sort of dogsbody.'

Donovan reached towards the silver cigar box on the table but stopped when Annie slapped him on the wrist and clucked disapprovingly. 'Don't even think about getting married, Bob,' he said. 'Bloody women take over your whole life.' It didn't seem to bother him, though.

It was a soft, warm, golden evening. Not quiet, because the sound of traffic in Berkeley Square, though muted at this distance, drifted in through the open windows.

Donovan said, 'So I suppose Lacy knew this Roger Kale from the old days, back in the sticks when they were in the theatre together. Then he gave her the Minnie Mouse mask and roped her in to help him blackmail Archie.'

'Close,' I said.

'What do you mean, close? Am I right or am I right?'

I said, 'Look, this whole business was

about making sure Jack Klug got that government contract. After all, Jack's shares were right on the floor but if he landed a huge job like that, whoosh, they'd go through the ceiling. And the question is: who benefits? Well, Jack obviously but he had nothing to do with the blackmail. So I went over to Companies House this morning and looked through the list of shareholders. Very enlightening. All the people you might expect — you know, Kale and his two mates — had invested heavily in Klug Construction.' I took a deep breath. 'And so had you, Donovan. You're a very, very big shareholder.'

He watched me, poker-faced. Annie glanced up at him and then across to me with alert interest.

'Well, of course I bloody am,' Donovan said. 'Soon as you told me what was going on I grabbed every share I could. Christ, didn't you?'

I sighed. 'No, as a matter of fact I didn't.'

'More bloody fool you then.'

'Yes, I suppose so. Anyway, some other interesting people had become big investors, too. Birgit Cassidy, for instance. She bought her shares the day after Klug put in his tender.'

Donovan removed his arm from Annie's shoulder and leaned forward. 'Oh? How d'you know that?'

'She told me. I asked her this afternoon. Her story is that she overheard something of a row between Archie and his Permanent Secretary about Jack's belated bid, realised she was onto some hot inside stuff and went out and bought. Clever girl.'

'You can say that again.'

I gave him a nod. A wise one. I was beginning to feel like Hercule Poirot. 'Thing is, though, that Lacy didn't have any shares. The chances are she didn't know Roger Kale either. They both worked in rep at the same time but he was up North and she was in the West Country. And though their TV programmes were put together on the same night there was no real reason why they should ever have come into contact. They worked for different BBC departments and anyway the Television Centre's a big place.'

Donovan looked exasperated. 'I don't know what the fuck you're getting at. Do you know what the fuck he's getting at, Annie?' Annie frowned and shook her head. She didn't know what the fuck I was getting at either.

I said, 'All right. We all spent a lot of time wondering about Minnie Mouse. Who was she? Why all that disguise? Was she perhaps somebody Archie knew or somebody Twill and Richards knew? Or both?'

'So?' Donovan said.

'So what I should have been wondering about was something else: the fact that Mickey Mouse — all right, Roger Kale — knew all about me. He knew from the start that I was working for Archie. He seemed to know where I was and who I was talking to and what I was doing at any given time. And he could only have got that information from someone on the inside.'

There was a pause and I let it hang there.

'Like who?' Donovan said softly.

I put my wine glass down carefully on the table, taking my time. 'Like you, Donovan,' I said.

There was another pause in which Annie shot a startled glance at Donovan and he stared at me with a look of pure venom. 'I didn't even know fucking Roger Kale,' he said.

'Oh, yes, you did. He was in two shows in the West End, a play with Carly Shawn and a musical . . . Well, the musical Annie was in when you first met her. And you backed both of them.'

'That's right, you stupid sod. I backed them — I put money in them. It was a business deal. I didn't hang out with the fucking cast.'

I picked up my glass again and took a sip, enjoying the tension, stretching it as far as it would go. Eat your heart out, Hercule, I thought.

'I had a word with Alex Twill yesterday,' I said. 'He used to be in rep with Roger up North. I mentioned some names to him, asked him if he could remember them. Margaret Thatcher, for instance.'

Annie laughed. 'You asked if he could remember Margaret Thatcher? How could anyone ever forget her, after what she did to this country — '

'Not that Margaret Thatcher,' I said. 'Another one, a.k.a. Carly Shawn. But she wasn't in the rep company, not under either name. So then I asked about Felicity Beckway.'

Donovan looked at me, shaking his head in disbelief. 'What are you saying?

That you thought Felicity Beckway
might be Minnie Mouse?'

'Well, it was worth considering. Felicity used to be on the stage, remember.
She could have been in rep somewhere.
She could even have been in rep with
Roger Kale. But no, she wasn't. She'd
never worked with him; as far as I can
make out she never met him. So she
wasn't Minnie Mouse. Truth of the matter is, Annie, that the only name Twill
could remember from way back then
was yours. You were Minnie Mouse.'

THIRTY-FIVE

First there was stunned silence, then there was uproar, Annie all outraged innocence, Donovan veering between bewilderment and a look which suggested that he wanted to kill somebody, preferably me. I waited until the tumult had died down.

Then . . . 'I didn't really think Donovan could have been behind all this because of the killings — Marcus and Kale. Not Donovan's style at all, much too crude, all that head bashing. He'd have got Shitfer to take them away somewhere, waste them and lose them for ever. But if not Donovan then who was giving Kale the inside dope? Archie? Hardly. Felicity? No, she didn't know anything about it, neither did Lacy. Birgit? Possibly, but there was nothing to suggest she had ever met Roger Kale either. So that just leaves you, Annie. You knew Roger all right — you were his girlfriend, the girl in the pictures he used to blackmail that councillor in the North, you and he were both in the musical Donovan backed. Also, no matter how much or how little Donovan told you, just living here, overhearing conversations, listening to the messages I left on the phone machine you could have picked up all the information you needed to keep Kale abreast of what I was up to. What's more, you own well over £100,000 worth of shares in Klug Construction and if Jack gets his contract that could be worth close to half a million in about a month's time.' I stopped, waiting for her to say something.

She was sitting up, alert, staring at me. Donovan, his expression alternating between confusion, anger and dismay, was glancing rapidly from her to me. He said, 'Annie?' his voice almost beseeching, as though he were begging her to tell me I was out of my mind, or maybe to laugh as if it was all a weird practical joke that she and I were playing on him. But she did neither of those things. She just kept looking at me with a hurt, puzzled frown as if a trusted friend had suddenly betrayed her.

I said, 'I'll tell you what I think, Annie — I think Roger Kale killed Freddie Marcus and I think you killed Roger. So what are you going to do? Tell me I'm wrong? Go for it — please. Convince me.'

Again Donovan said, 'Annie? Annie, tell him.'

She said, 'You're wrong,' but the response was automatic, resigned, as if she didn't expect to be believed. She got up, refilled her wine glass and sat in an armchair away from Donovan and me, making the apex of a triangle, she at the head of a long, low occasional table, Donovan and I on either side of it.

'Bobby Lennox, boy detective,' she said. 'What's your next trick, Bobby? Do you snap your fingers as a signal to Inspector Plod to come out from behind the curtains?'

I shook my head. 'What am I going to tell the police? I can't prove anything. It's all circumstantial. Doesn't make it any the less true, though. You know that as well as I do. I think Donovan knows it, too.'

She nodded thoughtfully then smiled across at Donovan. 'Are you disappointed in me, Donovan?' she said. 'Or are you going to stand by your woman? Come on, tell me you love me no matter what I've done. I mean, hey, all right I killed a guy but you've killed people, too. You've killed a lot of people. Why is it so much more awful when a woman does it, when I do it?'

Donovan said nothing, just sat there staring down at the carpet. I had never seen him so out of control of what was going on around him.

She nodded sadly. 'Men,' she said, as if that one word explained everything, as if nothing was ever to be expected of such creatures, certainly not understanding. She glanced around her, almost as though she were looking at an audience of other women, invisible to everyone except her, all offering silent agreement. 'I didn't mean to kill Roger. We had a row and he got violent. He was jealous, that was the trouble. He punched me. Right here.' She put her hand on her left breast. 'He was very strong and he was completely berserk. I'd never seen him like that before and I was terrified. I really thought he wanted to kill me. He started chasing me around the room. It was like some dreadful French farce except that he was in such a rage. Anyway, I grabbed this statuette, a bronze thing, quite heavy and very ugly, I'd always hated it. And I hit him with it but he kept coming at me and I hit him again. Then I ran for the door and he came staggering after me and when I'd got out and slammed the door behind me I heard him fall.'

'Jesus,' Donovan said.

I said, 'Why was Roger jealous?'

Annie gave me a wry, ironic grin. 'Because I was going to marry Donovan.' She frowned, fidgeting around in her chair. 'Shit, I wish I still smoked. I could really use a cigarette now. I suppose neither of you . . . ?' Donovan and I shook our heads. She sighed. 'I'd been sleeping with Roger on and off ever since we were in rep. When I first met you, Donovan, Roger and I had just finished one of our flings. Actually, he'd already moved on to Carly Shawn because her legs are even longer than mine. He was always a leg man.' She hesitated. 'I can't say all this to you, Donovan, I just can't.' She shifted in her chair so that she was looking directly at me, blotting Donovan out of her line of vision. 'I'll talk to you, Bobby. It's easier. So . . . Well, at first with Donovan everything was great, I was very happy. But then he was away a lot, in America and places, doing God knows what kind of business that he didn't want me involved in and I got lonely and a little bored. I had nothing to do here. Then, one day, I bumped into Roger and we started up again, only somehow this time it was more serious than before. I don't know, we were both getting older and, well, we started talking about marriage.'

Donovan said, 'You were living with me and you were talking marriage to somebody else?' He seemed back in control now. Thoughtful. Cold.

She nodded. 'All right, I'm a bitch. It wasn't that I didn't love you, Donovan, because I did. I still do. But I knew about you and the women you'd had and I reckoned all I had to look forward to was another few weeks with you and then, bye-bye, darling, here's a lovely cheque, don't spend it all at once, have a nice life.'

I said, 'How did Carly Shawn fit into all this?'

'She didn't. Roger said that was all over, that he was just going out with her because the publicity was good for them and the show but they weren't going to bed together any more.'

'You really believed that?'

'Yes!' She hissed the word at me. 'You can think I'm gullible if you like but I believed him. I knew Roger, I knew him very well.' She watched as Donovan reached for a cigar. This time she didn't try to stop him. 'Well, anyway, Roger and I started thinking how we might use my situation to make a little money for ourselves and, suddenly, it all fell into place. Donovan and I had dinner with Archie one night and he was talking about this big building contract that was going through his department. And then, a couple of nights later, we were with Jack Klug and he was whining on about how his firm was going down the toilet and I just put two and two together. The funny thing is, I bet Donovan and Archie and Klug didn't even know that I was listening or that I could understand what they were talking about. Men always think good-looking women are just brainless bimbos.'

So between them she and Kale concocted this theatrical plot to compromise Beckway. They knew he would be on *Speaking Out* that night because it had been announced the previous week; they knew about Beckway's weakness for pretty women, and Kale had heard about Lacy's reputation with men. The anonymous bouquet of flowers had been Annie's idea, as had the fake message to lure Lacy from the hospitality room. True, they were banking on the flowers having the desired effect, on Lacy putting out to Beckway and Beckway responding but they felt the odds were good. Besides, if none of that had worked they would have tried to grab Beckway when he went back to his dressing-room. All they really needed was for Beckway to be alone for a few minutes in the basement corridor and the use of the unwitting Lacy was just one possible way to fulfil that object. And if none of it had worked and they had failed that night, then they would have sought another opportunity at another time.

'We could wait,' Annie said. 'We had a few days, we'd have got him somewhere. I know it sounds a crazy plan but it wasn't really. There was very little risk for us.'

Very little but some nevertheless. The one thing they hadn't allowed for, couldn't allow for, was Freddie Marcus roaming the building in search of the absent Beckway.

'He saw me going into Roger's dressing room,' Annie said. 'I'd gone there to get dressed after we left Beckway in the loo. I wasn't wearing the mask, obviously, but I was still wearing the coat. He only saw me for a moment but I knew he'd recognised me. Donovan and I had met him a couple of times at dinners and things. So when Roger came in I told him and he said not to worry, he'd handle it.'

'How? How was he going to handle it?'

She shrugged. 'He didn't say and I didn't ask him. I left it all to him.'

Kale had followed Marcus home that night, had seen him and his wife rush from their house and had followed them to the airport. If he had planned to silence Marcus then the opportunity didn't present itself.

There followed a few deeply anxious days for Annie. If Marcus had told Beckway whom he had seen and what she was wearing and Beckway had told Donovan . . . The slice of luck for Annie and Kale was that Marcus had had no chance to pass on what, to him, would merely have been a piece of gossip.

'But then,' I said, 'Marcus came back and rapidly turned up dead. I bet you were surprised.'

The look she gave me was cool, even a touch disdainful. 'Roger had no choice. We were in much too deep by then. He didn't enjoy killing Marcus. It was simply something he had to do. It was just unfortunate really.'

And with Marcus out of the way the little blackmail caper would have worked if the unexpected hadn't happened, if Donovan hadn't asked Annie to marry him and if Kale hadn't astonished her by throwing a fit of jealousy. She had gone to see him the weekend after the engagement party to tell him there would be no more blackmail and to get the photographs and negatives from him.

She had been confident that Kale could be persuaded to see things her way, that eventually he would be satisfied with the money he would make from his shares in Klug Construction; if necessary she was even prepared to let him have her shares. But she was wrong. He wanted the money, yes, but he wanted her as well. In the past he had always been the one who started and stopped their intermittent affairs and to be thrown over by her for Donovan was something he would not accept.

As he saw it, Annie, finding herself now with two fiances, had simply taken the better offer. When she had told him, on the morning after the engagement party, that it was Donovan — not him — she was going to marry, he had sent the photograph to Felicity Beckway out of spite, out of rage, out of God knew what emotions. In some twisted way it had seemed to him that Beckway was getting off lightly; if he, Kale, was going to lose his woman then so, goddammit, would Archie.

It was when he told Annie what he had done that the row and the fight started.

'But you didn't intend to kill him?' I said.

'No.'

'Of course, if Kale hadn't been content with simply screwing up Archie's marriage, if he had also decided somehow or other to let Donovan know who Minnie Mouse really was, you'd have been a lot worse off financially, no matter how much your shares were worth. But none of this went through your mind while you were beating him about the head with that statuette you hated so much?'

Angrily she said, 'No — it was nothing to do with money. Not then. It was Donovan. It had never occurred to me that he would ask me to marry him but when he did . . . Well, there was no choice. Not as far as I was concerned.' She made a small, exasperated sound. 'Don't you see? I love him. Roger was exciting and fun and very good in bed but I didn't love him, not as I love Donovan.'

She shot a quick, appealing look at Donovan but he simply stared back at her. There was no expression on his face at all that I could read.

I said, 'So what happened to the photographs?'

'Sorry?'

'Somebody removed the pictures and the negs from Kale's flat. Twill and Richards didn't and the police didn't, so it can only have been you.'

She looked once more at Donovan but still there was no help or support from that direction. She said, 'Well, all right, yes. I was outside the flat when I heard him fall. I waited for a bit and there was no sound from him so I let myself back in. I could see he was dead, anyone could see he was dead. So I took the pictures. What else should I have done?'

'Good to know you didn't lose your head,' I said. 'Someone else who'd just accidentally killed a man might have panicked, run away. You know how silly people can be. But not you, Annie. You stayed cool.'

'Are you saying you don't believe me?'

'I'm not sure it matters what I believe. It's what Donovan believes that you should be worrying about.' But whatever it was Donovan believed he was not about to tell us, not then. He gestured to me to carry on and I did. 'How did you expect to get away with it, even if everything had gone according to plan? You and Kale and the others all bought shares in your own names. What if Donovan or Archie had done what I did and checked the register at Companies House?'

She shrugged, wearily. 'So what? OK, they might have had a shrewd idea that I had something to do with the blackmail, but I'd have been long gone by then. I'd have been living abroad somewhere. I told you — I thought Donovan was going to kick me out, not propose marriage. If I'd had any idea he'd do something like that then . . .' Another shrug. 'Anyway, there was nothing to connect me to Roger or the other two. So they'd have been all right and I didn't think Donovan would do anything to hurt me.'

Again she looked at Donovan. Again he just stared back at her. Then he got up and said, 'I'll handle it from here, Bob. Better if you left now.' To Annie he said, 'And you, don't you dare move from this room.'

He walked with me down the stairs to the front door. The house was quiet and peaceful, the servants out for the evening.

'So what happens next?' I said.

'Don't worry about it, Bob. I'll take care of it.'

'How? You can't go to the police because, one, you don't have any evidence and, two, you don't want to get yourself publicly mixed up in anything like this. But the fact remains that Annie killed somebody. Is that all right with you?'

'I said don't worry about it. Annie won't cause any more trouble.'

'What are you going to do, for Chrissake? Are you going to kill her? Is that it — eye for an eye? And for what? Because she killed Roger Kale — or because she was sleeping with him while she was living with you?'

He shook his head. 'I don't care who she killed. I don't even care who she slept with — well, I do a bit. Never pleasant to be a cuckold, specially at my age. But there are more important things to consider. When you come right down to it, it's very simple really: I trusted her and she betrayed my trust. And I just can't have that. So Annie's finished. One way or the other she has to pay.' He opened the door and eased me out. 'I'm not happy with what you've told me tonight, Bob, but I'm grateful. You've saved me making a fool of myself. Now get out and mind your own business. You don't have to worry about Annie any more.'

He closed the door behind me.

I hesitated a moment then walked to my car. As I got there I glanced back at the house. Annie was looking at me from the first-floor window. She gave me a sad smile and a small wave of the hand.

I never saw her again.

THIRTY-SIX

Linda called me from Barcelona the next morning. She would be in London for a few days on her way back to California: could we have lunch or dinner or something? I said, OK. A few hours later she called again to say everything had changed; she had to go straight to Los Angeles, no stopover, but she'd be finished with the film in a couple of weeks. Would I go to LA to see her, spend some time? I said I'd think about it.

In the post that morning there was a cheque from Beckway's accountants, a retainer for my services. Some service I'd provided. All right, I'd discovered who was blackmailing him but the man was dead. It wasn't my fault that he died but he was still dead.

A couple of days later I cashed the cheque and sent the money to a charity.

As for the rest, well, it was officially announced soon afterwards that Klug Construction had landed the contract to build the prison and every morning

I would turn to the financial pages and watch the share price rising. I had a personal interest in this because I was a shareholder, wasn't I? No, I hadn't bought any myself but my partners, without benefit of inside information and acting solely on the takeover rumours, had acquired a hefty chunk on our behalf. It had never occurred to me, when I was searching through the list of shareholders, to wonder whether we were among them. But it just shows, doesn't it — sometimes the sun does shine on the righteous.

I called Birgit a couple of times but she was very busy. She had odds and ends of Beckway's business affairs to tidy up and besides, let's face it, she wasn't all that interested in me in the first place.

I talked to Felicity two or three times a day and two weeks after Beckway's death I went to the Hertfordshire house when her daughters were back at school and spent the weekend consoling her.

And then, of course, there was Annie and I still have no idea what happened to her. For all I know Donovan had her killed; he was capable of that. Equally he might have banished her from the country on pain of death if she ever returned; he was capable of that, too.

One day, when everything had quietened down, I went again, just out of curiosity, to Companies House to check the shareholders in Klug Construction. A lot of the names I had found before were missing, among them Annie's. When I asked Donovan who had sold her shares and what had happened to the money he simply said, 'What are you worrying about? I told you — it's not your problem.'

So maybe she's abroad somewhere, not daring to return to Britain until and unless Donovan gives permission, living on whatever money she has and dreaming of what might have been.

You know, looking back on it all, what surprises me is the lengths to which people will go for comparatively little. What Annie stood to gain from blackmailing Archie Beckway — £300,000, perhaps £400,000 — maybe isn't all that little but in the overall scheme of things it's not such a hell of a lot either. As it turned out, hers was a fairly modest scam but small greed can lead to big crimes and blackmail and murder are both big crimes.

They may not be the biggest or the worst in the world these days; maybe drug trafficking is. Blackmail and murder usually destroy only one person at a time and murder can be unpremeditated; a drug pusher can start the destruction of a score of lives in one night. And yet there is still something particularly shocking and cowardly about blackmail.

Even giving Annie the benefit of the doubt about the death of Roger Kale, even if you excuse her for the passive role she played in the murder of Freddie Marcus, she had still coldly, calculatedly set in train the events that led to the fear and mental agony that blackmail can bring and had brought to Archie Beckway.

Like I said, I don't know what Donovan did, or had done, to her. But whatever it was I hope it caused her pain. I don't mean physical pain: I mean grief, anguish, deprivation of something she badly wanted.

At the very least she had that coming to her.

We hope you have enjoyed this Large Print book. Other Thorndike Press or Chivers Press Large Print books are available at your library or directly from the publishers.

For more information about current and upcoming titles, please call or write, without obligation, to:

Thorndike Press
P.O. Box 159
Thorndike, Maine 04986
USA
Tel. (800) 223-2336

OR

Chivers Press Limited
Windsor Bridge Road
Bath BA2 3AX
England
Tel. (0225) 335336

All our Large Print titles are designed for easy reading, and all our books are made to last.